PRAISE FOR THE

"A fast-moving story, and a great start to an intriguing new series."

—Sheila Connolly, *New York Times* bestselling author of the Orchard Mysteries, the Museum Mysteries, and the County Cork Mysteries

"Holmes creates the perfect contemporary cozy—with a smart and engaging heroine, a quirky and mysterious Berkshires town, and a cast of characters to rival any who live in Cabot Cove. Don't waste another minute—this is your new favorite series."

—Hank Phillippi Ryan, Agatha, Anthony and Mary Higgins Clark award-winning author of the Jane Ryland series

"You will be on the edge of your seat until this murder is solved."   —A Cozy Girl Reads

"Delightful . . . The story, with a hunky barber, Ruth's childhood friends, and conflicts between the new town manager and the 'old' Orchard, winds up to a suspenseful and satisfying end."

—Edith Maxwell, Agatha Award–nominated and national bestselling author of the Local Foods Mysteries

"Take one tightly wound plot, a charming clock shop in the Berkshires, a woman you want to be your best friend, and you have *Just Killing Time*."

—Sherry Harris, Agatha Award–nominated author of the Sarah Winston Garage Sale Mysteries

"With its bucolic setting, engaging characters, and clever plotting, Julianne Holmes has crafted a mystery to stand the test of time."

—Jessie Crockett, national bestselling author of the Sugar Grove Mysteries

"An intriguing premise, a fun mystery, and a town and heroine with heart."

—Barbara Ross, author of the Maine Clambake Mysteries

chime
and
punishment

JULIANNE HOLMES

BERKLEY PRIME CRIME
New York

BERKLEY PRIME CRIME
Published by Berkley
An imprint of Penguin Random House LLC
375 Hudson Street, New York, New York 10014

ISBN: 9780425275542

First Edition: August 2017

Printed in the United States of America
1 3 5 7 9 10 8 6 4 2

Cover art by Cathy Gendron; *Clock Face* © by harlowbutler/Shutterstock
Book design by Laura K. Corless

To all who call me Aunt Julie:
Chase, Mallory, Becca, Tori, Harrison, Emma, Evan,
Alex, and Brandon. I love you all to the moon and back.
Always remember—dreams do come true.

acknowledgments

Writing this series has been a true delight. While writing is a solitary activity, getting published is not. Were it not for the following people, you would not be holding this book in your hand.

Tom Colgan, Sarah Blumenstock, Stacy Edwards, Randie Lipkin, Grace House, and everyone else at Berkley Prime Crime. Writing a series at Berkley Prime Crime was a dream of mine for many years. You've helped that dream come true.

Allison Janice, thank you for helping Ruth come to life.

Cathy Gendron, thank you for your wonderful cover art.

My agent, John Talbot. He helps me navigate these waters.

The Wicked Cozy Authors: Jessica Crockett Estevao, Sherry Harris, Liz Mugavero, Edith Maxwell, and Barbara Ross. Your friendship, support, encouragement, and tough love mean the world to me. WickedCozyAuthors.com

The Wicked accomplices: Sheila Connolly, Kim Gray, and Jane Haertel.

My blogmates at Live to Write/Write to Live (nhwn.wordpress.com) and Killer Characters (killercharacters.com).

David and Susan Roberts. My trip to the clock tower was invaluable—thank you both. David and his brother run the

Clockfolk of New England, in case you want to visit real clock-makers.

Sisters in Crime, especially the New England chapter. I am so grateful and proud to be part of this organization.

Mystery Writers of America, another wonderful support organization.

Jason Allen-Forrest, my first reader and dear friend.

Scott Forrest-Allen, thank you for your title help!

The mystery readers I've met while writing this series. I've met you at Crime Bake, at Malice Domestic, at Left Coast Crime, at Bouchercon, online, and at book events. You are the reason I write. Thank you for loving the folks in Orchard as much as I do.

My friends at StageSource, and in the Boston theater community. I love that you are so excited about my alter ego, the mystery writer. Thank you for your support.

Last but not least, I am blessed with an amazing army of friends and family. Thank you all for being part of my life and being part of this adventure.

A special thanks to my parents, Paul and Cindy Hennrikus, for being supportive of my dreams. I am so lucky that you are my parents.

chapter 1

"Time isn't going to move any quicker with you staring at the clocks, Ruth," Nadia Wint said, looking up from her laptop to throw me some side-eye from underneath her black bangs and heavy makeup.

"Today is winding day. Maybe I should get a jump on it," I said. I reached under the front counter of the Cog & Sprocket for the winding keys to the row of banjo clocks we had displayed on the left-hand wall of the shop. They ranged in age, in manufacturer, and in worth. But they were all my pride and joy. Especially since they were all synchronized and running like, well, like clocks.

Nadia reached out and grabbed my upper arm. "Ruth, stop. Dealing with you is bad enough this morning. If you wind all the clocks, Pat is going to jump out of his skin, and I don't need that."

Our social media/communications/marketing maven was right, of course, in her hipster, twenty-going-on-forty way.

Pat, the Cog & Sprocket's general handyman, took his jobs at the shop seriously. Winding day was his, and had been ever since my grandfather died last October. At the very least I needed to wait until Pat came in, then offer my help. Problem was, he wasn't coming in for another hour, and I had nothing else to do. The shop was clean, my apartment upstairs was tidy, and I was too distracted to take on a repair job.

"Why don't you go out for a run?" Nadia said, biting the inside of her cheek. Three times a week I got in my running outfit, filled my water bottle, and stepped outside, determined to get past week two of my 5K running program. Something always distracted me, usually the inevitable temptation of a steaming cup of coffee at the Sleeping Latte. In March I decided to call it my Running for Coffee program, but I hadn't told Nadia that.

"I'm showered and dressed," I whined, slumping gracelessly onto the counter and feeling utterly useless.

"The party starts at noon. Not sure why you felt the need to get dressed by eight. You're not usually a morning person," Nadia said, steadily typing away.

"Nor are you, Nadia."

"You're right. I'll own it," she said, ceasing her relentless typing for a moment to look up at me. "I'm a nervous wreck. I was lying in bed, going through lists in my head, and decided I may as well get up and come over here, where I can actually do something. Tell you what—I could really use one of Nancy's breakfast sandwiches. Would you go down to the Sleeping Latte to pick one up for me?"

Eggs, cheese, bacon on fresh Italian bread, oozing butter. My stomach gurgled at the thought of the sandwich, and I realized I was hungry.

"All right. You win. I'm going to take a walk and stop bothering you," I said, tossing my phone into my going-down-the-street bag with a flourish and a sigh. My going-down-the-street bag contained money, an ID, a notebook, and lip gloss. It weighed twenty pounds less than my normal ready-for-anything bag. It also made a dramatic exit much easier. "I hope that makes you both happy."

The effort was lost on my other morning companion. Bezel, the gray cat who lived with me in my clock shop, gave me a cold, hard stare and then blinked her eyes, hard. Her yowl was less "It will all be okay" support, and more "For the love of Mike, get yourself together, Ruth!" She was, as always, correct. I needed to pull it together. After all, today was just another day. Another day on the path to my dream coming true.

The Clock Tower Signing Ceremony was scheduled for noon. Of course, Nadia was as nervous as I was. This whole extravaganza was her idea, after all.

Well, not the whole thing. The idea of restoring the clock tower, thereby ensuring that my grandfather's dream came true—that was mostly me. Thomas Clagan, G.T. to me—for "Grandpa Thom"—left me his shop, the Cog & Sprocket, when he died last fall. He also left me his lifelong dream, a dream he'd been trying to make a reality for the last few months of his life. How could I not take up that mantle? Especially when it seemed like there were a few people in Orchard who didn't want it to happen. That got my back up and hardened my resolve.

Dreams like this came at a price, and fund-raising had been tough. We'd gotten a few influxes of cash over the past few months, but clock towers are expensive even when we're donating the man power. We were close to cutting the dancing figures—a huge part of the design—when Nadia had had her brainstorm on a dreary April day: "Let's get sponsors."

"Sponsors? Like have banners hanging out the window? Have the figures that come out on the hour carrying signs?"

"No, not those kinds of sponsors. But honestly, that's not a bad idea. I'll file it away in case this doesn't work. No, I'm talking about people paying to etch their names on clock parts. We'll figure out which. Maybe we could have people sign strips of metal with their names and weld them on something? Would that screw things up?"

"What makes you think folks would be willing to pay to have their names where no one could see them?"

"People want a reason to be proud of their town, a part of their community. They want to be a part of that. They want to leave a legacy. And we would social media it up, of course."

"Social media it up" was a Nadia term for taking pictures, writing clever captions, sharing them, and generally creating a buzz. I may have doubted her at one point, but in the past six months, I'd seen what Nadia could do. Not only was the Cog & Sprocket busy beyond any reasonable expectations I may have had, but other businesses in the area were benefiting as well. Nadia had adopted Orchard, and its inhabitants, as her new hometown. She still tried to pretend she was too hipster chic to really care, but I knew better.

"Nadia, I'm not sure . . ."

"Ruth, when are you going to get it? This isn't just about a clock tower. This is about Orchard getting its heart beating again."

"Orchard getting its heart beating again? Did you just come up with that?" I'd said, cocking an eyebrow at her.

"No, Freddie Hamilton wrote it on her blog last week."

"Freddie Hamilton has a blog?" Freddie Hamilton— Orchard native and rising baking superstar over at the Sleeping Latte—was a bit of a flibbertigibbet, mildly put. She and

Nadia were the same age, but whereas I'd trust Nadia with my life, I wouldn't trust Freddie to hold a thought. I couldn't imagine her writing a paragraph, never mind an entire post. She could barely hold up her end of a conversation. That said, the girl could bake.

"You've got to get with it, Ruth," Nadia'd said, smoothing her fingers over her sleek ponytail. "Having a blog isn't that big a deal. In fact, it can be a little old-school. But Freddie is mixing it up, posting photos. Anyway, she took a picture of you polishing up the old bell, and posted that. Not sure if it was you, or the clock tower, but it went viral."

Nadia bent over her phone for a moment and then handed it to me. Sure enough, a lovely picture of me, wild red hair half clamped down by safety glasses, a shop jacket covering my dress, leggings tucked into my Doc Martens.

"It would be swell if someone let me know they were taking my picture," I'd said, feeling a bit exposed. "This is a little frightening."

"Swell? How old are you, anyway? Half the reason it works is because it's an action shot."

"Great. Ruth Clagan in action. Anyway, tell me more about this idea."

"We get some folks to sign up in advance. Make it more expensive closer to the day—let's call it Signing Day. Then the day of, we can get those things Pat uses all the time. The things with the different tips—"

"Dremels?" I said. Not as precise as some of the tools I used, but very handy for a lot of the restoration work we took on.

"Dremels. Right. With the engraving tip. We'll get a few of them and have people etch their names on these strips of metal. We can attach them to something, maybe the clock weights, later. We'll charge different amounts for different-sized panels. Make it a party. Raffle off something or other. It will drum up interest. May get folks to contribute more to the fund."

· "But that sort of etching won't last forever," I said, thinking about the handheld tool we planned to use.

"Of course it won't. But they're easy to use, and that's important. For the next fifty years, people will walk by the clock tower and tell people that their name is up there."

I had to learn never to question Nadia and her schemes. We'd announced Signing Day for the first Saturday in June. Today. We'd thought we would have a dozen or so folks sign up. Instead, we had close to fifty, with dozens more making donations to the fund. It was overwhelming on so many levels. No wonder I hadn't been able to sleep past six this morning. Now Nadia and Bezel were kicking me out of my own shop. Fine. The Sleeping Latte called to me, and who was I not to listen?

"I'll be back," I said, heading out the front door. Nadia barely looked up from her laptop on the counter. Bezel turned and offered me a generous view of her backside as she sauntered lazily toward the back of the shop.

I walked out the front door and stood on the front porch for a full minute, letting the fresh air and small-town charm of Orchard wash over me. The Cog & Sprocket wasn't the largest shop in town, but we did have the best view. We were on the corner where three roads intersected. A river ran behind the shop, the roaring current a constant layer of white noise. I'd come to depend on that sound to help me sleep at night.

Across the street, Been Here, Read That, the newest business on the block, was still dark. Beckett Green, its owner, would be in soon enough to open up. Hopefully our paths wouldn't cross until I'd had a little more coffee. Beckett was trying to be a better citizen of Orchard, but trust was still an issue.

If Been Here, Read That was quiet, the Corner Market was anything but. Ada and Mac Clark's grocery store was open from seven thirty in the morning to nine o'clock in the evening, six days a week. On Sundays they closed at six. The success of the business was both welcome to the Clarks, and overwhelming, especially since their son, Jack, was just six months old. They had hired some help, but I wasn't surprised to see Mac Clark himself sweeping off his front porch. He looked up and waved when he saw me. I waved back and smiled a genuine smile.

The old Town Hall sat in between the two stores. I looked at it, and as it always did, my heart skipped a beat. As a result of a series of legalities I still had trouble wrapping my brain around, I had inherited the building last fall. Kim Gray, the town manager, and I had wrestled over what that ownership meant, but since the New Year, the path had been clear. I created a nonprofit so we could apply for grants. Both Harris University and the town of Orchard were tenants, helping with operating support. I'd used the opportunity to start the renovation of the clock tower. From here, that work was barely visible since the clock wasn't running yet. But I knew the hours that had been spent on this project already, and smiled in anticipation.

The Winding Ceremony was set for June 21, and I knew all too well that the timing was tight. Really tight. The last of the clock pieces had been finished and assembly was set to begin on Monday. My hands ached to hold the tools and to get started. I'd maintained clock towers, and wound them, but I'd never assembled one before. I was thrilled at the opportunity.

Our clock tower wasn't just a clock tower, though. I'd seen only pictures of what it had looked like in its full glory. During World War II, the clock workings had been taken out and melted down to help with the war effort. When they were being put back in the tower in 1953, a spark had caused a fire. The old stone building had survived, but the old wooden clockface had been destroyed, and the clock parts all collapsed in on themselves. When we'd talked about rebuilding it we'd considered just fixing the clock for a minute. But only for a minute.

The rest of the clock tower—the hourly bell, and the figures that came out of the doors one level down from the clockface, on the street side of the tower, welcoming the new hour—were what made our clock tower so special. The craftsmanship of that tower was more European and had been designed by my great-great-grandfather Simon Clagan, one of the founding fathers of Orchard. His son, Harry, hadn't inherited his father's skill as a clockmaker. For some reason, that seemed to skip generations. My father was proof of that. But my great-grandfather Harry had been a good salesman and had convinced the town elders that putting the community to work building the tower was a public good and that it would bring in tourists. He'd been right on both counts. The loss of the tower, less than a generation after it had been completed, had become less painful as time went by, since so few people remembered it in operation, but my family always remembered. Rebuilding it had been an obsession that my grandfather had passed down to me.

Now, here I was, trying to pull it off in six months. Fortunately, I wasn't working alone. Far from it. I had two other clockmakers on the case. My stepgrandmother, Caroline Adler, was working in the shop, keeping up with repairs and inventory. Her mentor and friend, Zane Phillips, had moved down to Orchard to recuperate after a difficult December, and he'd stayed on to help. In fact, he'd moved into the guest quarters G.T. had put in his workshop out at the cottage where Caroline lived.

I worried that Zane was working too hard, but Caroline assured me that she hadn't seen him so happy in years. Not only was Zane helpful in getting the clock workings ready to go, he had taken on the responsibility for manufacturing the figurines that would come out on the hour. He'd been carving them based on old schematics, and on my grandfather's drawings. He wouldn't let me see what they looked like, though today was going to be the unveiling of a model of one of them.

"Good morning, G.T.," I said softly, looking up at the top of the tower. "We're almost there."

So many folks thought I was being altruistic in my efforts to rebuild the clock tower, but they were wrong. I was being selfish. Working on this made me feel closer to my grandfather and helped me feel like he was still here, supporting me. I took a deep breath, a little ragged this time, and stepped down the front stairs onto the sidewalk.

chapter 2

I strolled toward the Sleeping Latte, slowing down in front of the barbershop and peering through the window. I wasn't surprised to see the building empty, but I was still disappointed. Not that I needed a haircut. Far from it. Flo made it her business to keep my curls somewhat at bay. No, it was Flo's nephew, Ben Clover, whom I hoped to see. The tall, handsome barber had become the de facto general contractor on the clock tower project after his aunt had decided to start cutting hair again, and he wasn't needed in his shop as often. Well, that wasn't the only reason he'd been helping me with the clock tower.

Ben and I had shared a New Year's kiss that had started the year off right, if unexpectedly. We went public with our relationship on Valentine's Day, when Ben kissed me in front of the clock tower, a bouquet of wildflowers he gave me pressed between us. Since Nancy Reed, Pat's wife, was walking by at the time, it was all over Orchard within the hour. By now it was old news.

Old news for Orchard. Not for me. Not for Ben. Both of us had been divorced and had come back to Orchard to recover and regroup. Neither of us talked about our exes except in the broadest terms. We focused on getting to know each other for who we were in the present, undefined by those old relationships.

"Isn't that weird?" Moira Reed had said after she'd asked about his ex-wife, and I had no new details to offer her. Moira and I had been friends since we were kids, when I'd spent summers in Orchard with my grandparents. Moira and I had a shorthand for conversations that I didn't have with anyone else.

"Weird?"

"Anytime I date someone, I want to know all the details of his past," she'd said, breaking off a piece of the cookie on my plate and swallowing it before I could protest.

"Why? What does it really matter? My husband left me for someone else. Ben doesn't need to know every detail of our marriage to know that hurt me deeply."

"Don't you want to know why his wife left him?"

"It doesn't really have anything to do with me," I'd said, taking a pious sip of my tea.

I'd been lying, of course. I wanted to know more about Ben's ex-wife. Beyond the fact that her name was Martha Esme and she lived in New York. But he'd been reticent to talk about his past, and his mood had gotten dark when I'd probed. So, I'd stopped, too happy to risk ruining our time together. Even when I saw her name on the return address of a birthday card to Ben two days ago, I'd brushed it off. Especially since it had arrived three weeks after the big day. Yesterday, when Ben said he had to make a trip overnight, surely that was a coincidence? He'd texted me three times and promised he'd be back this morning. I believed him.

I needed to believe him if this was going to work.

"Ruthie, give me a hand, would you?" Flo's hybrid SUV pulled in along the curb.

She turned on the flashers and jumped out, going around the back of the car. Flo's outfit today was subdued. Well, subdued for Flo. Black leggings, yellow and black tunic, purple scarf in her hair. Her hot pink sneakers were the final clue— this wasn't the outfit Flo was going to wear this afternoon. Public events warranted at least three-inch platforms. Despite the early-morning hour, it was busy enough in Orchard that a double-parked car on a two-lane street was challenging. I looked over at Been There, Read That convinced I'd see Beckett peering out, cell phone in hand. Double-parking was one of Beckett's favorite reasons for speed-dialing the Orchard Police Department. So very neighborly of him.

Flo had spared no expense on her car, and the back hatch rose slowly at the push of a button. I walked over and peered in the back. Bundles of towels, a couple of boxes of supplies for the shop.

"I was going to drive around back and unload, but then I saw you."

"Beckett would have a fit," I chided gently, reaching in and grabbing one of the boxes.

"Beckett can suck an egg," Flo said, picking up a pile of towels. "Pile it up by the front door. Don't look at me like that. He's a pill of the first order—you know that. Anyway, I need help. I'm an old woman."

"You're an old woman." I laughed. Flo was anywhere between fifty and eighty, but I'd never call her old. "Puh-leeze." I picked up another box and carried it over to the front door. The boxes were heavy, and I was glad Flo had asked for help. I walked back and picked up the third box. Flo didn't try and stop me. As soon as I cleared the hatch, she lowered it.

"Do me a favor—stay with this stuff while I go park the car and open up the shop," Flo said, pulling out without waiting for an answer.

I looked down at one of the bundles of towels, which were deep purple. The transformation was complete. Flo had retired over a year ago, leaving Ben to run the shop. As I'd recently learned, it was as much to give Ben something to focus on after his marriage broke up as it was because Flo was ready to move on. Ben had renovated the shop and opened for business. Problem was that he'd renovated the charm right out of the shop, and Flo's client base stopped visiting. It was just a little too hip for Orchard.

When she came back last fall, she made noises about running a drugstore on the other side of the shop and leaving the haircuts completely to Ben, but that didn't last long. She started cutting a few of her old clients, and by March she was taking care of most of the hair appointments. The black and gray décor in the barbershop didn't last long either. She'd painted the walls right after the New Year, and moved the furniture around. Slowly but surely color was creeping back in. I noticed the other bundle of towels was a celadon green. Maybe color was doing more than creeping.

I looked over at the shop next door, Flo's Emporium, named for Flo but run by Ben, theoretically. They'd hired Jason Scott to help out, and he'd taken over the day-to-day operations, including hiring part-time staff. Not that the shop was that busy. Flo and Ben were careful not to overlap with the Corner Market or Been There, Read That, which meant that the shop carried a variety of over-the-counter medications, crafts, greeting cards, office supplies, and hair care supplies. Jason had a relationship with a pharmacy in Marytown, and he'd bring over prescriptions for pickup—a service that meant a lot to the older residents in town. He offered advice on alternative remedies as well, and provided advice and a friendly ear for the residents. Though he'd been in town for only two months, he was starting to rival Nancy Reed for the position of town gossip.

I saw the lights in the barbershop start to come on, and I picked up one of the boxes. I stood as Flo opened the door.

"By the sinks is fine," Flo said, picking up a bundle of towels and carrying them toward the back of the shop. "I'm going to run these through the washer before the day starts. New towels always have a bit of lint on them. Just doesn't do to add lint to a wash and set."

"I like the colors. Was pink sold out?"

"Oh, you. Green and purple are very hip. You taught me that. The gray ones have seen better days."

"Can you give us some of the old ones for the clock tower project? They'd be helpful to have around."

"Already thought of that. Ben grabbed a couple of stacks. He's recycling the rest."

"Ben's here?"

"Of course. Got back early evening. Stayed out at the house with me, since I needed his help picking out tiles for the new bathroom. We had plenty of time, since he was home so early. He was barely gone, come to think of it."

Subtlety was not a core value for Flo. Part of me wanted to jump in. Did he visit his ex-wife? What was she like? Did Flo think he still loved her? But I stopped myself. If I wanted to have these questions answered, I needed to ask Ben myself.

If I asked him, though, it meant that I needed to be willing to answer questions about my ex-husband. The fact that he'd left me for another woman was known around town, thanks to Nancy Reed, so people didn't pry about more of the details. Thinking back over the last six months, since Ben and I officially starting dating, it was odd that we'd never talked about the what-went-wrong angle of our marriages. I'd been so careful not to talk about Eric that I'd stomped down my curiosity about Ben's ex-wife.

Eric Evan. Eight years ago I'd promised to stay with him for better or for worse. As it turned out, Eric ended up being the very definition of the worst. When he left me for his graduate student, I'd been devastated. But now we were closing in on a year since our divorce was final, and thinking about Eric no longer hurt. In fact, I'd realized recently that what I mostly felt about my divorce was relief. I'd thought I was happy being a faculty wife, living on campus, working on clocks as an avocation that was tolerated, but not fully supported, by my husband. I'd learned the art of small talk, wore a uniform of tasteful, well-fitted clothes, tamed my hair into a bun every day, and plastered a smile on my face. Dinner was ready every night we were home, and my social life was worked around his schedule. I'd made some friends, but Eric got most of them in the divorce.

The few friends I had retained were nothing but supportive of my new life. I wore leggings and dresses. My Doc Marten boots had been upcycled by Moira, who stenciled cogs on them in soft silver. Sometimes I ate crackers and cheese for dinner and didn't feel even a little guilty. But most meals were shared with my new hometown folks: Ben, Caroline, the Reed family. Or I ate at the Sleeping Latte, where you are never really alone. Recently I'd decided to get rid of my old faculty-wife wardrobe. Partly out of necessity and partly as a symbolic final act of shutting the door on my previous life. If I am honest with myself though, few things from my past life fit me anymore.

"Ruth, could you hand me that bundle of towels?" Flo said, standing in the door of the laundry area.

"Sure, sorry," I said, shaking myself back to the present and picking up the bundle and bringing it over.

"Since there's still room, I may as well run a full load," she said, adding the towels into the front loader. "This high-capacity washer is really something, isn't it? I never would have sprung for one this nice, but I'm glad Ben did. Saves water in the long run."

"Will you need all these towels?" I asked.

"It's Saturday. Busy all around, but since we're closing at noon for a couple of hours, we've got an extra busy morning. Ben is even coming in to give a hand."

"You're closing for the Signing Ceremony? That is so sweet," I said, touched.

"Ruthie, by now you know me well enough. Nothing about me is sweet. I wouldn't miss the Signing Ceremony. I can't wait to get my name on one of those clock weights. I also wouldn't miss seeing Kim Gray's face for anything in the world."

"So, you think she'll really show up this time?" I asked. Kim Gray, the town manager, had somehow avoided coming to any events hosted by the Cog & Sprocket.

"She's an idiot if she doesn't. Course, she *is* an idiot, so maybe she won't show her face. Don't look shocked—you think she's an idiot too. Time she came around and realized that she's been outplayed. Everyone in town wants the clock tower to get operating. You've made it a symbol of Orchard.

She needs to get on board and enjoy the ride." Flo closed the door of the washer and walked over to get the laundry detergent. Low phosphate, earth friendly. No doubt Ben's handiwork, trying to make a beauty shop as green as possible.

"Well, if it's the symbol of Orchard, that's Nadia's work, not mine. She has been social media–ing every step of the way. We have people who come into the shop to see the model in person, because all she shows on Instagram and Facebook are parts."

"She may be good at marketing, but she's got something to market, and that makes all the difference. You've made folks care about something good." Flo closed the detergent door and hit a few buttons.

I walked over and gave her a hug. "What would I do without you, Flo?" I said.

She gave me a quick squeeze and then pushed me back, holding on to my shoulders.

"You'll never need to know, because I'm here for good. Now, let me take a look at that hair. I've got a few minutes, so let's get it tamed. No buts about it. We need you to look your best today."

chapter 3

My walk to the Sleeping Latte had a spring in my step. As much as I resisted Flo's fussing with my hair, I loved the way it looked after she was done. Instead of the barely tamed mop I now had an artfully designed do that looked like I'd pulled it back and casually pinned it up. She'd added enough hairspray to ensure it would last through the rest of the day. After I promised twice and crossed my heart that I would wear more makeup than normal, Flo let me go, taking only another hug as payment.

Flo, and others, gave me credit for pulling Orchard together, but I didn't deserve it. Orchard had always been a place with a lot of heart. The Clagan Clock Tower project was something we could all focus on. Besides that, it was fun for people to think about. A lot of work for those of us in the trenches, but a lot of fun. Fun was underrated. I hadn't had a lot of fun in my twenties. Turning thirty started a new adventure, and I'd found out that fun was a big part of that.

"What have I said to you about always carrying your water bottle with you?" Jason Scott stepped out of the doorway of Flo's Emporium.

"Jason, you're going to give me a heart attack one of these days!"

"Sorry about that. First time I've ever been accused of being stealthy. Maybe I should thank you for the compliment?" Jason was a big man. Solid and broad shouldered, with a graying goatee and shaved head. He was a fitness freak and was thrilled when Beckett offered free "Been There, Read That" water bottles after the town banned the sale of bottled water. They were nice bottles, so we all used them. Jason was the water cheering squad, reminding us to refill our bottles three times a day.

I knew that Flo and Ben thought the world of Jason, but I didn't share their enthusiasm. Something about him reminded me of my ex-husband. Lovely to talk to in person, but guaranteed to start up the gossip mill the minute you were out of earshot. Butter wouldn't melt in his mouth. I didn't trust that much charm in a man. When he wasn't wearing his uniform of flat-front khakis and button-down shirts he was wearing athletic tights and cycling shirts that put his heavily muscled frame on neon display. I was grateful he was wearing a button-down—the shirt of the day was lavender and white striped—since the image of Jason in his skintight cycling clothes was something I didn't need to see this early in the morning.

"Earth to Ruth. You were a million miles away. Usually are."

"Am I?" I said, determined not to get defensive. Were I to be completely honest, I'd have to admit Jason was right. Daydreaming was my special skill. I preferred calling it "unencumbered thinking." I found that not grounding my thoughts let me come up with unexpected solutions, a useful trait in a clockmaker with high aspirations.

I realized that Jason was waiting for me to continue the conversation. He usually was. He was a pleasant person and quite gregarious, but never overshared about himself. I always assumed if someone wanted me to know something they'd tell me in due course. Jason tested that assumption, but I held firm.

"Are you coming to the Signing Ceremony today?" I asked.

"I'm going to try," he said. "As soon as business calms down I'll put a sign up and run over. Everyone who's anyone is going to be there."

"All the requisite speech-makers will be there," I said. "It's a warm-up for the Winding Ceremony at the end of the month. Orchard comes out to support its own. And we love a reason for a party."

"It starts at noon?"

"The speeches start at noon, then we'll have folks signing and eating cookies until around two. Then a cleanup, and the cocktail party at five out on the portico. We need to set up the hall right afterward. There was a glee club concert that had to be rescheduled—"

"The director got sick," Jason said. "I volunteer with them. It was a nightmare, having to tell folks that we were canceling at the last minute." He shuddered at the memory.

"Yes, well, Jimmy Murphy asked if they could use the Town Hall tonight. We needed to move things around a bit and create a gap in the afternoon so we could help turn the space into a concert hall."

"I know the glee club is really grateful," he said. "There's a call out for folks to come by around four and help set up."

"That's good. We'll have a lot of tables that need to be moved. And the refreshments will need to be cleaned up, of course."

"What's on the menu?"

"I'm not on that committee," I said. "That's up to greater talents than I. Speaking of which, I should stop by the Sleeping Latte. See you this afternoon?"

"I'll try my best," Jason said, giving nothing away.

Coming into the Sleeping Latte always made me smile. The building itself had always been an aberration in our sleepy New England town. Neon pink, blue, and lots of chrome in a sea of white clapboard, stone, and brick. The warm diner décor was hipster cozy, working with the most recent renovation that had made it look like a '50s hunting lodge. Moira had bought it at a bargain price when the previous owner had realized high-end coffee with pretentious food didn't work in the Berkshires, especially in the off-season. Moira still served the high-end coffee, but added regular coffee and a variety of teas. She recently started serving Italian sodas and shrubs—a specialty drink made with her father's homemade syrup concoctions. Shrubs were my new favorite discovery. Vinegar, fruit, sugar, herb mixes, made into syrup and mixed with seltzer water. I was always happy to be one of Pat Reed's tasters, and was delighted to give him a shelf in my refrigerator for his experiments. Who knew his latest seasonal concoction—cider vinegar, rosemary, and blueberry—would be so delicious?

My favorite part of the Sleeping Latte is the smells. Nancy Reed had been part of the success of the shop from the beginning, and her breakfast sandwiches were to die for. When Nancy got a seat on the Board of Selectmen, however, her time became limited. Then Jack Clark was born, and Mac asked Nancy to help run the Corner Market, and she had even less time. Moira was forced to hire someone else to help in the Sleeping Latte kitchen.

I took a deep inhale. Yum. The gates of heaven surely smelled like this. Cinnamon, caramelized sugar, tomato sauce, bread—the mixture shouldn't be so intoxicating. I caught a glimpse of the kitchen magician herself, Frederica "Freddie" Hamilton, as she came through the kitchen door with a tray of goodies to replenish supplies. She looked as harried as ever, with her hair held up and back with a bandanna, her face brushed with flour marks, and her apron covered with smears of food. She caught my eye and went to wave. Unfortunately, one of the scones she was holding tipped off of her suddenly unbalanced tray and landed in front of the counter. She had the good grace to look embarrassed and went back to the task at hand.

Moira Reed appeared from behind the curtain and picked up the errant scone. She turned and looked at me, shrugging her shoulders. "She's a flipping disaster," she said, leaning in and whispering in my ear.

"Maybe. But she's a genius baker," I said, eyeing the pastry display. "How long was that scone on the ground? Do you think it's safe to eat?"

"You're not eating food off the ground," Moira said. "Let me get you a fresh one. And a cup of coffee?"

"I really shouldn't," I said, patting the slight roll at the bottom of my stomach. Freddie's baked goods were taking their toll.

"But you will. Go sit by the window. I'll be right over. I could use a break."

I walked over to the table by the window and put my bag on one of the chairs. I texted Nadia that I was going to be a little while longer. *Take your time,* she texted back. I could sense her relief in her text. While Moira was getting the coffee, I noticed that a few of the tables hadn't been bused. This time of year was a tough one for businesses that depended on student help. The gap between the end of the school year and the beginning of summer term meant no student workers. I walked over and grabbed the tub that had been left on top of the wastebasket, inviting people to bus their own tables. Would that some people actually got the hint.

I gathered dishes and didn't stop until the tub was filled. I walked it back to the kitchen.

"What are you doing?" Freddie asked, squinting at me through a cloud of flour.

"A few of the tables needed to be cleared, so I took care of it," I said. I walked over to the dishwasher and opened it. Half-full. I couldn't tell if it was dirty or clean, but decided that the dishes on hand would make it full and soon enough they'd all be clean.

"Thanks, Ruth. You're a savior. I'm having trouble keeping up with it all this morning."

"Has it been busy?"

"Busy? That's one way to put it. I'm trying to get food ready for the party this afternoon and also keep the front of the shop in stock, plus special orders. I keep thinking I'm getting ahead, but then someone else comes in and buys a bag of scones or a dozen muffins, and I'm behind again."

"Your baked goods are famous," I said. I wasn't exaggerating. Freddie had become an Internet sensation when Nadia had uploaded a dozen short videos of her, calling them simply "Freddie Bakes." Bake she did. With her short, dark curly hair, brown eyes, carved cheekbones, and long legs, Freddie could have been a model. She seemed quite unaware of how stunning she was and did little to show her looks off, preferring to wear overalls, tank tops, and high-top sneakers instead of catwalk fashions and stiletto heels.

"Well, I don't really mind being busy," Freddie said, wiping her brow with the back of her hand and leaving yet another streak of flour on her face. "I can't keep up with today, is all. Thanks for helping out."

"My pleasure. I'm going to run the dishwasher through. Make sure to unload it when it's done. They probably need more cups out front."

I looked over and noticed Freddie back at her mixer, adding more ingredients to the large bowl.

"Freddie, did you hear me?"

"What? Oh, sorry, no, I wasn't listening. Trying to get these cookies in the fridge—they need to chill for an hour. I want to get them ready for this afternoon."

I sighed and wiped my hands on the dish towel by the sink. I grabbed the empty dish tubs. "The dishes will be done soon. I'll tell the people out front." I walked back out to the front of the store.

"Tuck, cups are in the dishwasher. Should be done soon," I said.

"Thanks, Ms. Clagan. We're running low," Tuck Powers said. He didn't look me in the eye, but kept cleaning the milk frothing machine. I sighed and didn't bother to try and chat. Tuck and Nadia had broken up a few weeks ago, and I knew Tuck blamed me. I guess I was partially at fault, since I never thought Tuck was good enough for Nadia, and the goings-on around New Year's proved that. While I didn't encourage Nadia, I didn't discourage her either. But I never wished Tuck ill. Hopefully he'd realize that soon.

"Where have you been?" Moira said, hitting a button on her phone and slipping it into the pocket of her apron. "Not busing tables again? How many times do I have to tell you, you don't work here?"

"Listen, you people keep feeding me for free. I need to earn my keep somehow."

"Well, today I'm not going to stop you," she said, following me to an open table, carrying two coffees and two scones. "Tuck and Freddie are the entire staff right now."

"What happened to, what was her name, Edith?" I said, peeking into the bag.

"Edith called in. Said she was sick. Sick of being inside on a beautiful day, more like it. At least Tuck is here. He is like two people out front."

"I'm glad he is working out," I said. "You were good to give him a job after everything that happened."

Moira shrugged her shoulders and added a spoonful of sugar to her coffee. "We all need to get a second chance at some point. He's a good kid, deserves a break."

"Kid? You realize he's only a few years younger than we are?"

"A few years that feel like a hundred. He makes me feel ancient. He calls me Ms. Reed."

"Calls me Ms. Clagan. Anyway, I'm glad he's here." I took a sip of my coffee and closed my eyes. I love a good cup of coffee, and this was one of the best. After a beat I opened my eyes again. Moira had turned her phone over and was checking it for messages. "How's Freddie working out?" I asked.

Moira sighed, gently tapping her finger on the table. "I still curse Mum every day for making me hire her," she said. She took a bite of the scone on her plate and chewed it slowly, taking a sip of coffee to wash it down. "Then I eat her food and thank the angels of baking for bringing her here so she can use her skills in the kitchen."

"Well, with Nancy being so busy around town, you need her in the kitchen, right?"

"I do, for sure. But it would be nice if she could multitask. Sometimes it's hard to realize she is Fred Hamilton's daughter. That man is the king of keeping a million projects going at once."

"He is indeed," I said. "We're lucky to have him working on the clock tower."

"He's lucky you gave him a job after Kim tried to have him blackballed." Kim Gray, the town manager, had the power to fire people from town contracts. Whereas her power would have gone unchecked a few months ago when she ended the Hamilton family contract, these days there was a strong contingent in town who took every opportunity to question that power publicly. Inadvertently I'd joined in with those ranks.

"Well, your parents gave him a good reference. Besides, he'd worked with my grandfather over the years, helping to do winding jobs when they needed help."

"Winding jobs. I'm glad he can help you with those. The day you had me help was enough for me. My shoulders still hurt. I can't believe people do that every single week."

"It isn't that bad," I said. I was lying. Pulleys and machinery offset some of the work, but the tension was still high. Hundreds of revolutions a week. It was hard work, but I loved it. She cocked an eyebrow at me over her coffee cup.

"We'll get you in winding shape soon enough." I laughed, taking a big bite of my scone.

"Who knew your job was so physically exhausting? I know it was a mental exercise, especially after that talk you gave last month at the library."

"I still think it was too much detail," I said.

"I don't. Harriet says they've had a run on all the books you talked about ever since. I think that's partly why today is so popular. Folks want to see the inner workings all laid out before you put them together."

"I can't believe Nadia is willing to wear a camera on her head for the next six weeks so she can get footage for a mini documentary," I said. Her first idea was to have me wear it, but between the curls and the other devices I'd be wearing on my head at any given time as I worked, we decided that wasn't a good idea. Nadia volunteered herself and insisted it was going to be video gold. Gone was the discontented twenty-year-old I'd met six months ago. Now she was one of the most valued parts of the Cog & Sprocket.

Moira and I both heard a light tap on the window beside us and saw Jeff Paisley give us both a wave, a wink, and a smile that crinkled the normally smooth dark skin around his eyes and mouth. Well, Moira got the wink. Orchard's chief of police is a job that, on paper, shouldn't be particularly taxing. But that was on paper. The last few months he'd seen more action than some small-town police chiefs see in their entire careers.

"How's that going?" I said to Moira.

"What?"

"Don't even try. You and Jeff. Remember, we promised we'd use each other as sounding boards."

"Well, then, be prepared, because I'm going to ask you about Ben. How are Jeff and I doing? Well, to say he is the kindest guy I've ever dated would be an understatement. He's incredibly thoughtful. And he's dead sexy."

"Sounds like it is going well, then."

"Yup. So, of course, I'm doing what I can to screw it up. Normally, I would have had a torrid affair and broken up by now. Jeff wants to take it slow, and I'm trying."

"Is his mother still planning on visiting?"

"She's here. Got here yesterday afternoon. I had dinner over there last night."

"What's she like?"

"She seems really nice, but very protective of her son. I got the distinct impression that if I hurt him, she'll take me out."

I laughed. My own mother was distant, at best, so I envied that fierce maternal love. But Moira's mother, Nancy, treated me like her own daughter, so I was getting used to the feeling of being loved.

As if she were reading my mind, Moira told me that her mother had picked up Jeff's mother this morning. "They're spending the day together," she said.

"Yikes."

"Yikes indeed. Mum's bringing her to the ceremony." Moira paused. "I hope Mum and Kim don't have a fistfight in the middle of the ceremony. Don't laugh. They've been going at it lately. I suspect my mother getting on the Board of Selectmen was the worst thing that happened to Kim in a long, long time."

"Nancy and Jimmy Murphy are quite the team."

"They are. He's got the political skills. Mum is trying to hone his killer instincts, so they can go after Kim and get her out once and for all."

"Nancy's been working on that for weeks."

"I know. She's stopped talking about it at home, but I know she's got something up her sleeve. All right, enough about all of that. How's Ben?"

I sighed and told Moira about Ben's trip and my suspicion that he went to see his ex-wife.

"What happened with them, anyway?" Moira asked.

"I don't know. We haven't really talked about our exes," I said, looking out the window at the passing cars.

"Still?"

"I know, I know. It's just that, the Ruth who married Eric Evan? I don't even know her anymore. I don't think Ben would have dated her. I'm so relieved that Ben is nothing like Eric, don't get me wrong, but Eric took the lead when we first met, and I let him. Ben doesn't take the lead, and I don't want to rock the boat."

"Ruthie, you have to talk to him."

"I do. My challenge is that he may say that he'd go back to his ex if he had the chance. And that might break my heart." I took a deep breath.

Moira reached over and grabbed my hand. "Hey, he's crazy about you. Everyone can see that. But you've got to talk to him if this is worrying you. You know that, right?"

"I know. It's only that things are going so well. I'm dating the nicest, best-looking guy in Orchard—"

"Hey there—"

"Fine. *One of the* best-looking guys in Orchard. My life is going really well with my work. I feel like I'm a part of this town. I don't want anything to screw this up, you know?"

"I do know, but you still need to talk to him."

"I will," I said, forcing a smile. "After today is over, I will."

chapter 4

A new wave of customers came in, and Moira had to go back to work.

"Want me to stay and help out?" I asked, stacking my empty plate on top of hers.

"No, I want you to go back to your shop and make sure you're ready for this afternoon. I know you have a million things to do."

"I don't, not really. Between Pat and Nadia, things are in good shape. But you're right, I should go back and check in. See you later?"

"Try and keep me away," Moira said, giving me a quick hug.

I walked out of the Sleeping Latte, considering continuing my procrastination tour by going over to the Corner Market. I held back. I might need something to do a little later.

As I turned toward the shop, I noticed a Mini Cooper pulling up beside me. My heart stopped for a moment, but then I exhaled. Eric's car was a different color. I forced myself to relax. I'd gotten a letter from him last week. A letter, not an e-mail or a note. Heavy-duty stationery, his initials in the upper left-hand corner, complete with his return address. I hadn't opened it yet and was still wrestling with the why of that. Our divorce was final, and I hadn't seen him in months. I really didn't want to. Did I?

Nancy Reed spilled out of the passenger side of the Mini, calling my name.

"Ruth, come meet Janet Paisley."

"I'd love to," I said.

I waited until the other woman got out of the car and walked around toward me. It gave me a moment to take her in. I could see where Jeff got his height. Janet was as tall as I was. Her short hair was natural, with flecks of gray weaving through her tight curls. Whereas her son was slow to smile, Janet's face broke into a wide grin as she walked toward me with both her hands outstretched. I took both her brown hands in mine and squeezed them.

"Ruth, how wonderful to meet you!"

"It's nice to meet you, Mrs. Paisley," I said, and couldn't help but return her smile.

"Mrs. Paisley. Bah. Mrs. Paisley was my mother-in-law, a formidable woman who scared me to death. I'm Janet."

"Janet, welcome to Orchard."

"Thank you. When Jeff told me about this Signing Ceremony, I thought, When better to go and visit his new home?"

"Are you alone?" I asked. I knew that Jeff's father had passed, but he had two sisters, and they both had families.

"Janet is on a reconnaissance mission," Nancy said.

"She's here to check us all out, especially Moira, and report back."

Janet laughed. "All wonderful things to report. Orchard is a lovely town."

"Wait until you meet Kim Gray," Nancy said.

"Between you and Jeff, I'm prepared to meet the Princess of Darkness." Both women howled at the inside joke.

"Well, even though we could sit and talk for hours, we have work to do," Nancy said. "We've got food to prepare."

"Freddie's working on it," I said.

Nancy sighed. "Of course she is. But I'll have to finish it, unless she's had a personality transplant. No worries. Janet said she'd help."

"Putting our guest to work, I see," I said.

"I wouldn't have it any other way," Janet said. "Now, let's get these supplies unloaded, and then you can show me the kitchen."

I offered to help, but both women waved me off. "You know what you could do? Move Janet's car out back in the alley?"

"Afraid Beckett will make Jeff give his own mother a parking ticket?" I said, taking the keys from Janet.

"Well, I'm never going to tell him this, but today he has a point. Better to leave the parking spaces for the visitors. Of which there will be many, so get back to your shop. This is your show."

"No pressure," I said as I felt the nervousness I had been ignoring all morning creep up behind me.

"Lots of pressure, for all of us. But we've got this," Nancy said, leaning in to give me a one-armed squeeze. I watched as the two women walked into the Sleeping Latte, chatting as if they'd known each other for years.

• • •

Getting into the car brought back a flood of memories. The squat and scoop was very different than me getting into my Scion xB, which was more of a slight bend of the knee to slide in. Much as I loved my green car, driving the Mini was fun. Nancy was smart to ask me, since getting to the access road behind the stores was a little challenging, and we'd need to park this car out of the way. Since it was so small, it fit between my store and the barbershop. The door didn't have a lot of clearance, but I was able to shimmy my way out of the driver's side.

As soon as I stepped into the alley, the jingling collar of Ben's dog, Blue, let me know he was close by. I turned and saw both of my guys standing back by the Dumpster behind the barbershop. Ben was holding Blue's collar, and I prepared myself for the full assault of the Australian shepherd. Blue launched himself at me the instant he was free, snuffling and wagging frantically as he wound himself around my legs. I stopped it the only way I could, by squatting down and putting my arms around the dog, nuzzling his neck and showering the top of his head with kisses. He dropped the ball he was carrying and returned a few of my kisses by licking my jaw.

"Hey, save some of that for me," Ben said, appearing next to me. He put his hand out and pulled me up into his open arms. His kiss was deep, and my knees were weak. I pulled back first, staying in his arms but looking into his blue eyes.

"It's good to see you," I said.

"Just good?" Ben said.

"Really good," I said, kissing him. "How was your trip?"

I was immediately sorry I asked. Ben's grip loosened and he stepped back, looking down at Blue and patting him absentmindedly.

"Complicated."

"I'm a good listener," I said.

"I know you are, babe," he said. "It's a long story, and I'd like to tell it to you. Maybe later tonight?"

"Sounds like a plan," I said, letting my breath out. "Do you need to work in the Emporium today?"

Ben smiled and looked relieved that the subject was changed. "Jason's on it."

"He's a big help," I said.

Ben looked over his shoulder toward the shop and then back at me. "He is. Honestly, we couldn't run the store without him. But he's way overqualified to be stocking shelves. We're going to lose him as soon as he gets his Massachusetts licensing straightened out and he can get a full-time job as a pharmacist. Better him than me though—my patience for worrying about the number of antacids to order is limited."

"Well, it is nice for folks to have someone around who can answer questions."

Ben picked up a tennis ball Blue had abandoned and pitched it into the woods. We both watched Blue run into the underbrush, his fluffy bottom wiggling with pure joy.

"Yeah, it is. He's knowledgeable about homeopathic medicine as well. The new service we're offering, where he brings folks prescriptions back from Marytown? It is going well, though not a ton of folks are taking advantage of it yet."

"Well, I know that Caroline and Zane are both grateful. Saves them the trip. Are you glad you hired him?"

"Sure, of course. We aren't ever going to be best friends, but he fits right into Orchard." Blue came running back with the ball.

"He's a font of information, that's for sure," I said.

"Information, that's a nice way of saying it. More like gossip." Ben wrestled the ball from Blue and threw it again.

"I did notice that he and Nancy are spending time together," I said, smiling. "Did you know Jeff's mother is in town?" I gestured to the Mini.

"Is that her car? Where is she?"

"She and Nancy are at the Sleeping Latte, cooking for this afternoon."

"So they are getting along well?"

"Seems so. Is the car all right parked here? I want to leave room in the back for Pat and Zane to both park."

"Yeah, it should be fine. I like the color. What would you call it?"

"Absolute Black Metallic. As opposed to Midnight Black Metallic."

"How do you know that so specifically?"

"My ex drove a Mini. He suffered over color choices for a week. As did I, since he was never one to suffer in silence." I looked down at my feet.

"Huh. You know, that's the most personal detail about him you've ever told me."

"Is it? Really? Ah, well, we can add that to the later discussion."

Ben smiled and drew me close again, running his finger down the side of my face. "Sounds like a plan. Speaking of which, are we meeting at the Cog, or at the Town Hall?"

"Why don't you come over to the Cog? I'm sure I'll have a ton of stuff to bring over. I've got to check in with Zane."

"Is he bringing the figures with him?"

We'd decided to recreate the dancing figures from the original clock tower, and Zane had taken on the project with gusto. In addition to mad clock making skills, Zane was an artist and had built most of his clock cases himself. I'd agreed, though the cost of creating the figures had added more to the budget. In order to pay for this aspect of the project, we'd auctioned off the final figure online, which would be carved to the specifications of the winner of the auction. It was another Nadia idea that was much more successful than I ever could have imagined, raising $25,000.

I still couldn't believe it. Twenty-five thousand dollars. Nadia's social media efforts helped and were picked up by several media outlets. The Berkshires had their share of well-heeled summer residents, and more than a few apparently liked the idea of having their face carved into a figurine on Orchard's clock tower. The last couple of hours of the auction had been wild, with the dollar amount going higher and higher until the last-minute winner came in. Once the bidding was over we got to see the name of the winner.

Beckett Green.

Those two words had taken the wind out of our happy balloon. I'd never forget Nancy's reaction to the news.

"I have to see *Beckett Green* dancing outside the clock tower every hour?" Nancy had said, her tone matching all of our moods. "Less than thrilled" was a polite way of putting it.

"He won't be dancing," I said. "More like coming out of the door underneath the clock and spinning around a few times."

"I have to see Beckett Green spinning outside the clock tower every hour?" she asked.

"Now, Nancy, Beckett's already invested a lot into this project," Pat said. "He gave us the grant match in December—"

"So we wouldn't run him out of town on a rail," Nancy said, obviously flustered.

"You're the one who got him to ante up," Pat said.

"True. I was hoping he'd learned his lesson, but he's still a royal pain."

"He is that," Pat agreed.

"Well, I guess the best we can hope for is Zane's creative license with the carving," I said. "Maybe he'll make him look not so Beckett-like." Not that Beckett was an ugly man, by any means. It's just that once you knew him, his personality made you wince every time you saw his face. I wasn't thrilled at the idea of seeing my dream project include a spinning Beckett, but a girl had to do what a girl had to do. The Clagan Clock Tower project needed an infusion of cash.

"Ruth, come back to me," Ben said, gently snapping me out of our memories. He was smiling at me, having gotten used to my zoning out. It was to his credit that he'd never taken it personally. "What are you thinking about?"

"I'm thinking about what I've done to get this project funded so far. And what I still have to do." I frowned slightly.

"It will be all worth it," Ben said, smiling encouragingly and taking my hand. "When do we get to see these figures anyway? What did he finally decide to do? Last I heard he was painting them. I can't wait to see what they are going to look like."

"Me either. He is bringing a model of the one of my grandmother Mae. The actual figures are going to be at least six feet tall. Zane wants to keep the final product secret as long as we like the direction he is going in. He hasn't even begun carving Beckett yet. He's still a block of wood."

"Ain't that the truth," Ben said.

Blue trotted toward us from the brush, ball triumphantly clamped in his jaws.

"Be nice. I'm going in. We had so much to do to get ready for today, we moved winding day to today. Pat and I have work to do." I gave Ben a quick kiss and turned to walk up the back stairs to the shop. I turned around, and Ben was still watching me. He smiled when he saw me, but I'd caught his expression right before. He'd looked a million miles away, with a peck of trouble weighing him down.

chapter 5

Walking into the Cog & Sprocket never got old for me. The workroom was very much like the shop my grandfather left me. Almost identical, but with two more workstations and a lot more clocks in process. Caroline had hung out her shingle again and was processing basic repairs. I was overseeing larger restoration work, along with Zane Phillips.

Zane Phillips. Six months ago I'd never heard of him. Now he was the newest member of the merry band of clock fanatics I considered family. Zane had retired, but it didn't take much to talk him into moving down to Orchard permanently and helping out in the shop.

"Zane, you've seen the inventory. We need help if we are going to get these clocks taken care of," I'd said to him in January.

"You have some real beauties, that's for sure. That French Charles X portico clock—I'd love to get my hands on her. I've worked on some like it, but never one so stunning."

"Tell you what—that can be your project," I said. I forced the smile on my face to stay in place, even though I was disappointed. I'd hoped to make the portico a post-tower project, but getting Zane to stay was more important. If I was going to pull this clock tower off, I needed his help. The only person who my grandfather had discussed his dream with more than me was Zane, as it turned out. That, and the fact that Zane had risked his life to save Caroline meant that he was a man I wanted to have around.

"Listen, you don't have to talk me into this. I've got nothing waiting for me back in Vermont, and you've got enough clocks to keep me busy the rest of my life. Plus, Thom's tower. Now, working on that would be a real privilege. No, you don't have to talk me into this. As long as I don't have to be in the store every day. You know, punching a clock. I'm done with that."

"You can stay out at the cottage, in the guest room out in the shop. You never have to come into the Cog & Sprocket if you don't want to."

As it turned out, Zane did visit the shop, fairly often. At first he and Pat Reed had circled around each other like a couple of old dogs marking their turf, but soon enough they decided to call a truce. Zane enlisted Pat to help him get more clocks ready for sale, teaching him what he didn't know.

"I feel like I'm back in school," Pat said one night after he finally got a grandfather clock put back together. "Zane is one hell of a teacher."

"Not too much of a know-it-all?" I asked. Sometimes I bristled at Zane's tone, but I tamped it down. Clock making was an apprenticeship business, and Zane knew a lot more than I did.

"Not on purpose. I've asked Zane to teach me some more about basic fixes, so I can do house calls on my own."

House calls for a clockmaker were actually fairly common, especially for large clocks. Sometimes we went out to see if we could do an easy fix. Other times we went out to give them an estimate for repair. If we were going to bring the clocks into the shop, someone had to get them ready to move. Then there were the winding jobs—winding long-cases in colleges or clock towers in town squares. Sometimes these were two-man—two-person—jobs. I wouldn't mind letting Zane and Pat handle some of them on their own.

"Hello," I called out as I came into the shop through the back entrance.

"In front," Pat called back.

"Happy winding day," I said. I went over to my workstation and took the ring of keys out of the top drawer. I walked through the gap in the cabinetry that blocked the front from the back of the shop. The workroom still had the aura of my grandfather's shop. That was on purpose. The front of the shop was very different. Also on purpose.

"I've got the clock map and the keys," I said, holding up the staples for winding day. The ring held the case key, and the winding key was left inside the clock. When we moved them, we knew to take out the winding key. We numbered the clocks and put the keys on the ring in that order. If locks stuck we changed them out until everything was perfect. There are never a shortage of keys in a clockmaker's shop.

We diagrammed the numbered clocks. Neither Pat nor I needed the drawing anymore, but we still pulled it out and laid it on the front counter anyway. I'd rendered the shop from the perspective of the front door and included scaled drawings of each wall. I'd also noted the type, year, maker, and any other information that helped each clock stand out. This document captured the shop as it was at this moment. Every time we wound the clocks, I recognized that next week, our job might be different. One sale took me back to the drawing board. I never threw out the drawings—instead I dated them and put them in a large portfolio case. Sketching each clock was relaxing for me, and Nadia used the sketches on the website.

On winding day, Pat followed me around with a pad and kept notes on each of the clocks. "Tension is off." "Door latch stuck." "The mechanism sounds off." Those notes became the to-do list for the next hour or so. Usually. Today, even though we pretended it was just another Saturday, we had a different to-do list that was hindering our concentration.

We'd gotten through a half-dozen clocks before the events of that afternoon came up.

"Still not sure how folks are going to sign their names," he said.

"We got a half-dozen Dremels to use for engraving."

"They aren't going to make very deep impressions in the metal," Pat said.

I sighed. We'd had the same discussion a dozen times before, but hadn't come up with a better solution. Pat was right, the names would be scratches.

"Let's have them write their names with Sharpies first, then they can scratch their name with the Dremel," I said. "Folks don't expect their great-grandkids to see the names in full. We'll take pictures and include them in the archives."

"Kim Gray will expect to see her name," Pat said, a smirk stretching the sides of his mouth.

"That's why we are having her sign the decorative copper piece. Kim, the Board of Selectmen, Jeff Paisley—they'll all be signing sheets of copper that we will use on the clock, as the flaps that slow the bell down after it has chimed. Kim will be fine." I couldn't look Pat in the eye. Neither of us believed that for a second.

"Flaps that slow things down. Sounds very fitting for her," Pat said. I tapped his upper arm and he laughed. We moved on to the next clock, and he opened the case.

My cell phone vibrated in my pocket. I took it out and looked down at the caller ID. Speak of the devil.

"Good morning, Kim," I said.

"What time do you need me at this signing thing?" she said without preamble. The ever-politic politician.

Kim Gray had been hired to be the town manager at the behest of the late Grover Winter, town benefactor and longtime member of the Board of Selectmen. He'd been the symbolic mayor for years, but as he grew older, he recognized the need for someone to come in and run things. Grover died before the full disaster of Kim Gray's being here had been realized. More's the pity. He could have made changes. I didn't know him well, but he and my grandfather had been great friends, and of like minds. I knew G.T.'s feelings about Kim, thanks to notes in his diary. They were cryptic, but I understood them, especially after Ben filled me in on what had been going on. Being G.T.'s granddaughter, I was marked as an enemy by Kim right off the bat. I'd stopped trying to change her mind, but did go out of my way not to aggravate her.

"It starts at noon. Your speech will be at twelve fifteen if we stick to the schedule. Could you be out behind the Town Hall at eleven thirty for—"

"I have meetings right up till noon. I may be a little late."

"That's a shame. I'm sure Nadia asked you to be there early for some press photos."

"Press photos?" Her voice perked up and I could picture her preening. Preening was one of the few things she did well.

"We have those reporters coming in from the *Eagle*. You've got a headshot, right? Maybe they can add you in later? I'll ask Nancy to hold up a broom or something and pretend it's you."

"Nancy is going to be there?"

"Of course. The entire Board of Selectmen is going to be there. So is Chief Paisley, and Jimmy Murphy, and . . ."

"The Judas brigade."

"Judas brigade?" Kim's paranoia was in full bloom today. She'd be a real joy to be around.

"Don't act like you don't know what I'm talking about. The board tried to get me fired, but they came up short on the vote. A secret ballot, but I know who voted which way. Jimmy Murphy didn't count on my friends standing by me."

"Friends?" I asked.

"Yes, I do have friends, you know. Beckett Green, for one."

Did Beckett switch his allegiance again? I wondered. I would have thought he would have learned his lesson well over the New Year, but with Beckett you couldn't really tell. He was never going to get voted onto the board if he kept siding with Kim.

"And Harriet Wimsey always has my back," Kim continued.

The town librarian had to fight tooth and nail for every penny of her budget and blamed Kim for every broken computer and every book they couldn't buy. Privately. But as a member of the Board of Selectman, and the keeper of Grover Winter's memory in many ways, Harriet publicly supported Kim. She assumed that Kim had Orchard's best interests at heart. I wasn't convinced, but then again, I was Thom Clagan's granddaughter. That impacted my perception of Kim, and Kim's perception of me. My grandfather hadn't been a fan.

"Well, water under the bridge. Right, Kim?" I said, forcing a lightness in my tone that I didn't feel. I wasn't going to let Kim get to me—not today. "I'll tell Nadia you aren't going to make the press conference."

"Of course I'll make the press conference," Kim snapped. "Eleven thirty?"

"At the Town Hall. Out on the back portico. We're using it as a staging area. You'll be able to—"

"What-ev-er. I'll be there. Don't start without me."

Would that I could, Kim. Would that I could.

I stared down at my phone, watching her image disappear from the screen as the phone disconnected. It wasn't Kim's curly brown hair, brown eyes, and porcelain visage on the screen. Instead it was a picture of the Wicked Witch of the West. Nadia had added it. I lived in fear of Kim discovering it, but couldn't bear to change it. The caricature was too fitting.

Then the bells chimed, and I broke into a smile when I saw my other boyfriend coming through the front door.

"Jack," I said, shoving my phone in my pocket and opening my arms wide. Jack, born John Thomas six months ago, broke into a wide grin and didn't complain when his mother handed him off to me. "How are you, my darling?" I asked.

I had always liked children, but I'd never been baby crazy. This little guy changed all that. Maybe it was because he'd been named Thomas for my grandfather. Or because he was such a good-natured baby from the outset, coming on to the scene when we all desperately needed something wonderful to take our minds off the terrible events of October and December. But I suspected the thing that cemented our relationship was that we spent so much time together.

Jack's parents were small-business owners, just like the rest of us. Ada took some time off when Jack was born, and Nancy helped out at the Corner Market. When Ada came back after a few weeks, she carried Jack in a sling, nestled tight to her chest as she rang up customers or restocked shelves. But once Jack hit three months, that didn't work anymore. Jack was a social baby and enjoyed sitting in his bouncy seat, talking to the world in between his naps. That didn't fly in a grocery store, but it was fine in a clock shop. Or more precisely, a clock shop office.

Nadia was as crazy about Jack as I was. We talked it over, and I agreed to let her babysit him at the shop, as long as she kept up with her work for me. Bezel had decided that Jack was her own private playmate and was surprisingly gentle with the baby. She was even able to lightly bounce the chair when it had ceased and he was getting cranky. The only person who objected to the arrangement was Pat Reed.

"This is a business, not a day care center," he'd said dubiously, eyeing the package of diapers we kept on top of a cabinet in the office.

"It is a community," I said, "and we have to help each other out. What other options do Ada and Mac have? Especially now that Nancy's on the Board of Selectmen and can't work as many hours for the Clarks."

"She isn't even getting paid to be on the board," Pat grumbled.

"No, she isn't. But boy, how glad am I that she and Jimmy Murphy are able to team up and keep Kim at bay."

"Tuck Powers could take care of Jack," Pat said.

"Tuck Powers? I wouldn't trust Tuck Powers to take care of a goldfish," I whispered to Pat. At that point Nadia and Tuck were still dating, and I didn't want to upset her.

"Freddie . . ."

"Freddie? Freddie can't load the dishwasher without breaking something. No, my friend, you know that Nadia is the best choice, with us as backup. The Cog & Sprocket is close enough for Ada to come over and feed him, and they can chiefly stay upstairs."

Pat always grumbled, but I'd found him upstairs more than once, sitting in one of G.T.'s old chairs, rocking Jack. He'd quickly fallen to the wee one's charms.

"Jack loves you," Ada said, handing me a drool rag.

"The feeling is mutual," I said, kissing his bald head. "How are his parents doing today?"

"Tired, but what else is new?" Mac said. "Excited about today."

"It is going to be great," Ada said. "Mac and I are heading over soon to set up the beverage stand."

"Thanks again for doing that," I said. "It is really generous of you to donate the drinks for today."

"Listen, our vendors are the ones doing the donating. We're only throwing in the ice and cups. Beckett is also giving away more water bottles for folks who'd rather use those," Ada said.

"He's not going to be happy until everyone has a water bottle with 'Been There, Read That' on it," Mac said.

"I've got three. One for home, one for the car, one for the store. I wish they weren't quite so perfect," Ada said wistfully. "The right size. Dishwasher safe. Free of chemicals."

"Plus, they fit into the whole Orchard-going-green thing," I said. "It's nice of him to provide them to the folks at the party."

"Ever the diplomat, Ruth," Mac said. "Everyone is happy to be part of this. It's the event of the season."

"Well, the event of the week," Ada said. "The event of the season will be the Winding Ceremony June twenty-first."

"I still can't believe I let Nadia talk me into scheduling these two events so close together," I said, jiggling Jack a little in my arms.

"Nadia didn't talk you into anything," the woman herself said, coming down the stairs from the office. "The bank account talked you into it. We needed to make today happen so we could financially get over the finish line."

"You are a mad genius," I said. She shot me a "whatever" look and shrugged her shoulders a hair. I watched as she caught Jack's eye, and her face broke into a grin. He squirmed in my arms, and I relinquished the warm little bundle to her.

"Ruth's right, you know," Mac said. "You are really good at thinking—"

"Big. She thinks big," I said.

Nadia had started working for me late last fall. I'd let her run with some ideas for our reopening, and they'd taken off. Our business wasn't bust-the-door-down busy, but it was getting more robust. Clocks were getting sold at a decent pace, though the cash flow wasn't what I wanted, or needed. I hoped that Nadia's marketing of the clock tower opening helped with that. She assured me that our website had a lot of visitors. Nadia told me that my "Ruth's Clock Talks" had become a modest Internet sensation.

"I think *differently*," she said, looking me straight in the eye. "You're the one who thinks big. You're the one who wanted to get this clock tower working. I'm just trying to help make it happen."

"It is a team effort," I said, embarrassed. Mac reached over and gave my shoulder a squeeze. Our families had been feuding for years, and though we were working to bury the hatchet, this was still as close to a hug as the Clarks and Clagans got.

"Warm moment over," Nadia said, knowing the history. "Is Jack good to go?"

"Fed and changed," Ada said.

"Well, I'll check on the changed part before I bring him over. Is the baby carrier in the bag?" Nadia asked.

"Yes, but he really doesn't like it," Ada said.

"Ada, he and I have an agreement. Today he gets carried facing out, and charms everyone. We still have a few hundred dollars to raise, and Jack is our secret weapon. He'll be fine. If not, Caroline will bring him back here. I've got it covered."

"Well, we need to get moving," Mac said. Ada reached out and took Jack's hand, bringing it to her lips for a gentle kiss. "We'll see you over there in a few minutes."

I looked up at the banjo clock on the wall. It was one of my favorites, with a winter scene of Orchard painted on the glass door at the bottom. My grandmother had touched up the painting years ago and I'd watched her. Those memories helped make the clock my touchstone. For the first time this morning it seemed like those hands were finally moving. Time to go and get ready for the big event.

chapter 6

Nadia brought Jack to her office on the third floor. I took a minute to plug in my phone and turned to go upstairs, but then the back door started rattling. I ran back and peered through the blinds that covered the window. Zane Phillips stared back. I took a breath before I opened the door. The scars on his face were still a shock, even though I'd seen them daily for months now. They gave him a sinister look, which was belied by everything else about the gentle crafts-man. When I'd first heard about how he got the scars—he built a clock made out of knives and got too close to the swinging machete—I'd thought that was a crazy idea. "Not crazy," he'd said. "Just underdeveloped. I still think I could have corrected the balance. But they took it apart after the accident." Now it was all I could do not to ask him about the design and offer to help him build it again. He and I were both big clock dreamers.

"Zane, shouldn't you be over at the tower?" I asked.

"On my way," he said. "Just wanted to visit the facilities and clean up a bit."

"Is this her?" I asked, pointing to the large package he carried under his arm. It was wrapped in a sheet, was about two feet long, and looked heavy.

"It is. Show folks what we're working toward. That's another reason I came by. I didn't want to surprise you in case it's not what you had in mind."

He walked over to one of the empty worktables and proceeded to unwrap the figure. I didn't try to help, or to rush him, even though time was ticking. Zane worked on his own internal clock.

He stepped in front of the figure before it was fully unwrapped, partially blocking me from the view until he was ready. He used one end of the sheet to buff the figure a bit and then stepped aside. I felt my mouth open, but no sound came out.

"It's your grandma Mae," he said.

"The spitting image," I whispered, feeling tears prick at my eyes. I didn't try and stop them. "It's wonderful."

"Course you had to know Mae to know this is her. But I'm glad you see the likeness. The final product will be about six times bigger than this. There'll be more details, but I want those to be a surprise."

The figure was carved and had been stained rather than painted. Only a few details stood out—the winding bun on the top of her head, the roses that covered her dress, the pearls that she wore around her neck. If someone asked me to describe her, these are the three things I would have mentioned. The blue-gray of the hair, pink in the roses, white of the pearls—those were bright splotches of color on the wood. Zane had used stains to highlight aspects of the figure, show the details of some of the carving. The figure was unique, and I loved it. I ran my finger along the apron and smiled at Zane.

"She'll be the first one out of the door every hour. She will do a little spin, then the rest will come out and spin. I'd say 'dance,' but they've got nothing to dance to," Zane said, flicking an invisible speck of dust off the statue's hair.

"The bell will be ringing. We aren't going to have this fight again," I said. "The dancing will be plenty entertaining—"

"Entertaining," he scoffed as he dusted another invisible speck of something from the pristine figure.

"And historically accurate. You've seen the old drawings and heard that recording that Harriet found. One bell."

"The old clock tower had one big bell. It had gravitas. This one's pitiful."

"This bell is plenty big. A little lopsided, but that's why we got it donated. Don't look at me like that. The big bell has been value engineered out for now. We've had this argument a dozen times already. We can't afford the *really* big bell."

"It is going to be a mite quiet," he said, grumbling.

"It is," I agreed. "But I'll bet at three in the morning it will be plenty loud enough. Anyway, we're never going to agree on the bell."

"I'd love to see a full carillon," Zane said. "Something worthy of the amazing clock we are building."

"Zane—" I said.

"Fine. I'm done. For today."

"Thank you," I said. Truthfully, I agreed with him. But I had to be practical. No matter how I stretched, it wasn't in the budget. I looked over at the figure of my grandmother and stroked the side of its face.

"I love this. Her," I said.

Zane beamed. "You think it is a good likeness?"

"I do. I love the colors. How did you do that?"

"I thought about painting them, but that would be too much upkeep. But we needed some color, so I did a paint/stain technique I developed, and then I added some stain and lots of varnish. I tested some pieces outside this winter, and they held up. Running more tests this week, under different conditions. We want to find the best possible solution. Eventually we'll probably want to make duplicates so we can switch them out. These should work for a while, at least, though."

I walked over and gave Zane a big hug. He hesitated, but then hugged me back. I leaned back and put both my hands on the side of his wonderful face. "You are a good man, Zane Phillips. I feel G.T. looking down and smiling right now, don't you?"

"He'd be popping his top button, he'd be so proud of you."

"You really think so?"

"I know so," he said, letting go of me. "Now, you leave me be for a minute. I need to put on a clean shirt and try to remember how to tie a tie."

"You're wearing a tie?" I said.

"I am. I always wear a tie at important events. How about you?"

"I'm not going to wear a tie," I said. "But I am going to wear a dress. I know, shocking. In fact, I need to get a move on." I walked back to the staircase and turned back to look at Zane, my foot resting on the bottom step. "She's beautiful. Thank you."

Zane laid out the sheet and prepared to wrap her back up. I'd ask him later if I could keep her in the shop. I'd love to have my grandmother back where she belonged.

The staircase up to the second floor of the Cog & Sprocket was very wide, and gently sloped. Perfect for carrying clocks up and down for storage and repair. My little apartment had been part guest quarters, part storage facility when I moved in. Reconfiguring the space to include a wide hallway with banks of storage had cut into the living space, but added to the homeyness of my nest. The door to my apartment was slightly ajar, and I walked in.

Nadia was over by the stove, heating up some water so she could prepare Jack's bottle. The little man himself was sitting in his bouncy chair on the floor. I'd picked the chair up at a yard sale and was disappointed, but not surprised, that the electric bouncer didn't work, despite my best attempts at fixing it. I needn't have worried. Bezel served as sentry, and Jack was fascinated by her soft fur and pointy ears. Her patience with the baby was remarkable, and exclusionary. She held the rest of the world in slight disdain, though as her chief food deliverer and litter box scooper she gave me occasional love rubs. She also was the best listener I knew, and helped me talk through complicated business and life decisions.

"Sorry, Ruth, I'll be out of here in a minute. Just want to make sure Jack has a bottle ready to go, in case."

"No worries. I'm going to change. Take your time."

"I topped Bezel's dry food off too. I still think we should bring her to the ceremony. We have her harness."

"Yeah, that's been a terrific success. We can take her for a drag."

"Well, if I didn't have Jack, I'd totally bring Bezel. She's the star of some of our best social media."

"Still not sure how a cat pondering clock guts on Instagram is so popular. Letting a cat near them is never a good idea. Most can be bent, and cat fur wreaks havoc in gears . . ."

"Ruth, we are creating our own reality. Bezel is a star. So are you. Get used to it. After today, we're going to be trending. @ClaganClocks, #AllGearedUp."

I was hesitant, but not about to throw cold water on Nadia's plans. Six months ago I had trouble envisioning today, but I kept believing. Now the clock tower was a step closer to reopening.

"In Nadia I trust. I'm going to go back and put on my dress."

"I still can't believe you're wearing a dress."

"I wear dresses all the time."

"Sure, over jeans or leggings. But this is a *dress* dress."

"It reminded me of my grandmother when I saw it. But don't worry, I'm wearing bike shorts underneath in case I have to climb a ladder or there is a gust of wind. I'm a practical dress wearer."

I walked back to my bedroom area and drew the curtain for privacy. The '50s-style cotton dress hung by the closet door, freshly ironed by Nancy Reed yesterday, so that the collar was crisp and the skirt was full. The white cotton and large blue cabbage roses made me smile. The dress really did remind me of my grandmother. At the very least, I knew she would have loved it. Pretty, but practical, with strong pockets, a must-have in all of my clothing. I loved the mid-calf length as well.

Getting dressed was very quick, with the last step pulling on the bike shorts. People were used to me wearing my lace-up Doc Martens, but today called for special occasion shoes. My red gladiator sandals were insanely comfortable and balanced on the line between my style and appropriate for the occasion.

I opened the curtain dramatically and struck a pose, but Nadia and her gang were gone. Probably for the best, since my preparations were only halfway complete. The bathroom mirror helped me understand where the tweaks needed to be done. My hair was still a curly mass of red, but thanks to Flo, it still looked good. I knew better than to touch it myself. She'd futz with my hair as soon as she saw me. Makeup was minimal, but I'd spent more time on it than normal. At the last minute I took out a deep red lipstick and put it on.

My clock cog necklace and earrings, both of which I'd made, completed the ensemble. I picked out a white cardigan in case it was chilly and checked once more in the mirror. I was as tall as my grandfather, but in this dress I also looked like my grandmother. They were both with me today; I felt it. I glanced over at the carriage clock on top of the cabinets and felt my pulse pick up. I needed to be over at the clock tower three minutes ago. Running late, again, to no one's great surprise.

chapter 7

I walked over to the Town Hall, using the crosswalk and looking both ways before crossing the street. During the winter the only reason to follow this rule was that the crosswalks were dug out first so you didn't need to climb over snowdrifts. But traffic picked up right before Memorial Day, and there was a steady stream coming through Orchard these days.

The Signing Ceremony started in less than two hours. Overflow parking was going to be at the high school, and that was a good thing. All street parking was already full. I took my phone out of my pocket, and texted Ben.

Did you cone off the back alley?

Done, he texted back. *Where are you?*

Heading over, I texted back. *Where are you?*

Flo has me running errands. Will be there in 10.

The Town Hall was the oldest building in Orchard proper. It was clapboard covered, but underneath the building was made of stone, which had helped it weather the many trials and tribulations Orchard had faced over the years. Floods, fires, the Great Depression, neglect—through it all the Town Hall stood firm.

I looked around at the beautiful grounds, complete with gardens and paths, and remembered the sea of mud that had been there weeks earlier after Ben, Pat, and I spent a weekend pulling out old bushes, overturning flower beds, and pulling weeds. Ben and Pat had taken the last load to the dump, and I was cleaning up the site.

"What are you going to do here?" Harriet Wimsey had stopped to survey the progress, arms crossed over her chest, a vague tone of disapproval in her voice.

"I was thinking about having some mulch delivered to cover the mud," I'd said. "I don't have enough of a budget for doing anything else right now."

"I have a suggestion," she'd said. "Do you know about the Community Orchard Nature and Garden Association?"

"The Community . . ."

"CONGA. We're volunteer gardeners. Why don't you let us take care of outside the Town Hall?"

"There isn't a budget—"

"Don't worry about budgets," Harriet had said. "We collect leftovers from other gardens."

"Leftovers? But—"

"I promise you. Donations only, surplus from other folks' home projects," Harriet had said. "I want to do this, please. I haven't done much else to help you lately."

I looked at Harriet. Tall, thin, gray wiry hair held back with a headband, blue cat-eyed glasses. Harriet was the same age as Nancy and Flo, but while they positioned themselves against Kim Gray, Harriet sided with her, assuming that Kim knew best. Flo had explained that Harriet had thought the world of Grover Winter, and since he'd handpicked Kim for the job of town manager, it was up to Harriet to honor his memory by doing what she could to help Kim succeed. Harriet was one of the reasons Kim still had her job. Lately I wondered if Harriet's faith wasn't wavering, but I knew better than to ask Harriet herself. Her actions spoke louder than words, and she'd never share her thought process with me.

"Thanks, Harriet. It would be great to have the outside looking nice," I'd said.

"Then I'm going to schedule a CONGA line," she'd replied, smiling slightly and nodding her head. "Grover, rest his soul, would have wanted the hall to look her best."

"One more question. What, exactly, does a CONGA line entail?"

"A CONGA line is, if I may say so, one of the best things about Orchard," she'd said. "Wait and see."

On the Saturday of the CONGA line, five minutes before it had been scheduled to start, I'd stood out in front of the Town Hall, waiting to see what was going to happen.

The first truck of supplies pulled up as a stream of twenty volunteers descended, led by Harriet Wimsey herself. A few volunteers broke off to unload the truck, others laid out stakes and strings on the front yard to create a grid. A few dribbled into the Town Hall. The large vacuous space had been cleared of furniture after the last event that was held there, and the rugs had been rolled up. The slate flooring was cold, but practical, able to hold up to years of foot traffic. Whereas the outside had been covered up with white clapboard to fit into New England norms, the inside stone walls were kept in their raw state. In past years tapestries had covered the walls, but those had been removed and were being restored.

I followed the CONGA volunteers in and helped them set up a half-dozen six-foot tables.

"These three will be for food and snacks. The Reeds will be along soon to deliver those. Those two by the door? Those will be for extra tools. The last one will be Command Central," Harriet said.

"Command Central?"

"We'll lay out the diagram of the gardens and the updated task list of what needs to be done. You said this place had Wi-Fi?" Harriet said.

"Yes. I wrote down the log-in and password and the rest of the information you requested." I handed her the two-page document I'd created, which I'd laminated, per her suggestions. She looked it over and nodded. I may even have seen the hint of a smile, but I couldn't be sure. Harriet would never be accused of overenthusiasm.

"Did you make—"

"Extra copies. Yes, here's six more."

"I only asked for two."

"But I made extras. I'm sure they'll be helpful to have around here: emergency contacts, preferred vendors, log-ins."

"It is always helpful to arm people with information," she said in a serious, almost reverent tone. She lowered her reading glasses on her nose and looked at me over the rims. Her angular features were heightened in the shadowy light of the Town Hall. I remembered the look well, from the years Moira and I would go to the library and giggle. Harriet was never a shusher—she used "the look" instead. It still scared me.

"You think I am overly organized, don't you?" she asked.

"Actually, no. I was thinking how glad I am that you are on it."

"On what?"

"On *it*. On everything. Organizing today. Being support-ive of the loyalty card program last winter. Helping me with research. You are one of the cogs of Orchard. You help keep it running."

"You are lucky that I've learned enough from you to know that being called a cog is a compliment. I thought the world of your grandfather, Ruth. You're cast from his same mold." She gave me one of her rare smiles, which pleased me inordinately.

"How can I help today?"

"Don't you need to be at the shop?" Harriet asked.

"Caroline is running it today," I said. "She asked me to fill in for her. Her shoulder is still giving her trouble, so she can't help out."

"I hope it heals quickly. She's one of our best gardeners. Well, in her stead, why don't you help with the food and supplies?"

"Sure," I said. Harriet didn't trust me to help with the gardens. Her mistrust was well placed. I was known to kill cacti. "Wonderful. You're much more useful on Command Central," I said.

Harriet smiled slightly, and a bit of color rose on her cheeks. "Well, let's see how the CONGA line is progressing."

We walked out the front of the Town Hall into a hive of gardening activity. A grid had been staked out. Different shapes—lines, circles, squares, ovals—has been spray-painted onto the mud. More volunteers had arrived and were unloading another truck of supplies. Three more trucks were waiting behind them.

"Where did all this come from? My tiny budget couldn't have covered all of this," I said.

"No, the budget covered the gravel we are going to use

underneath the paths. We saved the old cobblestones for edging. The CONGA started early this morning, with volunteers going around to pick up the contributions folks had made."

"Contributions?"

"We take the community part of gardening very seriously. Everyone has leftovers from projects. The garden plan takes into account that not everything will match—that's why there are all these different shapes. Everyone donates leftover plants and things from their gardens. We make them work. That oval? The Browns had a lovely birdbath and some granite pavers that will fit in that spot perfectly. The Polleys had a lot of extra concrete pavers they didn't end up using on their driveway. They offered them to us for the paths. Not historically accurate, but the price was right."

"They just gave them to us?" I asked. I knew of the Polley family, but I didn't know them personally. The pallet of pavers had to cost a small fortune.

"We'll have a plaque outside, with special thanks to the contributors. All that is for another day. Is Pat bringing over the clock parts we'd talked about?"

"Clock parts? He did leave a pile of wheels and cogs, a couple of old weights, and some other clock parts out in the back. They're under a tarp."

"Good enough," Harriet said. "We want to incorporate clocks into the gardens. Now, we need to get to work if we expect to finish this weekend."

"Finish this weekend?" I looked around, wide-eyed. The workers were still unloading everything.

"Of course. That's what a CONGA line is, or rather does. It is fun, and busy. But it doesn't last forever. We'll get it done. Besides, we both know that if Kim Gray has a minute, she's going to put a stop to this, just to spite you."

"To spite me?" I said.

"Don't act like you're so surprised," she said. "It doesn't suit you. We both know that your moving back to Orchard was the beginning of a rough patch of road for Kim. She blames you for that. I've been trying to keep her in line, but I'm getting tired. That is for another day. Luckily for us both, she's in Boston at a conference. We'll get it done today, and she'll be none the wiser about it."

I looked around on this Saturday morning, and smiled. The CONGA line had, indeed, gotten it done. Paths wound around beds, each of which had its own personality. The path that led to the back of the Town Hall met a dead end of sorts. To the right was the side entrance to the Town Hall. Straight ahead was a six-foot fence with a trellis on top. There was a door in the middle of the fence that led to a hardscaped area, a portico edged with gardens. The idea for the back was eventually an outdoor performance space or gathering spot. Right now it contained a few tables and chairs that had been procured from yard sales and spray-painted to match the color palette the CONGA folks had chosen—white, black, gray, federal blue, and a lovely violet color. This afternoon it would be a holding pen for the VIPs, with food and drinks available to the large donors while we posed for a few pictures. We'd set out some of the clock tower inner workings for scale, and for context. We'd also set up a frame and hung the bell we were planning on using, so folks could ring it. That was Zane's idea—he hoped that someone would be so horrified by the muddled sound of our donated bell that they would open their checkbook and solve that problem. Tonight's cocktail party would be for the folks that helped make today happen, but we had hours before that took place.

I walked into the Town Hall through the front door. The old building was empty, with tables along the far end. A podium had been set up on the right side of the room. There was a configuration of pipes that framed the podium, and a black drape hung on it. It gave the area a sense of formality. Fred Hamilton was hanging a sign on the back pipe, alongside the town crest.

"Where did you get the sign?" I asked Fred.

"Whoa, Ruthie, don't sneak up on a man on a ladder," he said, grabbing the ladder as he held the pipe for support.

"Sorry, Fred. Didn't mean to scare you. It looks great in here."

Fred harrumphed acknowledgment of my comments but went back to the task at hand. He was midfifties, at the most, but was the sort of man who looked the same his entire adulthood, with more wrinkles and whitening hair the only signs of time passing. He was a few inches short of six foot, trim build, and a full head of wavy hair. His hair was his best feature. I knew well enough by now that I needed to let him finish before we could continue to talk, so I cooled my heels and took a walk around.

Pat had asked if we'd hire Fred on to help us get the clock tower project in gear. "He's fallen on hard times since Kim canned him," he'd said. In February Kim Gray had fired Hamilton Plumbing from all municipal projects. The official reason was that his most recent bids weren't in the ballpark. Unofficially, Kim and Fred had never gotten along, but his contracts were long running and hard to break. She'd argued that the transfer of ownership of the Town Hall changed the terms of all her contracts. She'd been renegotiating contracts ever since.

"Fallen on hard times" was code for "the reasons don't matter, but if we can help we should because that's what decent folks do," the credo that Pat Reed adhered to and that my grandparents had raised me on. By his suggestion, Pat was vouching for Fred, and that was good enough for me.

Fred was a plumber by trade, but he had a lot of other building skills that we'd put to good use. *Taciturn* was a nice way of describing Fred's personality, but he never groused about what he was asked to do.

"That even?" he asked. I looked over at the sign and backed up so that I could assess it. The sign had the Cog & Sprocket predominantly featured, but it included other businesses that were supporting the Signing Ceremony.

"It looks good. Sorry you had to do that on your own."

"No worries. It is made of foam core." Fred grabbed a roll of duct tape from the podium and ripped off a piece. He fished around in his pocket and grabbed a few coinlike items, putting them on the tape.

"What are you doing now?" I asked.

"I'm going to add some weight to the bottom so it doesn't flap around. Added some washers, going to put the tape on the back of the sign. Figure folks are going to be coming and going for a few hours, so there's bound to be a breeze."

"Good thinking," I said. "This looks pretty official."

"That Nadia, she's a sharp one. I was making fun of her for her arts and crafts projects, but it looks terrific. Wait till you see what she's got in store for the front of the lectern. Pat's working on that out in the side offices."

"Why did you set it up over here, not in the middle of the hall, along the back wall?" I asked. This side of the room wasn't used often—behind the walls were dead storage and the building mechanics like the furnace.

"Traffic patterns. Folks will pay attention to the speech-ifying, and then we'll get them moving in the right directions so they can do their signing."

"What's the weight doing on the platform?" I asked, pointing to the heavy metal doughnut that was sitting on a stool on the corner of the podium.

"Demonstration purposes. Since we're going to have the VIPs sign their strips today, Nadia thought it would be a good idea to show them how it will look. We'll turn the weight around, like this, and show folks a sample of the finished project."

I walked over to the podium and looked at the back of the weight. Metallic strips with names were glued in rows.

"Turn it," Fred said.

I put my hand on the top of the weight and let it twist. It took a little force, but it did turn around. "This is terrific," I said.

"Yeah, well, the final product will look a lot better, but this will give folks an idea."

"I'm so glad that you figured out the best way to get these weights signed. Soldering the metal strips is a great so-lution."

Fred shrugged his shoulders. Different-sized donations got different-sized signing plates. We were going to use Sharpies to do the signing and then shellac them before attaching them to the weights. But then we decided that etching would feel more official, so we added the Dremel step. There was something about using a tool that made folks feel like they got their money's worth.

Fred turned the weight back around, away from the au-dience.

"What time are folks starting to show up?" he asked.

"We're going to meet out back at eleven thirty to have some pictures taken. The doors to the auditorium are going to open around then, so that folks can come in and wander around a bit. Would you mind—"

"Nadia's asked me to keep an eye out in here, answer questions. Pat Reed too."

"I want to get a picture of you—" I said.

"There'll be plenty of time for pictures. Nadia's got a team of folks taking pictures, doing that social media thing. Besides, I don't want to run into Her Majesty Kim Gray if I can help it."

"From the sounds of it, she won't be around for too long. I hope she makes it here in time for the press photos."

"Can't imagine she'll want to miss those."

"Neither can I. Hope seeing her will be . . . all right."

Fred shrugged his shoulders. "Small town. We're bound to run into each other." Fred walked over and adjusted the black drape, then turned back to me. "Ruth, I've never thanked you for taking me on this winter."

"Fred, you—"

"Let me say this. I know Pat put you up to it, but you didn't have to do it. I've done pretty well in my business, but Patty's illness, well, it wiped us out. When she died, I stopped paying attention to the business and paid more attention to feeling sorry for myself. And drinking. Guys who worked with me, they tried to cover for me, but I wasn't up to par. That doesn't mean Queen Gray had any business firing me. None. You folks helped me get back on my feet and gave Freddie a job to help out with the bills. I appreciate it. And uh, yep. That's that."

"You're welcome," I said. I wasn't tempted to give Fred a hug or say any more about it. If you looked up *cranky*

Yankee in the dictionary, Fred's picture would be there as an illustration.

"I hear the selectmen are trying to get rid of her," Fred said, completely moving past the emotional speech he had just given.

"Think they'll be successful?" I asked.

"I think Kim Gray will get hers, one way or the other. That's what I think."

chapter 8

"We can't wait any longer," Nadia said. It wasn't a question. I looked at the clock on the wall in the Town Hall. The press photographers had pushed us to start taking photos on the portico as close to eleven thirty as possible so they could reset up in the Town Hall. We'd agreed, and were done by ten of. We moved inside the Town Hall to mix and mingle. Ben had suggested that folks move along to signing their metal strips, which they had done after a bit of demonstration from me and Pat on how to use the tools properly. Activity was beginning to wane a bit. We needed to make our speeches, and soon.

"Still no sign of Kim?" I said.

"No visual sighting. No text. No e-mail. No phone call. Not to you, or me, or Nancy, or Jimmy Murphy. No one. We're getting behind, and people are getting bored."

I looked around the crowd and saw Pat and Nancy talking to each other. Or she was talking and gesturing wildly, even by Nancy Reed standards. Nancy had run out right after the press photos were done, and I hadn't seen her since. Fred was over by the display of the clock parts, talking to Freddie. I noticed he'd changed his shirt and put on a tie. Jason Scott was helping Flo at the food table, and Ada and Mac were handing out drinks. Ben was walking around with a camera, taking pictures. He caught my eye and winked at me.

"We have to start the speeches," Nadia said.

"Where's Jack?" I asked, imagining a baby-crying fest breaking out in the middle of the speeches.

"Caroline's giving him a bottle. She's back at the Cog & Sprocket, so they could have some quiet time. Not sure who needed it more, Caroline or Jack."

"Okay, let's start. Of course, Kim was supposed to give the opening remarks. Maybe Jimmy will—"

"You're doing it."

"Nadia, I can't. We talked about this. I was supposed to stand on the podium while Ben talked about the Clock Tower Committee after Kim introduced him."

"Well, guess what? It's showtime, and you're the show. Go. Just go. I need to get everyone synced and make sure they're recording this."

I walked up to the podium and stood behind the lectern. I motioned to Ben, and he joined me. The members of the Board of Selectmen filed up as well. I surveyed the crowd once more, but still no Kim. Beckett Green was over by the model of the clock tower, talking to Zane Phillips, gesturing at the model of my grandmother he'd put on display beside it. I noticed Jeff Paisley standing in the back beside Moira, who smiled and waved. Caroline came in, carrying Jack, right before I started my speech. I smiled at her, glad she wasn't going to miss this. Ada walked over and took her sleeping son.

"Hello, folks," I said, and then jumped back a bit at the echo of the microphone. "I'm Ruth Clagan, and I own the Cog & Sprocket." Everyone applauded, which was nice but also unnerving. "Thank you for being here to help us launch the clock tower project. Are you having fun? Has everyone signed something?" Some cheers erupted, and there was more applause. "This is a community effort, and I am thrilled that three of the members of the Board of Selectmen—Jimmy Murphy, Nancy Reed, Harriet Wimsey—are here. I'm also grateful to our friends at the Corner Market and the Sleeping Latte for providing refreshments. You all noticed the gardens as you came in. We were CONGAed, and glad of it." A smattering of laughs went throughout the crowd, and I noticed a lot of the community gardening volunteers. "There will be time for more thanks later, but right now I'd like to introduce you to the chair of the Clock Tower Committee, Ben Clover."

I stepped back to make room for Ben at the lectern, and then I got in line with Jimmy, Nancy, and Harriet. Lots of applause greeted Ben, but he waved it off.

"I'm sorry that Kim Gray is missing this party," he said with a charming ease that belied the sting of his statement. Her absence may have gone unnoticed before he said it, but not anymore. "Now, I know that Ruth thinks that the real party will be the day we wind the clock, a couple of weeks from now. But I think today is the day we celebrate. Three years ago Grover Winter and Thom Clagan formed this committee to help realize Thom's dream of rebuilding the clock tower. It was a committee of two. Right after I moved to town, they signed me up to join them. How could I not? Grover had the charm and Thom had the passion. It was impossible to say no to the two of them together.

"Last year we lost them both, and I thought the dream had died with them. But I hadn't met Ruth yet. Ruth has Grover's charm, and Thom's passion. Even though the current committee has only been working together for a few months, with Ruth's vision, we're going to make this happen. Imagine that, folks. By the end of June we'll be able to look up and see what time it is in the center of town. Next December we'll be ringing in the New Year with a clock tower show.

"Today you are all here to sign your name to the strips of metal that are going to be attached to the clock weights that keep the machine running. Now, I've been told by a reliable source that we can add as many weights as we want to, so keep on signing, and send your friends down. Over there, you can see the display model of the clock that is going up in the tower, and Pat and Zane can talk you through how it works. The bell is out back, ready to go up into the tower on Monday. But the parts are just parts without the artists who put them together. So let's give a big thank-you to Ruth Clagan, Pat Reed, Caroline Adler, Zane Phillips, and Fred Hamilton. Without these folks none of this would be happening. I'm going to ask everyone to come up to take a bow."

Pat walked over and took Caroline's hand, guiding her to the front of the room. Zane came from a different direction, and Fred left his post to come to the front of the room. I stepped off the podium to stand with them, because that's where I belonged. With them. I put my arm around Caroline, and she put her arm around my waist.

"Now, before we finish up for the day, there are three more pieces of business. First order of business: I'd like a voice vote on the following, that we start calling this the Clagan Clock Tower. All in favor, say 'aye.'"

"Aye!" the room thundered. I started to wipe the tears away, but I couldn't keep up with them, so I stopped. The Clagan Clock Tower. G.T. would have hated it—too showy for an old New Englander—but I was secretly thrilled. And grateful for waterproof mascara.

"Second order of business: I'd like everyone to take a look at the image of Mae Clagan that Zane Phillips has carved. She's a prototype of one of the figures that will be dancing in December. The final sculptures will be six times this size. We'll reveal the other figures at the Winding Ceremony in a few weeks. Just a reminder that Beckett Green donated enough money to choose what one of the figures will be. There may be other opportunities for you to bid on figures, so stay tuned.

"Third and final order of business: the carillon dreams of Zane Phillips. We've got the hour bell outside for all of you to see. But Zane wanted to have you listen to the carillon that could play when the figures come out to dance. He's offered to do a demonstration if you're interested."

Zane would never stop wanting a separate set of chimes for the figures to dance to, rather than dancing to the methodical, muddled chime of the solo, lopsided bell. For now, the plan was for the bell to activate the figures to come out and dance at the same time as the clock struck. They'd be activated by the clock, but they wouldn't differentiate the time by doing anything special. Every hour would have the same dance. No one was happy about the lack of chimes, but I'd been the least unhappy. Maybe it was because I lived across from the tower.

"Pat, maybe you can explain what we are going to hear?" Ben said.

Pat walked up to the lectern, carrying his phone.

"Thinking about what bells sound like, and how they

operate, has been quite the learning curve for me," Pat said. "The Clagans are clock people. They like gears and cogs and winding. I've learned a lot from them over the years. But clock tower bells? I had no idea how complicated that conversation could be. Here's one example of a carillon in Europe." Pat hit a button on his phone. A cacophony of bells sounded, playing a piece of classical music I couldn't place.

"We don't want anything fancy like that for our clock," Pat said.

"Good thing," someone said. "That's a lot of noise for Orchard."

"Yup. We need a little more of an Orchard sound." Folks laughed. "There are a lot of options in the bell world. We could have gone for electronic bells, but where's the fun with that? For now, we've just got the one bell. But Zane is pricing a carillon to be installed at a later time. Today, for a special treat, he's asked the Marytown Handbell Society to give us a short demonstration. They've just arrived and will be performing soon."

"Would electronic chimes be cheaper?" Beckett Green asked the question from across the room. The question he knew the answer to, since he'd been in the room with us as we talked this through.

I walked up to the podium. "No, not necessarily cheaper."

"But they would be more versatile—is that correct?"

"Yes. We could change the tunes."

"And the volume?"

"No, not the volume. That is something we'll need to discuss when that phase of the project is ready to start."

"Can't bells be played by people instead of by the clocks?" someone else asked.

"There are some that can be played manually. That may

be an interim solution for special occasions. We don't have a budget for someone to live in the clock tower and ring the chimes every hour." The audience laughed, and Pat looked down at his phone. He stepped up to the mic.

"It appears to be showtime," he said. Sure enough, the handbell choir came in, eight people in all. They lined up near the front door and rang their handbells. They played a lovely waltz, one of my favorites. Nadia held up her phone, and I noticed a few other people filming it. The queen of social media would never let a moment like this pass.

As soon as it began, it was done. The crowd cheered. I exhaled, happy that this surprise twist didn't end the day with a thud. Zane certainly kept me on my toes. I got off the podium and walked over to the choir to thank them. "Happy to do it," the choir director said. "Sorry we can't stay, but we are on our way to another event. When Zane asked us to come, we couldn't refuse."

"How did Zane find you?"

"He's one of our biggest fans," she said.

Of course he is, I thought. I made my way toward the food stations, saying hello to as many people as I could. The day couldn't have gone any better.

I walked around to the signing stations, answering questions about the clock parts, posing for pictures. Who ever thought people would be so excited about using a Dremel to barely etch their name on a place no one would ever see it? The town of Orchard had caught clock tower fever, and I was thrilled.

"Hi, everyone. Could I have your attention?" Jimmy Murphy was on the podium, using the microphone. "I hate to rush you, but tonight is the Orchard Glee Club concert, and we promised we'd have the room cleared by midafternoon so they could set up. We won't leave until everyone has signed. Don't worry. But I wanted to let you know that we're on the clock." People laughed at his terrible pun. Nadia walked over, and he leaned down so she could whisper in his ear.

"Folks, just a reminder. Pictures from today will be on the Cog & Sprocket site this weekend. Nadia wants you to tap—is it tap photos?"

Nadia took the microphone, but didn't go up on the platform. "Hi. I work over at the Cog & Sprocket. Make sure you tag us if you share your photos. Thanks so much for coming by today and for helping us get the word out. Remember to use the #AllGearedUp."

There was a final rush, but within twenty minutes, right before three o'clock, the room was clear, except for members of the Board of Selectmen and the volunteers who had helped us pull today off. I looked around and clapped. Ben joined me, and everyone else soon joined in. Nadia came over to me and gave me a big hug, which I returned.

"Thank you all so much!" I shouted. "Now, we do need to get this place cleared out. But why don't we move things out to the back portico and raise a toast to ourselves before the VIP reception starts at five? Or is it too early to start drinking?"

"It's five o'clock somewhere," Jimmy said. Everyone laughed, and then Pat and Fred each went to one end of a table and prepared to take it outside.

"Need help?" Ben asked.

"That would be great, Ben," Pat said, stepping away from his end of the table. "We're going to lock the tables in the side room laid out like they are, so we can keep track of what goes where. Fred and I have a system. If you'll help him move the tables, I'll go out back and grab a dolly for the clock weights."

I realized how hungry I was, and I looked around for some food. As if she read my mind, Nancy pulled out a tray of pastries and lifted off the plastic wrap.

"I saved some food for all of you," she said, offering the tray around and smiling knowingly. "There's more back at the Sleeping Latte."

"Maybe we should move the VIP party to the Cog & Sprocket?" I said. "It's tight timing with the concert."

"We can keep the events separate," Nancy said. "Besides, there's all that clock stuff Pat's been putting around the portico."

"Right, I forgot about that," I said. Pat and Zane had been creating some demonstration pieces for the VIP reception so folks could get a sense of how the clock would work. The display included a stand that we hung the bell on, so folks could hear how it would sound.

"Anyway, we've got time to take a breath. They need to set up the stage and get the chairs loaded back in. Here, eat something," Nancy gestured to a tray of desserts. "I'm going to bring Caroline a couple of cookies to tide her over." Nancy opened up a napkin and put a few cookies in it. She made her way across the room to where Caroline was seated.

Just as I was about to reach for a particularly sugary-looking cherry tart, Pat rushed into the room.

"Where's Jeff?" he asked me—his face white and his eyes wide.

"Jeff? Probably with Moira. Why?"

"I went back, and at first I noticed that the clock tower bell had tipped over. I was surprised . . . It was supposed to be so steady . . . Then I walked over . . . It was behind the table, by the gate door, so I didn't see it at first . . . There's someone under the bell."

"Someone? Do you know . . . Can you tell . . . who?" I asked, swallowing hard.

"Kim Gray's dead."

I gasped in shock. "I'll text Jeff."

After I sent the text, I followed up with a call. I kept my voice low as I told him what happened, relieved to find out he was across the street, walking his mother to her car. Seconds later Jeff burst through the door and headed straight back to the portico.

"Don't move," he said to Pat and me. "Nobody moves. Make sure, okay?" We both nodded, and Jeff went out the side door.

I put my arm through Pat's and leaned my head on his shoulder. Poor Pat. In December, I'd been the one to find a dead body, and it took me a long time to get that image out of my head. Some nights Mark Pine, one of my former employees, still haunted me.

"Okay, Ruth?" Jeff was speaking to me, and I hadn't heard a word. I hadn't even seen him come back in.

"Sorry. Say it again. I was a million miles away."

Jeff reached a hand out, took mine, and gave it a squeeze. "Do you have a list of who was here today?"

I disentangled myself from Pat and stood. "Yes, Nadia had a sign-in sheet, so we could contact donors who didn't make it. She also wanted to get the names of folks who came by, so we could follow up with them."

"Good. Get those lists and add the names of anyone else. Write down the timeline. Everything you remember from today."

"You want me to help?" I said.

"I want you to cooperate," he said. "Pat, come back and

show me what you found. Talk me through it. You up to that?"

"Of course," Pat said. The two men walked out toward the back of the room.

"What's up?" Ben asked. He and Fred had continued to move the tables into the side room where we were going to store them. They were both about to grab the last table and had stopped when Jeff rushed past them. "Where's Jeff going?" Everyone stopped what they were doing and turned to look at me.

"There's a situation out back. There's been an accident. Kim . . ." My voice broke.

"Is she all right?" Ben asked, concerned.

I shook my head and blinked back tears. She wasn't my favorite person, far from it, but still. Everyone stared at me, and I cleared my throat. "I think we should hold tight while we wait for Jeff, Chief Paisley, to come back. Or until someone else official arrives."

At that moment the scream of a siren came closer. "Speak of the devil," Zane said. The cavalry, in the guise of Officer Ro Troisi, had arrived.

Out in the Berkshires, towns have their own police force. But nights and weekends, the state police were usually on call. Not in Jeff Paisley's Orchard, though. Jeff Paisley was always in charge, along with three officers. Ro Troisi was the only full-time officer, and Jeff's right hand. She had grown up in Orchard, which was both an advantage and a burden. An advantage because she could fill in gaps for Jeff and explain town connections that an outsider might miss. A burden because she was known as the youngest Troisi, the only girl with five older brothers. Her family nickname, she confessed to me one night after we'd finished a bottle of wine, was Princess. The name suited her. Ro had dark, curly hair she clamped back in a clip. She didn't wear makeup, but she didn't need it. Off duty, she looked like a princess, but not the frilly, big-dress sort of princess. More the take-no-prisoners, rally-the-troops sort.

Ro came into the Town Hall and walked over to Ben and me.

"Jeff's out back," I said. "He told me to pull together lists—"

"I know. We've got Wilson and O'Malley securing the perimeter. Marytown is sending over a team to help. They are going to be here in a few minutes."

"State?"

"We've had to call them in as well," Ro said. "But this is our investigation." She looked up and cleared her throat.

"Listen, folks, I'm going to have to ask you to stay put for a few minutes until someone comes in to take your statement," she said.

"I'm sorry, but that won't be possible," a voice said. I turned to see Jason Scott standing beside the table with the last of the signed strips. One hand was on his waist, the other hand held his water bottle, which was half-full. "I have to get back to the shop and then run back to Marytown to pick up some supplies. You have no idea how quickly we are going through allergy meds these days. They tell me it's because of the winter we had, whatever that means. Anyway, I'm sorry that there's been an accident, I really am, but you can't keep us here. There's a concert tonight. I have to go get dressed—"

Ro muttered, "Give me strength" under her breath— so quietly only I could hear—and turned toward Jason, addressing him but speaking loudly enough that everyone could hear.

"Friends, thank you all for your patience. I'm sorry to say, there won't be a concert tonight. Not here," she said. "This is a crime scene."

chapter 9

Pat Reed and I sat on the edge of the platform and sipped the coffee that Moira had asked Tuck to send over from the Sleeping Latte. We were all waiting for Jeff to tell us when it was time to go home.

"I don't suppose it might have been an accident?" I asked Pat.

"I don't think we're supposed to talk about it," he said.

"When I found Mark in December, I wrote everything down so I wouldn't forget it, and to help me think. I also talked it through with Jeff, point by point. He helped me process what I had seen. You may end up telling Jeff everything in your statement, but I know that he wouldn't be your first choice for a confidant."

"No, not likely." When someone arrests you for murder, that's a hard thing to get past, though I know Pat was trying. For Moira's sake.

"You could always talk to Nancy," I said.

"Even less likely," he said, looking over at his wife. She was deep in conversation with Jimmy Murphy, but as if her sixth sense kicked in, she looked up and met Pat's gaze.

"You need me, Pat?" she asked.

"Wondering if there were more cookies."

"I'll text Tuck and have him bring over what's left. May be a while—he has to close by himself tonight."

"No rush," I said, but it was too late. Nancy's fingers had been flying while we talked and she was already back to her conversation with Jimmy.

"Pat, why don't you tell me what happened. I'll write it down and give it to Jeff. It will help settle your mind, I promise." I sat back and took another sip of my now cold coffee.

Pat still didn't say anything, but I had to keep trying. "How do you think the bell fell over on her?" I asked. "Maybe she was having some sort of attack and she grabbed it for support? Pulled it over on herself?"

Pat took a deep breath and ran his hand over his chin. "The thing of it is, Ruthie, I don't see how it could be an accident."

"Why do you say that?"

"You've picked up a few bells in your lifetime."

"Tried to with some of them." Bells could be awkward to pick up. Heavy, weight not evenly distributed. Wrestling a bell wasn't simple.

"So what are the chances of a bell falling off a stand and the mouth covering her face perfectly?"

"Not good," I said, putting my hand on his. "Tell me what you saw."

Pat flipped my hand over, gave it a squeeze, and then let it go.

"I went outside, making sure the bell was set up like we'd

talked about. Then I saw a pair of legs around the corner of the table. I knew it was Kim—I recognized those ridiculous shoes she insists on wearing. At first I thought she'd passed out, so I started to go over to her, but then I saw the bell . . . and that she wasn't moving. I checked her pulse to be sure. Then, well, you know the rest."

"Poor Pat. I'm so sorry."

"I'll be fine. But I won't forget it, not for a long time," he said.

"Can I ask you a gruesome question?"

Pat screwed up his face, but didn't look away. "What?"

"The scene must have been a real mess."

"A real mess? What do you mean?"

"You're going to hate this, but I've been reading a lot of crime novels lately—"

"Bad enough you're living one—"

"Enough. Anyway, head wounds are really bloody. Plus, everything else. But you don't look like you got any blood on you."

Pat closed his eyes. "There wasn't a lot of blood," he said.

"Maybe you missed it?"

"Ruthie, I'm going to tell you something I'm not too proud of. I can't stand the sight of blood. Back when the kids were little, Nancy was in charge of Band-Aids. Nope, if there'd been a lot of blood I wouldn't have gotten close. But I walked around and checked her wrist for a pulse. Got close."

"Make sure you tell Jeff where you walked, just in case there are footprints," I said. "I'm sure it's important for him to have every detail. Did you see anyone else?"

"Zane was going to go up to the tower to check on something, lights or something, just as I was coming into the vestibule area. I told him something had happened to Kim and that he needed to make sure no one went back to the portico. I saw Freddie unwrapping a tray of cookies in the corner. Jason was coming in from the kitchen area. He may have been looking for the water tap to fill up his blasted water bottle. He looked like he was going to head out the side door, but I told him not to go out there."

"I wonder why he was heading back there?" I asked.

"No idea, unless it was to sneak out so he didn't have to clean up. I wouldn't put it past him," Pat said gruffly.

The back portico to the Town Hall was blocked from the front path by a fairly sturdy door. It could be opened, but was usually locked to keep folks from wandering around the grounds. The side door led to a good-sized vestibule that provided access to all parts of the Town Hall. One door opened to the staircase up to the clock tower. Another led to the kitchen and office areas. A third let folks into the Town Hall itself. It was quite ingenious, actually, controlling access while keeping the Town Hall itself wide open. If the gate door was closed and locked, the only way to get back there was through the Town Hall.

"Maybe he was going to get his bike? Isn't the new bike rack out there?" I said.

"Other side of the fence, along the 'Dumpster shack,'" Pat said. The Dumpster shack was nicknamed by Mac Clark, who had designed and built the structure, with Pat's and Ben's help, in order to keep the peace on this side of Washington Street. The shack was more of a storage shed. It was behind the Corner Market, parallel to the Town Hall. The fence was attached to it on both sides. Beckett had strong feelings about food Dumpsters, potential rodents, and smells, and complained about the Dumpster

lineup behind the Corner Market. Mac agreed to the building now referred to as the Dumpster shack, partially as an
excuse to step up his recycling game. The structure held
a food Dumpster and recycling bins. Off to the side, out
of Beckett's line of sight, was a compost heap. Mac tried
for 0 percent food waste, preferring to donate to soup
kitchens and shelters when he could, or compost rather
than tossing it.

Mac installed some bike racks along both sides of the
Dumpster shack, part of the agreement he'd made with Kim
to get the Dumpster shack approved and not tied up in permit hell. Kim loved tying things up in permit hell, and keeping her hands on the strings. She wasn't going to be doing
much of anything anymore now though. I shivered.

"That side door used to be one way to get outside to the
back of the building, but now it's the only way, with the
fence."

"Was the gate closed?" I asked.

"And locked," Pat said. "Besides, she was lying right in
front of the door. I don't see how anyone could have gotten
out that way."

After a moment, Pat cleared his throat. "Anyway, that's
all I remember. Once I got back in here, I found Jeff. You
know the rest."

"I wonder if gap in the fence by the 'Been There, Read
That' side was open?"

"Nope," he said. "Beckett's Dumpster was tight up
against his side of the fence." The fence on the Been There,
Read That side of the back grounds was six feet tall, with a
three-foot gap for egress. Beckett pushed his Dumpster up
against that gap, moving it aside only when specifically
asked to. Likely he also parked up against it, to make sure

no one moved it. No one could access the back portico from outside, only from inside the building.

There were a dozen questions pecking my brain cells into action. How did Kim die? When did she die? Why did someone kill her? I ran my hands over the raised gooseflesh on my arms. If someone killed Kim, the only way they could leave was through the Town Hall.

Then, *why* someone killed her was the most important question. That would be the only way to figure out the who. Because the list of possible suspects was long, and likely included me.

The concert was moved to the school gym. There was some talk about canceling it outright out of respect, but then a suggestion was made to do the concert in honor of Kim, and the show went on.

"Thank you all for your patience," Ro Troisi said. "We've got preliminary statements from all of you, and we'll be getting in touch tomorrow to go over them with you."

"Tomorrow's Sunday," Jason said.

"Yes, it is," Ro said, smiling benignly at the big man. "The next day is Monday."

"I just mean, I don't work on Sundays. I spend the day in Marytown."

"Will you have your cell phone with you?"

"Of course."

"Then we can reach you when we need to. And we'll need to, I'm sure."

Ro and Jason had a brief staring contest, but he blinked. I made a mental note to invite Ro over for a cup of coffee. She had a story to share. I could feel it.

"We need to finish cleaning up," Ben said, starting to reach for a stray cup that someone had left on the edge of a table.

"No, we're going to ask you all to leave everything set up just as it is. You need to leave everything here."

"But the leftovers—" Freddie said.

"There are no leftovers. Only evidence," Ro said. Fred put his arm around his daughter, and she buried her head in his chest.

Jason Scott scurried out as soon as he could, mentioning "volunteer usher" issues that needed attending. He fussed when Ro made him leave his knapsack, but he finally agreed once she let him take his helmet, water bottle, and bicycle wheel so he could ride back home. He scurried off, shirttails out, pants clipped at the ankles. I was grateful he hadn't changed into his bike shorts. That was a sight I didn't need to see tonight.

No one else made a move, so I stood. "Well, friends, I hate that this is how today ended."

"Me too," Nancy said. She put her arm around Caroline's shoulder. "What should we do next? Head over to the Latte?"

"It's late," Caroline said. "I for one am exhausted. How about if we all meet at the Cog tomorrow afternoon?"

"That sounds like a good idea," Flo said. "Perhaps we should have a meal of some sort?"

"We could use a Grandpa Harry high tea," Nancy said. My great-grandfather Harry wasn't as gifted a clockmaker as his son or his father but he was a real town leader, getting Orchard through Prohibition, the Great Depression, and World War II. Rumor had it he got the town through Prohibition by running a speakeasy in the back of the shop on Sunday afternoons. He called it "high tea." Everything was served in china teacups, but it was seldom tea.

"I think that could be arranged," I said, looking at Caroline. She nodded.

"I'll send out an e-mail when I get home, coordinating food," Nancy said. "Caroline, can you take on the tea?"

"Nancy, I didn't mean for you to take over—" I said.

"I'm not taking over. I'm helping. You don't mind me helping, do you?" she said, looking hurt. "Because—" Pat shot me a look, and I understood.

"Of course not, Nancy. You know I can't pull these things off without help. Let's plan on five—"

"There's a game at four," Pat said. The game was, of course, the Red Sox. I had learned opening day that the Red Sox and their games were a major part of Pat Reed's summer entertainment. *Entertainment* was probably too mild a word. His summer obsession. It was quickly becoming one of mine as well.

"The game will be on," I said.

"Then I'll be there at four," Pat said.

"You two are impossible. I doubt that everyone wants the play-by-play . . ." Nancy stopped and put her hand over her mouth. "What are we doing? Kim is dead. We're planning a party, and Kim is dead."

"Let's call it the business owners of Orchard gathering to show respect," Flo said. "That's appropriate, isn't it, Caroline?"

"I should think so," Caroline said. "A wake of sorts."

"You see? If Caroline says it's fine, it's fine. Now listen, Nancy, I'll be in touch. Ben, would you drive these old bones back home? I don't think I can do it."

"Of course, Aunt Flo," Ben said. He walked over to me and squeezed my hand. "Are you okay? I'm going to drive her home, then I have an errand to run. Not sure when I'll be back."

I squashed down my disappointment and forced a smile. "Call me when you get back," I said. "Maybe come over?"

"It may be really late. But I'll see you tomorrow, I promise."

chapter 10

I unlocked the front door of the Cog & Sprocket and took a deep breath. The faint scent of motor oil, cleaning solutions, old furniture, and family history never failed to calm my nerves, no matter what state they were in. The front counter was up, and the curtain that blocked the pass-through between the open-backed shelves that divided the workroom and the shop itself was open. The shelves held some of our stock—the carriage clocks and shelf clocks that deserved public viewing and were for sale. We made it a point to have clocks at all price points, and some featured in-progress work to let folks know what was possible for their family heirloom. I always left a clock being repaired on the front counter. My secret was the clock, and three others like it, were never going to be fixed. They were there for demonstration purposes or as conversation starters.

Instead of heading to the back stairs, I walked over to the right and sat on the settee. It was an old piece, one that my grandmother had had in her bedroom. Camel backed, with mahogany claw feet that grasped orbs. Some value had been lost after years of refinishing and reupholstering and everyday use. But that was as it should be. I ran my hand over the black fabric with its white, '50s-inspired starburst pattern. The entire room was like that—old furniture recovered with midcentury fabric in black, white, and grays, with an occasional red or yellow accent. Everything was meant to be sat on and used, rather than admired. The furniture matched my clock philosophy. It may be valuable, but it couldn't be so precious that it couldn't be used. In my opinion, there was nothing sadder than an old clock that was only a piece of furniture, rather than a wondrous machine that continued to keep time.

I leaned back on the couch and closed my eyes. There was much more comfortable furniture upstairs in my apartment, but I wanted to process this down here, where the ghosts of the Cog & Sprocket regularly gathered to inspire. I felt a push against the side of my foot and opened my eyes to look down. Bezel roughly pushed her face along the length of my foot. She looked up at me and headbutted my knees. I patted my lap, but in typical Bezel fashion she ignored me and jumped up beside me instead. After she'd settled down she did reach out and put her paw on my lap. At least there was that.

Bezel was usually kept captive up in my apartment, but Saturday night into Sunday was her roaming time, when the pet door that was installed on my apartment was unlocked. Cat dander wasn't good for clock parts, or for Caroline's allergies, but thirty-six hours of Bezel didn't cause too much damage, especially since we had an air filter on all the time.

"Bez, Kim Gray was killed today," I said.

She squeaked at me and tilted her head. "You're right, I

don't know that for sure. But she did die. Someone crashed her head in with the bell we were going to use in the tower." Another squeak. "Good point, Bez. That wasn't a perfect bell, but still. I hate that part of the clock is involved in this." I petted her head and then ran my hand down the length of her body. She sighed and closed her eyes. I did the same thing, but kept petting her. Bezel had taken my grandfather's death as hard as any of us. It took her a few weeks to trust me, but now we were a unit. Even with Ben and Blue in our lives, Bezel still owned me, and knew it.

There was a slight rapping on the glass door to the shop and I instinctively shrunk down on the couch. I should have gone upstairs. Lights on meant an open shop to a lot of folks. I sighed and stood. "I'll be right back," I said to Bezel.

I parted the old-school metal venetian blinds that covered the front door. Like others items in the Cog & Sprocket, these blinds were well used and had been both repaired and restored over the years. Opening and closing them had been part of the daily routine of the Cog & Sprocket for as long as I remembered, which was the primary reason I didn't get rid of them in the rehab. I didn't see anyone at the front door, but suddenly Moira Reed's face appeared. I jumped back, and then I opened the door.

"You scared me to death," I said, wincing at the word *death*.

"I wasn't sure you were here," she said. "I thought maybe you'd gone out to the cottage."

"No. Caroline invited me, but I wanted to be alone."

"Do you want me to go?" she asked, gesturing behind her out the door.

"No, come in."

"Do you have wine?" she asked.

"I do, upstairs."

"Well, that's good. We need something to go with all this food." She held up two canvas bags, both of which were loaded to the very top.

"This is really good," I said for the third time. Other than that sentence, we'd eaten in silence for fifteen minutes, devouring a fig-and-cheddar-melt panini with a side of homemade potato chips in between sips of a particularly hearty Malbec.

"A Freddie special," she said. "I tried to tell her that no one wanted to eat a melted sandwich that wasn't piping hot, but she told me they'd eat these. She melts the cheese on both sides, then puts the fig jam in the middle, and it seals it up. I've gained five pounds since she started working for us. Sandwiches aren't even her best thing. Try this." She took a cardboard to-go container out of her bag and opened the lid. She grabbed a spoon and added a dollop of coleslaw to my plate.

"I like these to-go containers, by the way. Recyclable?" I took a fork and dug into the slaw. Bacon, blue cheese, red cabbage, grape tomatoes. A vinegar-based dressing. Yum.

"Indeed they are. Make Orchard Green. Just like the bags. The only thing Beckett, Ben, and the Clarks have ever agreed on."

"When I first heard that tag line I thought they meant Beckett Green, and it made me a little sick to my stomach."

"My mother said the same thing," Moira said, laughing. "I hadn't even thought of that."

"Now that it's in your head you won't be able to see his new T-shirts without feeling a little nauseous. The 'Green' part of the logo is five times the size of 'Make' and 'Orchard.'"

"Well, he's contributing the recycling garbage cans to downtown, which is great," Moira said.

"It is." I nodded. "One a block, though. How many folks visit Orchard in the summer? Seems like overkill to me."

"Well, we have a fair amount of traffic since we're on the back route between Tanglewood and Marytown. Plus the students over at Harris University tend to wander over here during the summer."

"What's the attraction?"

"Aside from excellent food and coffee? The river adventure."

"The river adventure?"

"I keep forgetting you haven't been around for a few summers. The Hamiltons have a kayak/canoe rental outfit that runs Memorial Day to Labor Day. Did run. Kim shut them down this year. Claims they didn't have permits to run the business."

"Did they?"

"Probably not. The whole point of Orchard is that it isn't a permit kind of place, you know? Needs to be safe, and compliant with laws, of course. But Kim added layers of bureaucracy to everything. You know that better than anyone."

Indeed I did. She kept me hopping with the clock tower. Or rather, she kept Nadia hopping. My patience with Kim had worn out before the spring thaw. Long before.

"Is the Hamilton family Fred's family?"

"Yup. The Hamiltons do a lot to cobble together a living out here. So do most folks. All the pieces work together to make enough to get by."

"Kim made it harder," I said.

"She did. It's like she had it out for them," Moira said, grabbing a handful of chips. We ate in silence for a bit.

"What's Kim's story?" I asked.

"What do you mean?"

"She isn't from here, is she?"

"No, and that was a big deal when she got hired, trust me. Grover Winter met her when he was a state representative, and he hired her to work in his office. After he retired, he stayed in touch with her. She went up to Vermont, then over to upstate New York. Municipal jobs. When they decided to create the position for Orchard, he suggested she throw her name in the ring."

"Did Grover know she was a nightmare before he passed, or is this new behavior?" I asked.

"I remember him saying she'd changed since her husband died."

"She was married? Did she have kids?" I knew nothing about Kim Gray's life. I never bothered to ask, or thought much about it. I assumed that anything worth knowing would get to me via the gossip network.

"No kids, that I know of. Wow. I don't know." Moira took a cookie off the plate. She broke it into bite-sized pieces, but didn't eat any.

"I know. Ever since I heard the news, I've been wrestling with something. I feel badly that Kim died. Maybe it was natural causes—"

"Fat chance of that around here."

"Nice."

"Sorry, I didn't mean—"

"I know. But no matter what happened, I feel terrible that I don't feel terrible."

"Well, at least you're not celebrating," Moira said.

"What?"

"I hear that the rounds were on the house over at the Beef and Ale."

"Keeping it classy."

"Always. Anyway, I get what you're saying. I'm the same. Not to say that I'm glad she's dead, but I'm not mourning her loss. Not many folks will be. Jeff's trying to reach her family. Mum and Jimmy Murphy are figuring out a public memorial service, probably the end of next week. They're hoping whatever happened gets figured out by then." Moira sighed and went back to moving her cookies around the plate.

"I'm sure Jeff will get it all sorted out."

"Listen, I have complete faith in Jeff. I'm crazy about the guy. But here's the thing. The suspect list is really long if this was a murder—"

"Who do you think is on it?" I asked.

"Half of Orchard, for starters," she said.

"Seriously," I said.

"I don't know," Moira said. "I'm not good at this sort of thing. Jeff is. You are."

"Moira, I'm not—"

"Just stop. I'm just saying that Jeff's going to need some help."

"He's got Ro."

"You know what I mean."

"What?"

"Ruth, like it or not, you have a talent for putting more together than clocks. Do me a favor, get out ahead of this."

"Ahead of what?"

"This is the third death in a year. Four, if you count Grover. I'm worried about Orchard. There's a cancer that's been growing here, and we need to get it cut out. I know Jeff's up to the job, but you've got a different set of skills. He'd never ask, but he needs your help. We all do."

• • •

Moira had left around ten. I'd looked at my phone and saw that I'd just missed a text from Ben. *Won't make it tonight. Sorry about that. You OK?*

I had a rule of thumb about texting versus calling. Only cowards text rather than call to break a date. Sure, we didn't have firm plans, but I'd hoped he'd come by tonight. I'd texted him back. *See you later, unless you're busy.* Passive-aggressive, sure. But at least I wasn't a coward.

I woke up in a foul mood. Strong coffee, usually an elixir with mood-altering properties, didn't work its magic this morning. Even Bezel, being her loviest, didn't help, though petting her calmed me down. After I'd settled down at the kitchen table with my eggs, more coffee, and a new notebook, she sat underneath the table and put her paw on my bare foot. I made a note to get her nails clipped, but didn't move my foot. It was, after all, the thought that counted.

I unwrapped the new notebook and sighed deeply as I opened it. My grandfather had passed on the notebook habit. Large, black hard-backed notebooks. Blank pages, used for lists, notes, doodles. Sketches of clocks to fix and clocks to make. I'd found years' worth of his notebooks, and I kept them all upstairs. Nadia had been working on getting them in chronological order, and then she was going to start to index them soon. G.T. was a creature of habit, and that made the job a little less daunting. He started a notebook, put the date on the inside cover. Once the notebook was filled, he put the end date on the back inside cover, and then went to the next book.

All the years I'd been married to Eric, I hadn't filled up

one notebook. Even when I started making art pieces and clocks, I hadn't done a lot of daydream sketching. Life with Eric had boundaries, and even my imagination stayed within them. I don't think G.T. had limitations, but he was focused. Everything was about the shop, and clocks. Other thoughts were put in the same notebook, questions in the middle of a page, or lists that meant something to him, but would take years to decipher. Once I'd realized what had happened to Grover Winter I'd gone back and looked at G.T.'s notebooks. Now random sentences made sense, and lists showed the way he was putting facts together. But you had to know what you were looking for to find it.

Harry Clagan had been a different animal. He kept the books for the shop in ledgers. We'd used similar ledgers up until this winter, and Caroline still insisted on keeping them as backup for the computer system we'd put in place. I'd found other notebooks that told other sides of Harry. One was a journal, with a running history of Orchard from his point of view. That had been invaluable while reconstructing the story of the clock tower. I'd also gotten a glimpse into the complicated soul of Harry Clagan—the despair he felt when his wife died, leaving him alone to raise his young son. His concern for Orchard's citizens during the depth of the Great Depression. His pride in his son's great talent. His love for his daughter-in-law. The stories of Harry the bon vivant passed down from my grandmother to me, but he died long before I was born, so I hadn't gotten a chance to know him, until now. These days I felt his presence was as much a part of the Cog & Sprocket as my grandparents' were—three benign ghosts who watched over Bezel and me.

This winter I'd found another notebook hidden in one of the floorboards. This Harry notebook held accounts for the people of Orchard. I couldn't always tell what the accounts were for, but they weren't for clocks. I was still deciphering the codes he used, but I'd come to suspect that Harry may have been a bootlegger during Prohibition. And he may have run a card game. I kept this notebook, and its secrets, to myself, but I was determined to break the code.

Harry had been famous for keeping Orchard running during the hard times. Clock repair business hadn't been robust during the Depression, but Harry kept people employed in the shop, and in building the clock tower. The mystery notebooks helped me understand how. Surely the statute of limitations was done on any misdeeds Harry had done? Besides, he'd done them for the best of reasons. I didn't intend to judge, only to know more about my family history, sordid or not.

Once I'd moved back to Orchard, I began a new notebook in honor of this new phase of my life. But part of Harry had been passed down to me, and I'd started a second notebook that was more of a journal where I processed my feelings about the changes in my life, and listed five things I was grateful for every day. The inner-thoughts writings were skimpy, but I'd kept up with the gratitude journal. For the last two months, Ben had made the list every day. I sighed and ran my hand down the notebook.

I'd started a new notebook again when Mark Pine had died, and made notes of the investigation as it had progressed. I'd even made notes after the case had been solved, and then I put the notebook in the new hiding place I'd created in the bottom of a grandfather clock that was in my bedroom, along with Harry's secret notebook. This new notebook was my casebook for the death of Kim Gray. I didn't like polluting my other notebooks with my ruminations on murder, but found writing and drawing to be very helpful.

I laid out my pencils, my pencil sharpener, and a large

eraser. Then I started to write. I wrote down everything I remembered from yesterday. I made a timeline. I drew a diagram of the room, the vestibule, and the portico. I kept adding details on different pages, trying to categorize details into different lists, while keeping myself from jumping to conclusions. I wrote and drew. At one point Bezel left and went back into my bedroom, presumably to take a nap on my bed. And still I wrote. When I finally looked up I'd been at it for over an hour.

I stood and stretched. Almost ten o'clock. I'd put in the broad strokes. More details needed to be filled in. I wasn't sure if I could add them all myself. But I'd need to try. Later. Right now I needed a shower, and to start working on a clock, my favorite way to calm my mind.

chapter 11

"What are you up to?" Pat said as he came in the back door of the shop carrying a large wooden box. He hip-checked the back door to close it again.

"Working on Flo's clock for the barbershop," I said.

Flo had found an old tin barbershop sign and asked me if I could turn it into a clock. Of course I could. I'd spent some time figuring out how to make the clock work so that it would be aesthetically pleasing to Flo but wouldn't make generations of Clagan clockmakers roll over in their graves. I'd decided to make the clock guts, as Flo called them, visible on the front of the sign. Or seemingly visible. The cogs and wheels didn't actually run the clock, they only looked like they did. The real clock guts were in the back, with an eight-day winding mechanism.

Pat stood behind me and peered at the clock. "That looks terrific, Ruthie," he said. "She's going to love it."

"I hope so. I'm going to show it to her after I've got a

few more details working. You did a great job cleaning up the sign," I said. The sign had been slightly dinged up, with spots of rust and faded lettering. Now it still had weathered charm, but looked refreshed, with the rust spots gone, the lettering redone in black against a white background.

Pat smiled and went over to another worktable. He put the wooden box down on a stool and went over to grab a black cloth to cover the surface. The black helped us keep track of parts while we took apart clocks.

"What have you got there?" I asked.

"I went by the town tag sale in Marytown this morning. Picked up a few things."

Pat unpacked the box, and I let him lay out his treasures before moving in to look at them.

"Lovely," I said. I picked up one of three shelf clocks he'd laid out. I heard a *clunk*, and winced. Clocks shouldn't clunk.

"You can tell me if you think they're worth anything," Pat said. "I liked the look of them and thought they were worth trying to restore for the cabinetry if nothing else."

"Do you think they're worth anything?" I asked. If Pat wanted to become a clockmaker, he needed to start being able to judge these things for himself.

"Well," he said, running his palms down his jean legs, "as I said, the outsides are all worth trying to fix up, no doubt. This one"—he pointed to the clock on the far right—"this one looks like it may be in its original shape. The other two have been restored—you can see that the labels on the bottom have been removed and put back. I haven't had a chance to look inside, of course, but that one also looks like the clockface and maybe the crystal are also original." He sounded more sure than his nervous eyes let on.

"I agree. They are all terrific, and we can use them, but that one is a real beauty. We won't know until we look at it more closely. How much did you pay for them?" Pat quoted me a number, and I smiled up at him. "Wow, what a steal!" The color rose slightly on Pat's face, and he broke into a grin.

"I thought these might be good to use as lessons for me," he said.

"Perfect," I agreed.

We had dozens of clocks that could have served the same purpose, but Pat was an obstinate man. Another cranky Yankee, as it were. It was hard for him to ask for help, even when it was to learn my trade. So I'd let him set the tone and choose the path. But teach him I would. Pat had as much passion for clocks as any Clagan. I hoped the talent was there as well.

"Went by the Town Hall before I came over. Jeff asked me to meet him there and walk him through what happened." He took a steadying breath. "The building's still closed. Probably won't be open again today, but Ro said they're trying to let us back in tomorrow, Tuesday at the latest."

"I hope so," I said. "I know they need to do what they need to do, but we've already got an impossible time schedule on this project."

"At least she wasn't killed in the clock tower itself."

"No, just out behind the tower. Under the tower bell."

Pat screwed up his face, jutted his lips out, and pulled them back in. He and I locked eyes, and I didn't blink. I also didn't say anything. I knew Pat wanted to tell me something—the lip dance was a sure sign. I also knew that Pat abhorred gossip, likely a direct result of living with Nancy, one of the great gossip hubs of Orchard. I'd trust Pat with any secret, and hoped he felt the same way about me.

"Cone of silence?" he said.

"Cone of silence," I agreed. Our shortcut language for "just between us." I'd tell my notebook later, but only the notebook.

"Do you remember when you asked me about what I saw? Were you asking me about how much blood there was?" he asked. I shrugged my shoulders, afraid to respond with the truth. I hated my morbid curiosity and didn't want to admit to wondering why Pat wasn't covered in blood last night, especially after he'd told me he'd checked Kim's pulse.

When I didn't respond, Pat continued, "I worry about you, Ruth, I really do. Thinking about how much blood . . . Well, anyway, Jeff told me that she couldn't have been killed by the bell."

"But you found it on her head? How could that not have killed her?"

"It would have, but she was probably dead already. Otherwise, there would have been more blood. But you knew that. From your true crime reading."

"The books are more scientific than salacious . . ."

"On second thought," he said, shrinking back, "I don't want to know."

"So, she was dead and then someone dropped a bell on her? Even if they didn't intend to kill her . . ." I said. "I wonder, did she die there, on the back portico? Maybe she died somewhere else and got moved there?"

"How would they have moved her there? The only way to get back there was through the vestibule since the gate door was locked. Surely someone would have seen that. Besides, it looks like she was there for a while. They found cigarette butts. Jeff asked if anyone else had been out there smoking. I told him not that I knew of."

"Kim smoked? I didn't know that."

"These days it's hard to know that folks smoke, since there are so few places you can do it anymore. Back in the day, everyone smoked everywhere. Now you have to smoke in secret."

"You sound bitter about that," I said.

"Listen, I used to smoke. I loved smoking. If they told me I had two months to live, I'd take it up again. I went back to it during the troubles last fall. I didn't buy a pack, but I'd bum a cigarette, go out, and hide. That's how I knew Kim smoked. She gave me a cigarette one day before a town meeting. She'd started up again. Stress."

"Stress. Selling the town down the river is stressful, for sure," I said.

"You want to hear something funny? I actually felt sorry for her, at least I did back then. Before she declared war on you."

I smiled at Pat and put my hand on his forearm. "Of course you did," I said. "You're a good man, Pat Reed. Anyway, they found cigarette butts in the back portico, which means that Kim must have been there for a while. Why didn't she come in? Maybe she was waiting for someone? Or had a meeting? Do they know how long she'd been out there?"

"Jeff didn't go into details," he said.

"I'm sure he didn't," I said.

"He plays it pretty close to the vest, but he did tell me two things. First, she may have died of natural causes, and the bell may be a separate incident. So best not to jump to conclusions."

"I wasn't jumping anywhere," I said.

"Second, the suspect list is a mile long. And you're on it."

• • •

Though I was rattled hearing it aloud, I wasn't surprised. Of course I was on the list of suspects. But, as Pat pointed out, the list was undoubtedly a long one. Kim Gray did not go quietly through life. Who knew what enemies she'd made before coming to Orchard? Again, I was struck by how little I knew about Kim or her personal life.

I was about to ask Pat for more details when the front door of the shop shook on its hinges. I looked up. Noon. I hadn't unlocked the front door yet, but being late was my unfortunate trademark.

"I wasn't sure you were opening today," Beckett said as he came in.

"Sunday hours. Noon to five, or by appointment. Not that I expect a lot of traffic today," I said.

"I was thinking that we should all close down today, in memory of Kim," he said.

"I think that the best way to honor Kim is to keep the stores open," I said. "I don't think she'd want anyone to lose money in memory of her."

Beckett sighed and shrugged his shoulders. He turned to the side and looked at the shelf of clocks that were over my shoulder. I turned to look at them as well.

"Those are lovely," he said. "Originals?"

"They're all originals," I said.

"What I meant was, what are they worth? Sorry to sound so crass, but I'm trying to educate myself."

"Of course. The price point varies. I try and always provide people with a range of prices—it helps them understand that affording a fine clock isn't out of folks' price range. It also helps people appreciate the fine craftsmanship that goes into clocks and understand the value of that craftsmanship.

Pop quiz, Beckett. Which clock is the oldest?" Beckett sheepishly pointed to the center clock, and I smiled. "Got it in one."

Ever since Beckett had been tricked into selling fake antiques he'd been cautious with me. It had taken some convincing to prove to him that I could tell right away, but once I'd shown him how I'd known, he had acquiesced to my expertise. He'd come to every clock class I taught over the winter. His questions had gotten more sophisticated over time. I had to hand it to him, when he was curious about something, he dove into understanding it.

"What can you tell me about this?" he asked, lifting onto the countertop a "Make Orchard Green" bag he was carrying. He lifted a box out of the bag and pushed it across the counter toward me. Most of his stock had been taken back as evidence, but a few pieces had been returned. I wondered if this was one of them.

"Oh, isn't this lovely?" I said. I took the miniature Seth Thomas clock out of the box carefully. Ever since the transport lesson I'd given him, Beckett had taken care to carry the clocks upright and wrapped. "It's a Seth Thomas cottage clock. Rosewood. Tombstone shaped—see the rounded top? Thirty-hour clock. Probably around 1875 or so."

"Amazing," Beckett said.

"Were you testing me?" I asked.

"No, of course not. But I did some sleuthing and came up with the same information."

"It is worth a hundred dollars or so," I said. "Depending on whether it works."

"It works. I wound it up last night, making sure I didn't overwind it."

"Does it keep time?" I asked.

"It runs a little fast, but I can live with that for a while. I was reading up about them. Fascinating. Different shapes, different woods. Some in brass."

"I've always loved miniatures," I said, unable to take my eyes off the pretty little thing in my hands, turning it over again. "Grover Winter collected them. Did you know that?"

"I didn't. How interesting. Is his collection intact?"

"Intact is hard to say." I shook my head, trying to forget the image of a killer crushing a clock under their heel. "There were at least a dozen. We haven't sold them yet."

"I'd love to see them," he said.

"They are all packed up at the moment, I'm afraid," I lied, thinking of them up in my apartment, sitting on the sideboard in my living room. "When I have a chance to unpack that box, I'll let you know."

"Sounds good. I get obsessed easily."

"Well, wander down to the American Clock and Watch Museum in Bristol. They have some obsession-worthy clocks to look at."

"Sounds like a good day trip," he said, looking genuinely excited. "That is, if I can get some more staff to cover the store."

Beckett's unpopularity rivaled Kim's in some quarters. It did not help him hire local staff, though things were beginning to thaw. "I thought you hired three new people last week?"

"Only one of them worked out. I thought a bookstore would be a relaxing venture. Hah. In between keeping the inventory shelved, the store in order, and someone able to handle money, it turns out I am asking for the moon. Especially since I'm also looking for someone who likes books."

"School let out. There will be more people looking for jobs."

"I sure hope so. Listen, this may seem contrary to what

I just said, but I also need to get more folks into the store. I'm hoping you'll reconsider coming in and giving a clock talk?"

I sighed. Beckett Green had gone out of his way to make my life difficult last winter, but he'd come around. Been forced to, because of some issues with his previous business partner. He was one of the chief patrons of the clock tower. He never held that over my head, but I was waiting.

"After the Winding Ceremony on June twenty-first we can talk about it. Until then, I am going to be focused on that."

"Of course, of course."

"Though today we won't be able to do anything," I said. "At least nothing over there. We can still keep prepping things."

"Prepping?"

"All of the components of the clock tower are out at the cottage. We need to start bringing them into town and getting it ready to be put together. Maybe that's what we can do today?" I asked Pat, who had been bent over his clocks, looking them over.

"We only want to move them once," he said. "We'll need to wait until we can get back into the hall. But tell you what. I'll head out and check in with Zane. Then I'll be back here around four, if not earlier."

"Sounds good. See you then," I said, watching him go out the back door without a word to Beckett. I'd forgotten that people were coming over this afternoon. I needed to check in with Flo and Nancy. I was sure that all the planning was done already, but I should at least make an attempt at being a good hostess.

"Have you been over there today?" Beckett asked.

"Sorry, what did you say?"

"I asked if you'd been over to the Town Hall, offering to help the chief."

"What do you mean?" I asked.

"Well, your Nancy Drew routine has helped him out a couple of times, hasn't it?"

"Nancy Drew routine." I felt the color rise on my cheeks.

"No offense, really. I'm sorry. I stopped by and spoke to Chief Paisley this morning, to see what I could do to help."

"To help?" I asked.

"Yes, I know, it seems ridiculous, doesn't it? The chief is a good man, but I know how divisive Kim was. I thought it would be helpful to have him know that someone cared about her and wants justice to prevail. She needs a Nancy Drew to care about her too." He looked down at the miniature and started packing it back up. The breath he took sounded a little shaky.

"Beckett, I'm sorry. I know you were her friend. This must be very difficult," I said a bit awkwardly, realizing that he needed comfort and I was the only one around to give it.

"Who would want to kill her?" he said, still looking down.

"I heard they aren't sure it was murder."

"Jeff's operating on the belief that it was a suspicious death," he said, sighing as he lifted his bag off the counter. "I know she wasn't very popular. She was going to lose her job if Nancy had anything to do with it."

"Nancy and Jimmy Murphy," I said.

"Jimmy? I thought he'd changed his mind."

"What makes you say that?"

"He's the vote that let her keep her job at the last meeting."

"Are you sure?" I asked, surprised.

"I am. I noticed he was using a red pen the day of the vote. I am a bit ashamed to admit it, but I dug the ballots out of the trash, I was so stunned at the outcome. Even though he'd ripped them up and thrown them away, figuring out what Jimmy's ballot said was easy, because of the red. He voted 'no.'"

Jimmy helped her keep her job? After he seemed dead set against her? What game was he playing?

chapter 12

"What was Beckett Green doing darkening your door?" Flo said, the door barely closed behind her. The minute she'd shown up Beckett made his excuses and left quickly.

"Flo, he might hear you," I whispered.

"Nothing I wouldn't say straight to his face—you know that's true."

"I do indeed."

Flo was a woman of strong opinions, but a good heart. She was also, likely, still holding a grudge against Beckett for his antics last fall. I was forever grateful that she was on my side in life, and intended to keep her there.

"Has Nancy called you?" she asked.

"About this afternoon? I've been thinking . . ."

"As have I. I don't believe in crocodile tears, but Nancy and I wondered if we should turn this into a remembrance dinner."

"So I should call Beckett and invite him?"

"Don't push it," she said, leaning against the counter. "You decided to open the store today?"

"Yes, second week of my summer hours. Though I doubt we'll see many customers. I'm open till five."

"Tourists don't really pick up until later in the month, when the schools are out."

I looked out across at the Town Hall. "I'm surprised there isn't press here." I shuddered. It was terrible after what happened at New Year's. The only thing that got them to leave was a record snowstorm in February, the requisite reporting of stranded cars on the highways, closed MBTA lines, and the booming ski season.

"Haven't you heard?" Flo asked. She flopped onto the settee and fanned herself.

"Can I get you a cup of tea? Heard what?"

"Tea would be a delight. Do you have any more of that fancy Paris tea? I don't know what's in it, but it sure is tasty. Anyway, Kim had an allergic reaction—that's what killed her. Apparently, she was desperately allergic to nuts. Did you know that?"

"I didn't." Flo and I walked toward the back of the store together. She settled herself on one of the chairs and leaned back. I went over to the kitchenette and felt the side of the electric kettle. Still warm. I pulled out a couple of tea bags, putting them in two mugs. I didn't bother to ask Flo how she'd heard about Kim. Flo probably knew before Jeff did. "I've got to admit, I'm feeling pretty badly about Kim. How would I know she had allergies? I'd have to have had a meal with her to know she had allergies."

"What do you mean?" Flo asked, taking the mug of tea from me. She bobbed her tea bag in her cup, and I pulled a small stool over that we could both use as a table.

"I can't believe Kim died, and I don't know anything about her. Did you know she smoked?"

"What does smoking have to do with anything?" she asked, squeezing out her tea bag and putting it on a plate I'd put on the stool. Tea and coffee this close to the workroom. I doubt my grandfather would have approved, but it saved people coming up to my apartment and gave me a little more privacy.

"Never mind, Flo. I wonder what she ate or got into contact with that set off her allergies."

"I'm sure Jeff will find out soon enough. Anyway, Nancy told me to meet her here, so we could think about next steps."

"Next steps?"

"Next steps in Orchard. Who is going to replace Kim as town manager? I wouldn't be surprised if Beckett hadn't sent in his résumé for her job already."

"I don't think that's really fair, Flo. I think he was one of her only friends. He's pretty upset."

"How can you be so nice all the time, expecting the best of everyone? Isn't it exhausting?"

I laughed. "It is, as a matter of fact. But hoping for the best is how I roll. Sorry about that."

Flo laughed too. "Roll on, girl. Now, where's that nephew of mine?"

"Ben? He isn't here."

"He's supposed to meet up with us too. I wonder what's holding him up?"

"I wouldn't know," I said. "He hasn't been in touch since late last night. He texted me and let me know he couldn't get together."

"A text? He knows better than . . . You have to cut him some slack, Ruth. He's got some ghosts visiting him this week."

"Ghosts?"

Flo looked down at her cup and took a deep sip of her tea. "I love Ben, with all my heart. Nothing made me happier than when he decided to move back to Orchard, even though I knew the timing was off."

"What do you mean?"

"I'd decided to move, sell the business to Matt, wash my hands of it all. Then Ben needed to come home." Flo twisted her cup in her hand and then looked at me. "I know you think I'm a terrible gossip. I guess I am, but only if I think the gossip serves a purpose. Stirs the pot. Other than that, I'll take a secret to my grave. Now, though, I think I need to gossip a little about Ben. Did he ever tell you what he did before he came to Orchard?"

"He said he owned a business."

"Computers, software. I never really understood what exactly. All I know is that he sold one company for a lot of money. Then he invested all of it in another company. In between he fell head over heels with Martha, and married her."

"I knew he was divorced," I said. "So am I."

"Well, you play your cards pretty close to your chest about your ex, Evan?"

"Eric."

"Eric. But I don't suppose you'd be happy to see him, would you?" I shook my head. "I can tell—your past is past. But Ben, he and Martha have some unfinished business."

"Unfinished business?" I could feel all of the suspicions and doubts that I had been trying to desperately to tamp down rising up in the back of my throat.

"When his second business went bust, so did the marriage. Ben never saw either of them coming. It broke him, so he came to Orchard to regroup. She e-mailed him last week.

Did he tell you about that?" I shook my head. "Well, she wanted to see him. They had dinner, night before last. That's all I know."

"Dinner with exes is allowed," I said with a dry throat. I took a sip of tea, but it tasted like bile.

"They sure are. But I don't want her to break him again. I figure you can stand in the way of that happening."

Before I could respond, the front door opened and Nadia came in. "Is Nancy here yet?" she said as she burst into the shop.

"What's this about Nancy?" Flo said, turning to Nadia.

"No one's seen her all day. Moira's worried sick. So am I."

Nancy's missing? Was this Nancy drama, or was she really gone?

"Where's Pat?" Flo asked.

"He didn't mention she was missing. He went out to the cottage to talk to Zane. I'll text him," I said.

"Text him? Does he text?" Flo asked. "I barely text."

"He does now. With Nadia on the team, it's the only way we can talk to each other easily." Nadia doesn't e-mail, and I don't think she knows you can use your phone to talk. Texting was part of my generation, but I wasn't great at it. I reached into my pocket and took out my phone. Dead. I'd forgotten to charge it.

I sheepishly looked up and displayed my blank screen. I went over to a workstation and plugged the phone in. "My phone turns itself off when I am down to ten percent. For all I know Nancy's been calling me for hours. Sorry about that. I'm a little out of it today."

"It's been a roller coaster these past twenty-four hours," Nadia said.

I looked up at one of the clocks, my favorite banjo with

a painted panel of old Orchard on the lower half. One o'clock. Twenty-four hours ago we were at the Signing Ceremony, having a wonderful time with friends and supporters. What a difference a day makes.

"It should turn back on . . . Here we go."

Yeesh. I had six texts. Three of the texts were from Ben. I'd read them later. Two were from Ro Troisi, and one was from Jeff Paisley. Ro and Jeff had both texted in the last hour and asked me to come over to the Town Hall. The voice mail alerts woke up. I had three messages, and I checked recent calls. Ben, Ro, and Jeff.

"Jeff wants me to come over to the Town Hall," I said. "I don't have any messages"—I quickly checked all three e-mail accounts—"from Nancy."

"Wonder what Jeff wants?" Flo said.

"Probably for me to walk through what happened. He'll want to talk to all of us."

"He talked to me this morning," Nadia said. "I brought him a memory card with all of the pictures we took yesterday."

"Did you make a copy of them first?" I asked.

"Of course I did," Nadia said, looking at me like I had just asked her if the sky was blue and the grass was green.

"Tell you what. I'm going to go over there. Would you mind the store? We won't get any customers, but I'd hate to be closed, just in case."

"Sure. Can you leave me your laptop? I'll upload the pictures while you're gone. I'll also check in with Pat and Caroline, and keep looking for Nancy."

"Great. I'll walk back down to the Corner Market and check in," Flo said. "I'm sure we'll find her. Are you still okay to host an early dinner here in the shop, Ruth?"

"It's fine," I said. Like I had a choice in the matter. "I'm going to leave my phone here to charge, so I'm off the grid for a while."

"Please. Off the grid? In Orchard? You won't be able to sneeze without people saying 'Bless you' all afternoon," Nadia said, settling in to work behind her laptop.

"The joys of living in a small town. I'll take care of dinner, Ruth. Go on over and help Jeff."

chapter 13

Ro Troisi met me at the corner of the Town Hall, where the paths crossed to take you to either the front door of the hall or the side door. I looked up and saw a half-dozen bicycles on the rack on this side of the Dumpster shack. The gate door was closed. I wondered if I could finagle a way to get back there. Morbid, I know, but I wanted to see for myself.

The next project was dealing with the fence around the back of the Town Hall, so that folks could have access to the back grounds more easily. We were still working out the details. Beckett was against the idea—he was determined to keep boundary lines clear. He also didn't want folks who were coming to the Town Hall to park in his small lot. As if a fence would stop them. The Beckett fence, as it had come to be known, circled the back area of the Town Hall as well, delineating the property boundaries, which were tight. It butted up against the Corner Market.

"What are you looking at, Ruth?"

"I'm trying to figure out how Kim got out back without us seeing her—"

"She parked out beside the Corner Market, right up against the fence."

"So someone let her in to the portico, or she came in through the vestibule," I said.

"Looks like."

"Do you know what time?"

"I'll leave that to the chief to share with you. He's inside."

"You're out here because?"

"Just making sure we don't have more visitors."

"More?"

"The chief is waiting to talk to you," Ro said.

"Good afternoon, Ruth," Jeff said. "Thank you for coming over."

"Hello, Chief," I said, looking around. "Are you alone?"

"For now. Waiting for the next wave of techs to come in," he said. "Come on in. We can sit in here." He motioned me to the front cloakroom that he had set up as a makeshift office for himself, blocking me from seeing inside the Town Hall. There were two six-foot tables set up, a box of coffee on one of them, and a half-dozen folding chairs strewn around the room.

"The next wave of techs?"

"As you know, contrary to what folks see on TV, there aren't enough techs to do all the work we need them to do. Sometimes you have to schedule them. Especially when they don't think that your work is a priority."

"Murder isn't a priority?"

"Preliminary findings aren't conclusive. I suspect you heard that already?" I didn't react, and Jeff shook his head. "You're good, you know that, Ruth? Trustworthy as a tomb."

"That's why you like me," I said, smiling and taking a seat.

"One of the reasons, anyway," he said, sighing and shaking his head as he sat across from me. "We can't walk through the site, but I've set up a pretty good approximation. I've been meeting other people down at the station, but I thought I'd invite you into the inner sanctum." I looked around the makeshift office at the pictures on the walls showing every angle of the main room, compiled from dozens of photographs folks had taken that day. I had sent Jeff all the pictures I'd taken, and saw them included. It was disconcerting to see myself so many times. There was an architectural drawing of the room laid out on one of the tables. It showed the room itself, as well as the detail of electrics, plumbing, closets and mechanics that weren't visible to the naked eye. There were circular stickers with numbers at various locations.

"Will all of this help you figure out what happened to Kim?" I asked.

"It will help me think, and give me a better sense of the building, and where folks were yesterday. Since you're the owner—"

"Don't remind me," I said, thinking about leaky roofs and ancient bathrooms.

"Town lore has it that your family has a rich history with this building, so I figured I'd ask you to talk me through a tour."

"Since we can't walk through—"

"Right."

"All right," I said. I couldn't tell what Jeff was up to, but if a tour is what he wanted, a tour is what he'd get.

"Do you notice when you come in, the door feels slightly off-center?" I pointed to the diagram. "Well, it wasn't originally. On both sides of the room they built cloakrooms, but at some point they took the right-hand cloakroom and expanded it a bit so it could house the furnace. Eventually they built a narrow hallway along that entire side of the building, for storage and for more mechanics. See how the stones are just a bit different, more uniform in size, and up on the top the brickwork has holes in it? That was for venting." I pointed to the details on the brick wall.

"Can anyone get back there?"

"You need a key."

"Is it always locked?"

"Yes. The boiler is back there, and other tools. Things that could walk when renters are using the space. This side of the building had the cloakroom, then the vestibule toward the back. Both of these are original."

"How about that wall there?" Jeff pointed to the wall opposite the front door. "Was that always there?"

"Good eye. No, that wall is fairly recent. See how squared off the stones are on the bottom of the wall? They were built to look like the original foundation. The building itself was barely used until the mid-'70s, when Grover Winter bought it and moved his real estate business in here. He built that wall and the offices behind it."

"His business? Really? I was looking around earlier. Those offices did look more recent."

"But they fit the building, don't you think? Stone, brick, dark woodwork. Lots of built-ins. The kitchen area in the middle of the hall. The Winters outgrew the space within a year or so. Rather than raze the building or add on, Grover made a deal with the town to lease it to them."

"There's a basement," Jeff said.

"Yes, but it's got short ceilings. Tight space. A little damp. Mostly used for storage."

"Looks like it used to be some sort of a wine cellar."

"You have been looking around. I think it was used for special storage during Prohibition. I've been reading my great-grandfather's diaries."

"Harry?"

"You are good," I said.

"Not really. I found a plaque with his name on it."

"Really, where?"

"Come here, I'll show you."

Jeff stood, and moved a portable whiteboard he'd set up. Sure enough, a small brass plaque was on one of the stones. FOR HARRY CLAGAN, CHIEF OVERSEER OF OUR TOWN. MAY THE BELLS RING IN HEAVEN.

"That's lovely. I'd never seen that before," I said.

"I'm not surprised. I think it was behind that painting." He pointed to an oil painting in a carved wooden frame that was burnished with gold. It was on the floor, leaning up against the wall. "Someone took it down. I found it in the kitchen, lying on top of a counter."

"Really?" I'd passed by the painting dozens of times, but never stopped to really look at it and never thought to look behind it. I bent down and examined it more carefully. A painting of Orchard, circa 1950. The details were amazing, but tough to decipher while seeing it resting on the floor.

"This isn't a good place to leave it," I said. "Can we move it? I'd love to look at it more closely."

"Technically, this is still a crime scene," Jeff said. "I'll keep an eye on it, and as soon as I can I'll bring it over to you. Now, can we walk through what you saw yesterday?"

I took out my new notebook and opened it. "I thought you'd never ask," I said.

As usual, I gave Jeff much more information than he gave me.

"Is there any reason people didn't go out to the portico during the party?" he asked, his notebook flipped open.

"The plan was to have a cocktail party out there around five. So we were keeping folks out of the area until then, since the beer and prosecco had been iced in tubs out in the back. Oh dear—"

"It's still there. It looks like Kim had helped herself to beer and some food."

"Food?"

"There was a tray of sandwiches, and some tarts."

"That was the cocktail party food, from the Sleeping Latte."

"So there was different food for the cocktail party? Anything in particular?" Jeff took some notes.

"Just more substantive. Finger sandwiches, cheese plates. Nicer desserts. The party was for volunteers and donors, and we wanted to make it more special than the open-to-the-public ceremony."

"Would Kim have been invited to the cocktail party?"

"Yes, though not showing up to the Signing Ceremony, she wouldn't have been welcome."

"Given that crowd, she may not have actually been welcome anyway."

"True enough," I said, fumbling with my pen. Jeff needed

to know everything, so I looked at my notes. "Did you know about the vote?"

"The one they finally had to fire her? They didn't have the vote, from what I've heard."

I bit the inside of my lip and looked down at my notebook.

"What is it?" Jeff said. "You know I'll find out anyway, so you may as well tell me."

"They did have the vote. It was two to one in favor of letting her keep her job. The deciding vote was Jimmy's."

"Murphy? He voted to let her keep her job?" Jeff let out a slow whistle. "You're sure?"

"Beckett Green told me," I said. "He came by this morning, around noon."

"I wish the flow of information worked both ways in Orchard. Thanks to a leak the size of Niagara Falls, most everything about this case became public knowledge as soon as I'd heard it. I hope I've plugged the leak, or at least diverted it, by closing ranks."

"You're bringing in a team, asking for an autopsy?"

"My gut tells me something is hinky about the entire case."

"Your gut? Usually that's my excuse, not yours." He didn't even crack a smile, so I went on. "How can I help you?"

"Between photos and statements, I think I have a good sense of the timeline yesterday. We've even got the window when Kim died—between two thirty and three yesterday."

"That's pretty specific," I said. "How do you know?"

"She called Beckett Green and left a voice mail at two thirty. He told me that much, even let me listen to the message. She mentioned that she was parking out by the Dumpster, where we found her car."

"She was supposed to be here at eleven thirty," I said.

"From what her assistant said, and her calendar indicated,

she intended to be here then. So one of the remaining questions is, where was she during those final hours?"

"Does her cell phone help?"

"Not obviously yet. Aside from the call to Beckett, she didn't text or e-mail from ten o'clock on."

"So, you know she was outside at two thirty. Pat found her at three. Someone let her back through the gate and offered her something to eat. Is that what happened? Come on, Jeff, I won't tell a soul."

"Just curious, huh? Well, this is common knowledge by now. The Marytown PD has had a press conference about it."

"Really?" I said, perplexed.

"No, not really." Jeff sighed. "In that half hour it looks like she was waiting for someone. We found two cigarette butts with her lipstick on them. She must have helped herself to something to eat—"

"Or whomever she was meeting offered her something."

"Right," Jeff said. "It looks like she had some sort of allergic reaction and died."

"Then someone dropped the bell on her head. Why would someone do that?"

"I can think of a few reasons," Jeff said. "But nothing stands out, yet. That's what I'm trying to work through."

"Pat said it was the bell for the clock tower. Is that right?"

"I'd like you to confirm that," he said. "Chances aren't good someone brought another bell in, but I need to confirm it. I have a photo here. You up to looking at it?"

"I guess," I said. Jeff pulled out his phone and scrolled through the photos, settling on one and then pinching his fingers to home in on it. He handed me the phone. Though I was prepared, I wasn't prepared enough. He'd done a good job at limiting my view, but I could still see Kim's hair splayed out on the portico, the bell covering her face.

I took a deep breath and pulled in my view of the photo carefully. When I pushed it back out, I went too far and saw the entire photo. A little blood, but not much, around the body. The bell had done damage—it must have; it covered her entire face. I swallowed back the bile that rose and handed Jeff his phone again.

"It's the bell we decided to use for the clock tower. See here, how it looks flat? The bell isn't perfectly round. There are also jagged edges on the inside of the bell, more so than usual. That's our bell."

Jeff looked carefully at the photo. "Did that affect the sound?"

"A little. We needed to be careful about the placement of the clapper."

"Why are you using it, then?"

"It was donated to us. It isn't ideal, but we needed to make it work. The budget is tight on this project."

"The bell would be a lot to lift for most people," Jeff said.

"See the loop on the top? That is for chains or cables. You can use it to pick up the weight, but you're right, it would be a lot to deadlift for most people. But we had it set up on a frame, so that we could demonstrate how it would sound when it rang. Zane was hoping someone would ante up and buy a new one."

"So someone could have pushed the entire frame over, taken the bell off, and then put the frame back up."

"Yes, they could have. The frame was on wheels, so it was movable. Were there any fingerprints?"

"None that we could find."

"Did you just share a clue?" I said.

Jeff shook his head. "I'm tired. Off my game."

"Was she dead before the weight hit her?" I said.

"Most likely, yes."

"But you think she died from an allergic reaction?"

"Nothing is certain, but we found an empty EpiPen beside her, so the assumption is she'd been having an attack. That's enough for a lot of folks who'd rather see this case closed."

"Really? But there was a bell on her head," I said.

"Folks want to move on before the press finds out what happened. Especially since the season is about to begin."

"Folks? Season?"

"The Board of Selectmen. The Business Alliance of the Berkshires. Tourist season. Having Orchard known as the murder capital of the Berkshires makes a lot of people unhappy."

"Including you."

"Of course, but for slightly different reasons, I suspect. I don't like folks dying in my town. We're maintaining chains of evidence, forensics is doing their work, and we've got techs coming in today to look things over."

"I've heard she was allergic to nuts? Anything else?"

"You are well informed. Why am I not surprised?" Jeff sighed. I made a motion of zipping my lips, then crossed my heart. He nodded and went on. "She was also allergic to bee stings, according to her medical ID bracelet."

"There are bees out in the land behind the tower. The Clarks are keeping hives," I said.

"They're trying to verify if she's been stung. That could explain—" Jeff said, then he shook his head. "What am I doing? You didn't hear all of that."

"I won't tell a soul," I said.

"All of this is conjecture until the ME confirms cause of death. She did a preliminary exam already and is doing a full autopsy today."

"On a Sunday?"

"Kim was a town manager, and that gets some priority. Besides, after the work we did last December, a few folks owed me a favor."

"We did?" I puffed up a little bit. Though I took no joy from the experience, I was proud of my role in bringing some justice to Mark Pine and thwarting an insidious plan.

"We did. But let's be careful of the 'we' here, all right? Don't go investigating on your own. It might be dangerous."

"I'll leave the investigating to you," I said. "My main reason for wanting to know what is going on is that the sooner you figure it out, the sooner we can get back to the tower work. I know that sounds terrible, but the twenty-first is coming up quickly. Can we get back to it soon?"

"Depends on what we find. But I'd imagine we'll be able to release the building in a couple of days. Probably keep the back roped off, though."

"That's fine," I said. "We were going to use it to assemble the clock tower, but we can do it in the tower itself. Though that is a bit risky."

"What do you mean? Risky?"

"During the Second World War, they took out the clock parts and melted them down. Part of the war effort. It took a few years for them to raise enough money to rebuild it. My grandfather was a kid, but was helping out. One day a spark from a welder's torch hit one of the beams, and it festered. Later that night, fire erupted, and the tower was gutted."

"But the building was all right?"

"My grandfather's family lived across the street and saw the smoke and called the fire department. G.T. said his father ran out and grabbed a garden hose, trying to save what he could."

"Seems like he did a good job," Jeff said, looking around at the solid structure surrounding us.

"Well, it helped that the building was solid stone. Apparently the interior was wrecked, so the walls were taken down. That's why you can see the stone in here. The beams in the clock tower were a total loss. You remember how terrible the wooden clockface looked when we went up to clean."

"It still smelled like soot," Jeff said, seemingly happy to be distracted from the case for a moment.

"It did, didn't it? Structural fixes were made, but the clock tower was too expensive to replace."

"Maybe that's what the plaque was for? Thanking Harry for saving the building?"

"Maybe," I agreed. "From the stories my grandmother told me, Harry took the loss of the tower badly. My grandmother said he used to say that a part of him went up in smoke that night. He took the loss personally."

"Sounds like he passed that on."

"He did," I said, smiling a little sadly. "Not going to deny it. Do you need anything else from me?" I asked.

"No, you've been helpful—"

"By the way, have you seen Nancy?" I asked as he shuffled his notes and papers into a rough pile.

"Nancy Reed? No, why?"

"Flo says she's missing."

"Missing? Does Ro know—"

"I'm sure they've found her by now. People don't just go missing . . ." I didn't finish the sentence. We both remembered a couple of times lately when they had done just that. "Tell you what—I'll text you when I hear from her."

"Thank you, Ruth. For everything."

"You're welcome. Call me if you have any other questions. By the way, a few of us are planning on having Sunday dinner this afternoon at the Cog. You're welcome to join us," I said, standing from the table and heading toward the door.

"I doubt I'll be done, but thank you."

"Then I'll bring you a plate. You and Ro. Have either of you been home today?"

"We both got to go home, take a nap, and shower."

"Take care of yourself, Jeff. For the record, I trust your gut. Do right by Kim. She wasn't my favorite person, but she deserves your best."

And mine too, I realized.

chapter 14

Jeff locked the front door of the Town Hall behind me. I took a deep breath of fresh air, happy to be back in the sunshine. I checked my watch—two thirty. Twenty-four hours. I knew that Jeff would figure it all out soon, but I hoped it was soon enough. If Kim was murdered, the last thing we needed was another media circus. Especially since she died during the Signing Ceremony. I know it was irrational, but I wanted the clock tower to be a good talisman—a symbol of hope and pride for the town—not a bad one. Needless to say, Zane was getting his wish. We were getting a new bell.

I looked down the street, toward the Sleeping Latte. They were open until three on Sundays. Another half hour to go. I could stop by and get some food, since I was fairly hungry. Maybe Ben would like something to eat . . . Shoot. My phone was back at the Cog. Funny how naked I felt without it.

I walked down to the crosswalk and looked both ways.

"Ruthie darlin'! How are you?" Jimmy Murphy came up on my left. His white shirt was open at the collar with his blue tie loosened. His blondish red hair was flecked with more gray than I remembered, and the lines around his eyes looked more pronounced. My grandfather always said Jimmy Murphy could charm the paint off a barn. I never understood that until I'd gotten to know him better these past few months. Charming he was, indeed. Normally. Today the smile was a bit forced. Also, he'd been a bit mysterious these days. Where had he been? Been There, Read That? Maybe he'd been over by the graveyard? Wherever it was, I hadn't seen him coming.

"Whoa, Jimmy, you scared me," I said, putting my hand over my heart dramatically. "Where did you come from?"

"Been over to see Beckett," he said. "We had some ill waters that needed to be cleared up."

"Really? I thought you both were great friends."

"Great friends? I'm not going to pretend we've ever been that," he said. "Beckett is a little short in the friend department."

"Especially now that Kim's gone," I said.

"They were good friends, weren't they? Birds of a feather, I suppose. It's all water under the bridge now. I went over to make amends, talk things through. We both care a lot about Orchard."

"We all care about Orchard," I said.

"True enough. It's time to get on the same page. Things have changed. With change comes opportunity."

"Change being Kim's death?"

He had the good grace to look slightly abashed. "Ruth, I'm sorry for the way she passed. What a terrible thing, an allergy attack."

"She died of an allergy attack?" I looked Jimmy straight in the eyes and tried not to blink.

"Now, Ruth, don't even try that innocent act with me. You've been locked in there with Jeff Paisley for an hour. You can't tell me you didn't find out a few things."

"Jimmy, I'm a clockmaker, not a detective."

"Don't make me laugh. You're a fixer. You can't help it. Your grandpa was the same way, God rest his soul. Anyway, the Board of Selectmen have been kept in the loop about the investigation, or what they know so far. We're due for another update at six. I was inviting Beckett to the meeting."

"Beckett?"

"He's offered to step in for Kim while we look for her replacement."

"He has? Already? She's only been dead for a day." Wow, that was fast, even for Beckett.

"Well, truth to tell, he'd made the offer a few weeks ago, when it looked likely she wouldn't be keeping her job for much longer."

"I was surprised she didn't get the boot after the vote this past week. Do you know what happened?" Jimmy didn't even try to look me in the eye. What game was he playing?

"I can't say. If we'd taken the vote this weekend, it might have come out differently."

"Things have been changing that quickly?" I said. "I really need to pay more attention. I've been spending too much time with my head in clock parts."

"Where it belongs. You don't want to worry your pretty head about ugly town politics, now, do you?" Jimmy asked.

"It is ugly, isn't it? Have things always been this bad? I wasn't really paying attention to town politics when I was a kid, but I don't remember this much strife. Maybe my grandparents hid it from me."

"There's always been a lot of drama here in Orchard. The town hit some hard times, had to make some concessions. Memories are long, fuses are short."

"Do you think it's turning around?" I looked over at Jimmy, one of the happiest people I knew, usually. Today? Not so much. He usually didn't have a short fuse. But what if he was pushed?

"What, the town, or the bad faith?" he asked.

"Both, I guess."

"Ruth, my darlin', I believe we are on the ascent. I really do. The last year or so have had the darkest days yet, but daylight is breaking through. Finally." Jimmy stopped, and smiled. "Speaking of daylight, have you seen that ray of sunshine, Nancy Reed, today? I've been looking for her, but she isn't returning my calls." Jimmy put his hands in his pockets and rocked back on his heels.

"I haven't seen her, but I know Flo is looking for her too," I said.

"Good enough. Between the two of us, she'll be found. We have some coordinating to do, do Nancy and I."

"Coordinating? That sounds sinister."

"Nothing of the sort," he said, laughing. "We've got to set some things right now that the path is clear."

"I'll let her know when I see her. In the meantime, a piece of advice?" I said.

"What is it?"

"Don't look so happy. It's a little unseemly," I said, doing my best to furrow my brow.

"Right. You're right." He forced his smile into a neutral line, though he couldn't get rid of the twinkle in his eye. "I'll work on that. I promise. You take care now," he said, giving me a wink.

As he walked away, he did look more serious. But at the same time, I thought I heard him humming, "Ding-dong! The witch is dead."

Jimmy had unsettled me. I knew, from experience, that cookies would help, so a trip to the Sleeping Latte was in order. I walked down toward the Corner Market and then checked both ways before jaywalking in the direction of the Latte.

"Hey, Ruth," a voice said.

I looked over at Flo's Emporium. Jason was standing on the front stoop. He had a disapproving look at first, but broke into a grin.

"You scared me!" I exclaimed. I really was jumpy. Yesterday must have affected me more than I realized. "I didn't see you there. I didn't think you were coming into town this afternoon."

"Sorry, sorry. You did look a million miles away. I thought it would be easier for folks if I came in today," he said. "Have they opened the Town Hall up again?"

"No, not yet," I said. "I was heading over to the Sleeping Latte to get some cookies," I said.

"They are running low on baked goods. At least they were when I went over for lunch. Which surprised me, since it's been quiet as a graveyard around here today." I must have winced, though I tried not to. "Sorry, that was tasteless."

We'd both run out of things to say. With some people, silence was a sign of comfort. With other people, like Jason, it was uncomfortable. Mildly put.

"I hear you've been changing the shop around," I said, filling the space. "Got a lot done?"

Jason shrugged. "Trying to. Flo isn't totally on board,

but she was here helping today. We're trying to get more inventory in, boost sales."

"Ben was telling me about that. What kind of inventory?"

"Right now, seasonal stuff. Bug spray. Sunscreen. Over-the-counter meds, mostly allergy."

"Doesn't the Corner Market carry that sort of thing?"

"They don't have a huge variety. We're trying to fill a need. Make it so that folks don't have to leave Orchard if they don't want to."

"That's handy," I said. "I used to live in the city, and I was used to traveling around for dinner, groceries, you name it. Now I barely leave these two blocks. I'm okay with that."

"Well, they're nice blocks, that's for sure. Getting nicer all the time."

What did he mean by that? Now that Kim was gone? Or was I reading into this? I always felt like I was having two different conversations with Jason.

"—hope he has a chance to think about it."

"Sorry, I tuned out for a minute. What were you saying?"

"Ben and I met this morning to talk about a proposal I had. I'd like to get a license to open a pharmacy here."

"How involved is that?"

"It takes paperwork. I'm a licensed pharmacist, so that helps. We'd need more space, but we could make the barbershop into a storage facility—"

"Close the barbershop? What about Flo?"

"She could open a shop in her home. She's supposed to be retired anyway. This would let her off the hook so she could phase out."

"Ben wants to close the barbershop?" I thought about our earlier conversation and his lack of passion for his work. Did Ben want to change that much?

"Ben and Flo would still own the business, of course. Everything would be in their names. I'm willing to do the day-to-day grunt work. The stuff that bores Ben to tears, but I like it. I like Orchard. I wouldn't mind settling down here."

"Have you and Ben been talking about this long?"

"No, today was the first conversation I had with him. I've been working out the details myself, working on the proposal so that I had a full picture of what needed to be done and how to do it before I brought Ben in on it. I finally got the guts together to talk to Ben, and texted him this morning. Turns out he needed a ride back to Orchard, so the timing was perfect."

"Perfect timing," I said quietly. I wondered where Ben had come back from, but I didn't want to ask Jason. I'd find out from Ben. "So, did you make it to the concert last night?" Changing the subject seemed in order.

"What?" Jason looked confused and fidgeted with his right foot.

"Last night. Weren't you going to the concert that got moved to the high school? Did you make it in time?"

"Yeah, yeah, I did," he said. "Jimmy Murphy saw me on my bike and ended up giving me a ride back to my apartment. Good thing, since I had to go home first and get changed into my black and whites for ushering."

"Black and whites?"

"Black pants, white collared shirt. Plain white, no pattern."

"Do you even own a plain white shirt?" I asked. Jason always wore collared shirts, perfectly ironed. They always had a pattern.

"I own two for this very purpose. Anyway, I made it right before they opened the house, thanks to the ride home."

"Jimmy's a good egg. That was nice of him. Where's home again?"

"Marytown. I have a great studio over there. The price is right."

"You ride your bike from Marytown? That's a haul."

"I don't always ride it the whole way. Sometimes I'll park my car where I need to be that night, then I'll ride my bike. But it isn't that bad a ride. Especially if you take the back roads. You should try it."

"Maybe I will, though usually if I am heading over to Marytown I need something specific, and hauling it back on a bike would be tricky."

"You'd be surprised how much you can carry with the right gear. Happy to show you sometime," he said, and took a gulp from his ever-present water bottle. "Plus, it helps to stay hydrated. I make a homemade sports drink to make sure my electrolytes are balanced. I'll give you the recipe if you'd like."

"Thanks, Jason. I may take you up on that once the clock tower is ticking. Say, have you seen Nancy Reed today?"

"No, why?"

"Just wondering." Silence. "I should get back to the shop."

"I thought you were going to get some cookies?"

"Yeah, well, I changed my mind."

"Woman's prerogative," he said. "See you later, Ruth."

I walked by the barbershop and looked in the window. Ben was there, mopping the floor. I knocked on the window, and he came over to open the door.

"When did you get back?" I said, wincing at the slight reproach in my voice. I didn't want to be a nag.

"A little while ago. I had to go and get Blue, then we went

out for a run, and I came back here to get some of the supplies Flo requested."

As if on cue, the Australian shepherd bounded over, stopping short of knocking me completely over. "Hello, my darling," I said, wrapping my arms around his neck and nuzzling my face in it. The perpetual smile on his face was my favorite tonic. Blue was also a good role model for Bezel on how properly to love your person. Ever since they'd spent more time together she'd become much more affectionate. Lately, it even seemed like she was enjoying it.

"How come my dog gets more kisses than I do?"

I stood and put my hands on my hips. I was tired, and hungry, and sick of pretending everything was all right. "Well, let's start with you going out last night—"

"You said it was okay to go—"

"And then not coming back—"

"I didn't count on Betty breaking down. I hate to admit it, but I think I need a new car."

"Did something happen to Betty?" I asked. Betty was Ben's old VW bug, circa 1976. She'd been garaged for the winter and had been back on the road for only a couple of weeks.

"Got down to Hartford all right. But then she wouldn't start. I had her towed to a garage. Had to take a bus to get back this morning."

"You should have called me," I said. "I would have come to get you."

"With all that's going on, you don't need that," he said, smiling his dazzling smile. "Besides, I got a ride most of the way, then took the bus into Marytown. Jason gave me a ride to town."

"Did you have a good time, wherever you were?" I asked. Yeesh. Not what I was going for. I took another breath.

"I had dinner with my ex-wife," Ben said. He raked his

fingers through his hair and looked away for a moment. When he looked back, I tried not to show any emotion. "It wasn't a good time, trust me. It's hard to describe how screwed up Martha makes me," he said. A shadow washed over his face. He tried to shake it off, but I could see that it was still there. He sat on one of the barber chairs and put his elbows on his knees, burying his face in his hands. I wanted to go over and put my arms around him, but instead I sat on the chair by the hair washing station.

"Sorry, Ben. I didn't mean to sound like that. You don't have to—"

"Yeah, I do. Here's the short version. I was crazy about Martha. Being with her was like a drug, and I was addicted. I trusted her, and took the 'for better or for worse, for richer or for poorer' to heart. She didn't. Worse came, and she bailed."

"I'm sorry," I said. "I know how much it hurts."

"I know you do, Ruth. We've only known each other a few months, but I don't ever see you crumbled by regret. Nancy says that you've . . ."

"Blossomed since my divorce? It's okay, I have. Back when I was married, I was who Eric expected me to be. I was a great faculty wife and deeply entrenched in his academic life. My folks loved that, and loved him. Then Eric had an affair. He broke my heart, for sure. But now? I feel like I've rediscovered the real Ruth since I came to Orchard."

Ben didn't speak right away. I didn't try to fill the silence while he gathered his thoughts. "I'm a lousy barber," he finally said. "I wish I could care about the new store, but I don't. Not the way I need to if I want it to be a success. Not the way you care about the Cog & Sprocket and your clocks."

I sighed. It was true, I really loved what I did. I knew

how lucky that made me. I also knew better than to try and pretend that running a drugstore should be his passion.

"Martha had some paperwork she wanted me to sign. Seems like part of the old business may have some life in it after all. Apparently someone is interested in getting their hands on some of the technology we developed. The part I kept in the divorce. She offered to buy it from me. Had the paperwork and a nice check all set for me."

"Did you? Sign the paperwork?"

"Hell no. I called my friend Paul—that's who I met last night. We haven't talked in a couple of years, and I've pretty much fallen off the grid. Turns out that the work we did is useful as part of a newer technology."

"That's great, right?"

Ben smiled a sadder smile than I'd ever seen before. "That's what I've been wondering the last couple of days. When I heard about the app they were developing, I felt more fired up than I had in a long time. I could get my old life back. Last night, when I was waiting for the tow truck to come and get Betty, I realized I haven't felt that spark about work since I moved to Orchard."

"Maybe not about work, but you've cared about other things. You care about the Town Hall and the clock tower. You cared about G.T. and Caroline, and helped her after he died. You cared about the clock tower for months before I got here," I said.

"I care about you," he said. "A lot."

"So instead of staying with me last night you had dinner with a friend. And instead of calling me, you sent me a text." I hated how hurt and defensive I sounded. And felt.

"My buddy let me sleep in the other bed in his hotel room. I needed privacy to call you."

"To say you wouldn't be coming back? How long does

that take? Especially after everything that happened yesterday."

"Paul could only meet last night, and we needed to talk in person. I felt terrible about leaving you alone. I'm really sorry."

I sighed and then got up to walk over to Ben. He met me halfway. I threw my arms around his waist and rested my head against his shoulder. He returned the hug, and hung on. After a minute, I leaned back, but didn't let go.

"Listen, big guy, I'm sorry to sound like a nag. I was just getting used to flying solo, and then you came into my life. I'm trying to figure this out."

"I don't want you to feel like—" Ben started to say.

I put three fingers on his lips. "Don't. Let me say this. I still feel like I'm able to fly solo a lot. That suits me. But last night I did some thinking, and Flo helped me put some things into focus. I've been hesitant to talk to you about your ex-wife"—I felt his spine stiffen a bit—"or about my ex-husband. It's like coming to Orchard let me cut that part of my life out completely. Except for my friends Rick and Steve—they'll never be out of my life—but even they don't remind me of my years as Professor Evan's wife. My plan was to not deal with it, but then Eric sent me a letter, and you had dinner with your ex-wife. Flo's the one who told me about the dinner, by the way."

"She told me that when she dropped Blue off. I was going to tell you myself, I just didn't know how. It's all pretty complicated."

"Well, I'm a good listener when you're ready."

"I know you are. It's one of the things I love most about you. One of the many, many things . . ." This was the first declaration of love Ben had made aloud, though he'd shown me he cared every day. I hadn't said the word either. Ben leaned down and kissed me. I melted into his arms and returned the kisses. Then I remembered that we were standing in front of a plate glass window in downtown Orchard, and I pulled back.

"Maybe we should go somewhere more private?" I said.

Ben looked at the sun streaming through the window. He leaned down and put his forehead against mine. "I've got to get blinds for the shop."

"You really do." I sighed. I didn't move.

"What did the letter say?" Ben asked.

"Letter?"

"From your ex?"

"I haven't read it yet."

"Why not?"

"Because I've been so happy, and I didn't want Eric to ruin that."

"Wow, it sounds like there are a few unresolved issues there."

"You have no idea. I'll read the letter later. For now, how about if you come over to the Cog—"

"And have dinner with the people setting up tables in the showroom. Aunt Flo texted me the plan."

I sighed. Ben kissed the top of my head and let me go. I reluctantly followed suit.

"I'd forgotten about that," I said. "I guess I should head over—"

"*We* should head over. I'm not letting you face the inquisition alone."

Another reason I was crazy about the guy—he helped me run interference with the real power base behind Orchard.

• • •

Card tables are a wonderful thing, and a staple at the Cog
& Sprocket. Not the modern, cardboard versions. No,
our card tables were wooden, with felt tops. A throwback
to the days when Harry Clagan hosted Sunday afternoon
bridge parties at the shop. They were perfect when more flat
space was needed on a temporary basis—when a clock
yielded more parts than could be accommodated on one
workbench, or a repair had to be halted midway and moved
aside. Or when it was dinnertime at the Cog & Sprocket.

After my New Year's celebrations, I hosted meals a
couple of times a month at the Cog. My past as a faculty
wife helped make me comfortable in the role of host, a role
that caused Caroline no end of stress. Though the Cog was
a store, the point of the open floor plan out front was to make
it comfortable for visitors and make it possible to host different events. It was crowded, but it worked. My favorite
thing about the dinners is that they were potluck. I never
had to cook and was able to eat leftovers for the rest of the
week.

As we walked in, I saw Flo setting up a card table. Ben
put down his knapsack, walked over, and took over setting
the first table upright then setting up the second one. Blue
bounded up the stairs to the apartment to say hello to Bezel.
I followed him up to let him into the apartment, but when I
was halfway up the stairs I saw that the door was already
open. I could hear someone singing in the kitchen. I turned
and jogged back down the stairs to where Ben had begun
helping his aunt.

"Just these two?" he asked, motioning to the three other
tables leaning up against Caroline's workstation.

"Set up one more so we can put the food on it. Close quarters, but it will be fine. It's only family—no need to impress. Help me put these plastic mats down so we don't have to worry if Zane gets overexuberant with his wine."

Family was defined by choice rather than bloodlines for these dinners. The Reeds, Flo and Ben, they were related. We included Jeff in the mix, especially since he was dating Moira. Caroline and I were related by marriage—hers to G.T.—but the bond was by choice. Zane had cemented his place as family when he'd risked his life for Caroline. Sometimes the family dinners expanded to include others, like the Clarks and Nadia. I watched Flo set eight places.

"Where's Nadia?" I asked. "Is she upstairs? I heard someone up there just now."

"Nadia went home to work on the pictures," Flo said. "Nancy came in a few minutes ago. She's upstairs."

"I promised I'd send a plate over for Jeff," I said.

"Of course. There'll be plenty. Nancy brought a ham and a turkey breast."

"Both? Is that where she was all day—cooking?"

"Don't get too excited. She got them from that spiral-baked ham store over in Marytown. You know the one, where they cook it for you, but you can pretend you made it yourself if you slide it into your own pan and heat it up? Anyway, she got them yesterday. No sense in them going to waste, is there?"

"Where's Nancy been all day, anyway?"

"She isn't telling me, that's for certain," Flo said. "She's barely said ten words since she walked in."

"Why don't I go up and see if she needs some help?" I said.

"Good idea. Aunt Flo and I will get down here set up," Ben said.

"We can't do much more until the store officially closes

at five. A few minutes to go," Flo said. "It's been pretty quiet today, but best not to turn anyone away."

"Perfect. I want to go over some ideas for the store Jason told me about. I have his proposal here, and I want to see what you think," Ben said.

"Do we have to?" Flo asked. "I trust your business sense."

"This has to be a family decision. That's you and me," Ben said. "Come sit down."

chapter 15

Living above your shop meant that privacy was a moving target. My bedroom area was off-limits, and the living room area was open only if I was in the house. The kitchen area was a free-for-all for anyone who worked at the Cog. Since the apartment was technically one large open space, the boundaries were soft, but established early. The only two beings who ignored the house rules each had four legs, and were chowing down in the kitchen. Given the vigor with which they were eating, I doubted it was regular pet food. I saw Nancy bend down and scoop some more food onto each plate, and knew I was right.

"You're going to spoil them," I said.

"Ruthie, you scared me. I had a chicken breast that needed warming up, so I figured who would enjoy it more than these two?"

"Sorry about scaring you. I'm jumpy today too. Thanks

for thinking of the fur babies. I know Bezel and Blue would thank you if they could get their heads out of their bowls."

"Blue almost knocked me over in thanks, so I'm good. I'm going to put some more in the fridge for later. It's right here, beside the bowl of potato salad."

"What bowl of potato salad?"

"The one I put aside for you. There are never leftovers of my potato salad, and I know you like your leftovers."

"If it weren't for leftovers I wouldn't eat most meals," I said. This was partly because I didn't love to cook. It was also because lately my budget didn't allow for a huge range of meals, and I suspected my friends knew that. I followed Nancy to the refrigerator and took out the bowl, cracking open the lid and dipping my fingers in. "Holy moley, this is incredible," I said. I went in for another taste, but Nancy rapped my knuckles with the wooden spoon she was holding.

"Dinner is in less than an hour," she said in a scolding, motherly tone. "Can't you wait until then?"

"I really can't," I said, pathetically. "I think I missed lunch. Not sure if I ate breakfast, come to think of it. If it weren't for you, I'd be starving to death right here."

"How can you forget to eat? Answer me that," she said, handing me a small bowl and a spoon.

"Easy. I've got a lot on my mind, and food wasn't included," I said, dishing out a healthy scoop.

"A lot on your mind. You've been trying to figure out what happened to Kim Gray, haven't you?"

"Not really," I said, swallowing. "I—"

"Leave this one alone, Ruth."

She turned back to the sink and washed the cutting board she'd been using. She'd wear a hole in it at the rate she was going.

I was used to matter-of-fact from Nancy, but never angry.

I put my bowl down on the kitchen table, walked over, and put my arm around her shoulders.

"What's going on?" I asked.

"I'm cleaning up. That cat of yours will jump up on the counter if she smells chicken." I looked over at Bezel, who stopped eating for a minute and looked at me with a "What do you expect? I'm a cat" expression, then went back to her food.

"Where've you been all day?" I asked. I squeezed her shoulder and then let it go. I stepped aside and leaned against the counter, forcing her to see me.

Nancy rinsed the board and put it in the drainer, then looked up.

"I never wanted Kim Gray to die," she said. "I didn't like her, but I didn't want her to die."

I struggled to keep my face neutral. I never would believe Nancy was capable of killing anyone, but I also knew that she and Kim were far from friends. Best to let her talk this out with me than to hash it out with Jeff.

"Of course you didn't," I said.

"Trouble is, I can't say as I'm sorry she's dead. I mean, I'm as sorry as I am every time anyone dies young. Fairly young. But—" Nancy wrung the dish towel once more.

"I feel the same way. I knew nothing about her, not personally. I couldn't even tell you how she took her coffee."

"Skim milk, extra foam. No sugar."

"Do you know that from the Sleeping Latte?" I asked.

"I know that from meetings in her office. She never came to the Sleeping Latte. Why support the Reed family in any way?"

"I guess you're right. I did see her over at the Corner Market pretty often."

"Well, she had to use some local stores. Besides, the Clarks have all sorts of food and were willing to work with her food challenges."

"Food challenges?"

"She was very particular about what she could and couldn't eat. Some of it was diet—she was always worried about gaining weight. But she had some pretty severe allergies. Couldn't even be downwind of a peanut. Tree nuts were her enemy. She wanted baked, never fried. No butter. She avoided white flour and white sugar. She must have been a joy in a restaurant."

"You never ate out with her?"

"No. Always in the conference room at her office. She'd have the meals brought in from the Corner Market. Basically boiled chicken and lettuce. I tried to bring baked goods, but she'd only let them in once she approved the recipes. Jimmy always said that my tarts were the only thing that got him through our meetings."

"Tarts?"

"Oatmeal crust, nonwheat flour. Happily, dairy was all right, otherwise I don't know what I'd have done. Anyway, how did we get on to Kim's tarts?"

"Kim's tarts?"

"A nickname. Whenever a meeting got scheduled Jimmy would text me 'tarts for the tart' and I knew she'd be calling me eventually to let me know. Usually at the last possible moment, with a 'Would you mind bringing some refreshments?' tacked on. At first, she'd only complain about everything I brought, but then I brought the tarts. She loved them, inordinately. They aren't on the regular menu, so Jimmy's 'tarts for the tart' would give me enough of a heads-up to get them made. Mind you, he got the heads-up from her assistant. She always waited until the last minute and then expected me to drop everything. She was a mean, spiteful . . . Oh my. I can't believe I'm speaking ill of the dead."

"A lot of folks had complicated feelings about Kim," I said.

"I spent the day trying to find her next of kin."

"I thought Ro was working on that?"

"The Orchard Police Department has their hands full on this. Jeff is trying to keep the investigation local, to thwart too much publicity. The board is trying to help where we can, without damaging the investigation. Since all three of us are suspects—"

"Surely not—" I said.

"Don't be naïve. I'd put me first on the list, followed by Jimmy. Then Harriet."

"Harriet? Wasn't she friends with Kim?"

"Harriet tried to rein Kim in. Some misguided attempt to make one of Grover's last acts redeemable. Even she had begun to see the futility of that, but she kept trying, bless her."

"Harriet is a character—"

"A character in a town of characters. Both of us included. She's been trying to track down Kim's family too, but hasn't had a ton of luck. She found a sister in California, but I haven't been able to reach her. We're having trouble finding anyone else, so I've been going through Kim's résumé, trying to contact folks from her old jobs. Lots of unanswered e-mails and phone calls on a Sunday."

"I heard Kim was married?" I asked.

"Years ago. She was a widow, apparently. I only know that because Grover mentioned it when she was hired. Course, we can't find any records of that marriage. Harriet is trying to track it down."

"Was she dating? I thought maybe she and Beckett . . ."

"I used to think so too, but the last few times I've seen them together it's been frostier than an icehouse in January. They must have had a falling-out."

"He stopped by this morning and seemed pretty upset," I said.

"Nothing like the finality of death to realize you can't fix what was broken. Maybe he has some regrets."

"Maybe? Do you have any?" I asked.

"About Kim? No, I've got to say, I don't have a single regret. I tried, heaven knows I tried, but she was a miserable woman. My only regret is that I don't feel worse about her dying, but I suspect I'll get over that."

I started the dishwasher before I went back downstairs. Nancy went down ahead with some of the food. I told her to send Ben up to help me with the rest.

Ben bounded up a minute later.

"Well, that went well," he said. "Aunt Flo isn't taking too kindly to Jason's plans."

"I saw Jason earlier," I said. I was so tired I'd forgotten who told me what when, but I didn't want to play games with Ben. "He told me a little about the ideas he discussed with you this morning."

"Did he mention the barbershop becoming a storage room?" he said, cringing a little.

"Only briefly. Not sure why he told me anything. It isn't really my business."

Ben cocked his head to one side. "You at least have a semi–vested interest. Anyway, I ran it by Aunt Flo. Her attachment to the shop was underestimated. Mildly put. We promised to talk more later, but suffice it to say, she isn't ready to retire."

"So that means you won't expand the Emporium?" I asked. "Is that going to be the official name of it, by the way? Flo's Emporium?"

"It won't be Flo's anything. She's going to take over the barbershop. Officially. We just settled that."

"Which means you'll run the store?"

"Maybe?" he said. He shrugged his shoulders. "We could always make the apartment upstairs into storage if we need it."

"Then where will you live?"

"Babe, I don't know. With Aunt Flo? Maybe I'll rent a place closer to Boston, come back and forth?"

I blinked a couple of times, trying to keep my emotions at bay. "Go back into business?" I asked, throwing a basket of silverware on the tray to go downstairs, using a bit more force than necessary.

"We aren't going to fight, are we? I'm not up to a fight," he said, already looking beaten.

I looked at Ben, really looked at him. Handsome, charming, thoughtful, the same Ben I met back in October. There was a wariness now, though. Maybe it had always been there, but I was starting to notice. I didn't want him to be afraid to talk to me.

"Nah, we're not going to fight," I said. "I don't like fighting. But we're going to talk. Later though. Right now we're going to have dinner."

"We're not going to talk about Kim Gray," Caroline said.

The din of small talk that had been accompanying the food being passed around the table ceased.

"Caroline, what do you mean?" Flo said.

"We aren't going to talk about that poor woman's death."

"Poor woman?" Pat said.

"You heard me, Pat Reed. For whatever reason, she isn't going to see her fortieth—"

"Oh, I think forty was in her rearview mirror," Nancy said. "I was looking at her résumé today. She has professional experience going back twenty-five years. Unless that was a lie too."

"A lie? What are you talking about?" Flo said, scooching back in her chair to peer at Nancy. "And why were you looking at her résumé?"

"We're trying to find her family, if you must know," Nancy said. "There's no information in her files about next of kin. So I thought I'd try and track down previous employers."

"Any luck?" Ben asked as he ate a forkful of potato salad.

"None so far, but it's Sunday. Not many folks at work. I left lots of messages and sent a bunch of e-mails. I got a couple of e-mails back, but they didn't help."

"Didn't she fill out one of those next-of-kin things?"

"If she did, it wasn't in the office," Nancy said, spooning a few more veggies onto her plate. "I'm hoping her insurance will have more information. I'll check on that tomorrow."

"I wonder if Jeff has any more information about what happened," Flo said, looking pointedly at Moira.

"Don't look at me. You know how he is when he is on a case. All work, no play."

"No play?"

"None. He didn't even come by to say hello to his mother."

"Oh wow, I forgot she was here," I said, almost dropping my silverware. "We should have invited her to dinner."

"I did," Moira said. "Janet said she wanted to head back to Jeff's to relax, but that she'd see me tomorrow if we need her again."

"Need her? Are you putting the poor woman to work?"

"Janet helped out at the Sleeping Latte this morning," Moira said, straightening in her chair. "Mom didn't come in, and I couldn't track down Freddie. Luckily Janet dove right in."

"Jason mentioned that you were low on baked goods," I said. I realized too late that I should have kept my mouth shut.

"Oh, I'm so sorry Mr. Organic Only didn't like our selection this morning. As if this morning would be any different than any other morning," Moira said.

"Fussy, is he?" Zane asked through a mouthful of chicken. "I'm not surprised. You know, he's training for a century ride later this month. Has to pay attention to how he fuels his body."

"So I've been told," Moira said. "Freddie's been experimenting with gluten-free muffins, but so far they taste like piles of hay."

"Serve them to him anyway. He's a jackass, may be perfect for him," Flo said, giggling like a schoolgirl.

"All right, everyone, time out," Ben said. "Let's try and have a nice dinner. No more talk about Kim, or Jason."

"How about the clock tower?" Zane asked, serving himself some more ham. "I've been working on a new concoction for the figures that will come out every hour. I left the last test batch of treated wood by the river, hoping to mimic the wear and tear that would occur during rain. They didn't fare so well in the elements. I added more oil to this new batch. I hope they hold up a little better."

"Were your test batches on a whiteboard?" Ben asked. Zane nodded. "Square pieces of work, different colors of brown? I hope Blue didn't pee on them," Ben said.

"That would throw your results right off," Pat said, laughing a little. "Though birds can cause trouble, so maybe that isn't a bad test. Maybe we should move the test board to higher ground after dinner?"

"Good idea, Pat. I wish I'd known what your great-grandpa used on the originals, Ruth. You haven't found his secret recipes for paints and stains, have you?"

"No, just some of the ingredients so far," I said. "Walnuts, beets, blueberries, walnut oil, spirits. He'd write shopping lists in the margins of his notebooks. Hard to tell what was for the clock shop, what was for his cabinetry, and what was his shopping list for dinner."

"Careful you don't mix them wrong and blow up the barn," Flo said.

"Flo, be nice," Caroline said, rearranging her napkin in her lap. "There will be no blowing up of the barn. Not this week. Of course, there was a close call last week, when Pat and Zane decided to try and weld the nameplates to one of the clock weights for practice."

"Who knew the glue we'd used to tack them down would cause that many sparks?" Zane said, gesticulating wildly with his fork. Coleslaw went flying. I needed to remember to put plastic on the ground next time.

"We had it under control the entire time," Pat said.

Dinner conversation moved on then, away from Kim Gray's death to the safer topics of clock weights and welding. I almost brought up the fire in the old clock tower, but stopped myself. Zane was telling stories from his past adventures with clock towers. Only the funny ones, I noticed. I stopped thinking, and sat back and listened.

chapter 16

I woke up Monday morning, tired and alone. Ben had wanted to stay, but his aunt Flo was all wound up and made a few quips about losing her business during dessert. Ben and I agreed he needed to head this one off at the pass.

"I wish I'd never told her about Jason's proposal," Ben said, lingering in the doorframe of my apartment as everyone else downstairs got ready to head home. "It was borrowing trouble."

"Chances are he would have said something to her. He said something to me."

"The hard part is, I don't know what I think about Jason's offer. I don't know what I want to do. Besides be here with you," Ben said.

"You are such a smooth talker," I said.

Ben kissed me. "I've been practicing that all day."

"The kiss, or the line?" Ben smiled and kissed me again.

"Are you two done loading that dishwasher? Blue and I are ready to go," Flo yelled up the stairs.

"Be right down," Ben yelled back, and then asked Ruth, "You sure you're all right here alone?"

"I'm fine."

"Okay, let's meet at the Sleeping Latte for breakfast, before we both have to open up. Sound good?"

"I could make breakfast," I said, thinking about the omelets I could make with leftover turkey and ham.

"I promised Aunt Flo I'd get her a breakfast sandwich. Okay if we meet at the Latte? Seven?"

"Don't think we're not going to talk at some point, Ben," I said.

"I actually was planning on talking at the Latte. Being alone with you in your apartment is too distracting."

"You and your sweet-talking ways. I'll be there," I said.

It went without saying, I was late to breakfast. Of course. A terrible trait, but one that Ben had gotten used to, and he accommodated it by running a little late himself. The barbershop was closed, as was the Emporium. Not much was open at seven except the Sleeping Latte. Even the Corner Market didn't open until seven thirty, though I saw signs of life over there. I had no idea how Ada and Mac kept up the pace their business demanded, especially with baby Jack added to the mix.

If Orchard was quiet, the Sleeping Latte wasn't. I had trouble getting in the door, but since I was willing to wait the line out, I sidestepped it and moved into the seating area. Most of the tables were free. I looked back at the line and saw the problem. Freddie Hamilton was working the front counter by herself. Well, not quite by herself. Ben was frothing milk and pulling espresso shots like a boss.

I walked to the front of the line and stepped behind the counter.

"What's going on?" I asked Ben.

"All hell has broken loose. Can you go in and check the baked goods?"

"Should I run the register?"

"No, Freddie has to stay out here. Ro let me put some stuff in the ovens."

"Ro? What's she doing here?"

"Ask her. Sorry, I'm trying to keep up out here. If she won't let you back, come out and take over here."

"But what—"

"Ruth, my love," he said sweetly, looking up from his work for the first time since I'd walked in, "I don't have answers so don't ask questions. Muffins. Now."

I walked through the swinging doors to the kitchen, unprepared for what I found. Nancy was sitting on a stool at the center table. Pat stood beside her, his arm around her shoulders. Ro Troisi stood as well, trying not to look at them. I saw Moira through the back-door window, talking to Jeff. *Talking* might be the wrong word. Her face was about six inches from his, and her face was flushed.

"Ruth, the kitchen is closed down," Ro said in her most official police-business voice.

"Ben sent me back here for muffins?" I said tentatively.

"They've got two more minutes," Nancy said.

"Please, Nancy, don't say anything, all right?" Ro said.

Nancy glared in response.

"Ro, can I check on the muffins?" I said, shuffling forward. "We can't let them burn. I promise I won't touch anything else."

"Oh, all right," said Ro.

I went over to the ovens and checked the timer. Another minute to go. A minute is a long time when people are staring at you. Fortunately, the sounds from outside the back door diverted my attention.

"What is the matter with you?" Moira said. "You're going to arrest my mother?"

I heard a deep mumble, presumably Jeff.

I focused on the timer. Thirty seconds to go. What was going on in here?

"You want me to shut down my business? Are you freaking kidding me?" Moira shouted.

More mumbles, then the timer went off.

I pulled two trays of muffins and one of scones from the industrial oven. I'd never actually helped prep baked goods before, but I knew enough to move all three trays to racks to cool for a minute. I wanted to ask Nancy what I should do next, but I was afraid Ro would reconsider and kick me out, so I grabbed three baskets and lined them with a cloth and then with brown parchment paper. The muffins were wrapped in parchment paper, with corners sticking up. I lifted one out by the corners. Hot, but I could deal with it. I loaded up the baskets. I didn't look at Ro for permission. Instead, I carried the brimming baskets out front.

"I'll be back with the scones in a second," I said once I'd placed the muffins on the counters in reach of the hungry customers crowding the shop.

"I take it we're not serving hot breakfast?" Ben asked.

"Not likely. Let me go get the scones," I said, stealing back through the doors.

I went back to the kitchen, doing my best to ignore the quietly urgent conversation that was threatening to explode between Ro and the Reeds. I put the orange-cranberry scones—or were they lemon-raspberry, I could never tell one from the other without tasting them—on half the basket. The other scones had chunks of brown in them. Maple-walnut?

"Don't these need some glaze?" I asked, glancing up at Nancy and attempting to act as if it were a normal occurrence to be crammed into the tiny kitchen with three extremely tense people, watching two more outside.

Silence met my question.

"Maybe there's some in the refrigerator?"

"The fridge is off-limits," Ro said, her official voice in place again.

"Off-limits?"

"We need to inventory it."

"Ro, what's going on?"

"I'll let the chief fill you in," she said.

I didn't have to wait long. Jeff Paisley pushed the back door open, followed closely by a still-ranting Moira.

"If you can't trust my family—even after everything we've been through—then I guess it's over," she said, tears running down her face. "I can't believe you think my mother's a murderer."

"What are you talking about?" I asked Moira. Then I turned to Jeff, who was just staring at Moira. "What is she talking about?" I looked over at Nancy, who wouldn't meet my eyes. I hoped she hadn't mentioned her lack of remorse about Kim's death to anyone else. It sure could make her sound guilty.

Not unsurprisingly, Jeff ignored me.

"Nancy, would you mind coming down to the station so we can ask you a few questions?" Jeff said.

"Are you arresting her?" Moira said.

"Shh, Moira, keep your voice down," Nancy said. "I'd

rather go down there than stay here and answer questions. At least that way you can go back to work. Poor Ben, he came down for a cup of coffee, now he's—"

"We need to close the store . . ." Jeff said.

"What?" Pat said, incredulous.

"Hopefully not for long," Ro said, shooting a glance at Jeff.

"For as long as it takes," Jeff said. "Nancy?"

"Can Pat come with me?"

Jeff sighed. "Yes. I'm going to have to ask you not to talk to each other—"

"Oh, for the love of—" Moira said.

"Enough," Pat said. "He's doing his job. Your mother didn't do anything wrong. It will all be fine."

"Dad, how can you—"

"It will all be fine. Right, Ruthie?"

What was going on here? Why was Jeff closing the Sleeping Latte? I'm not sure why Pat brought me into it, except that I was the coolest head in the room.

"Nancy, I'm going to text Kristen Gauger and see if she can meet you down at the station," I said, fingers flying over the screen. Texting Kristen was the best way to get hold of her. I'd learned that the hard way.

"She isn't under arrest," Jeff said.

"Still, better to have her lawyer there, right?" I said, forcing a smile. "Jeff, we all trust you with our lives, but we've got to watch out for each other here." Jeff Paisley had a wicked glare, and I was getting it full force.

"So, when you say we need to close the Latte, what do you mean? Can the folks out there finish their coffee?" Moira asked.

"People are drinking coffee?" asked Jeff.

"And eating muffins," I said.

"Where did they get the muffins?" Jeff asked.

"I put them in the oven when I got in this morning," Moira said. "Thanks for taking them out, Ruth."

"No problem," I said. "These are the scones. I was trying to figure out how to get them frosted."

"What part of 'we need to close the store' was unclear?" Jeff asked.

"To be fair, you told her that you'd let the technicians do their work. You never said close the shop," Nancy said.

"Nancy, we need to process the Sleeping Latte," Jeff said. "An anonymous tip said that whatever killed Kim came from here. I have to take it seriously. We need to proceed carefully. If I don't shut the Sleeping Latte down and run tests, you will always be under suspicion. I'll probably lose my job because I showed bias toward your family due to my relationship with your daughter."

"So you think the food is poisoned? Or the coffee? Is that what you're saying?" Moira said, putting her hands on her hips and squaring off right in front of Jeff.

"Moira, I know you're angry. But I wouldn't be doing anyone any favors if I didn't do my job," Jeff said. I had to hand it to him, he met her angry gaze straight on and let the conflict show on his face. "For the record, of course I don't think the food is poisoned. But I have to proceed with caution. Where did this muffin mix come from?"

"The batter was from yesterday," Moira admitted. "All I did was stir it up and put them in the tins. They're fine. See?" Moira ripped a piece of muffin and put it in her mouth, chewing furiously. Before Jeff could stop her, she took a piece of the other muffin, then the scone, and jammed them in as well. Crumbs tumbled down her chin, and she put her hands on her hips, chewing furiously, glaring at Jeff.

"Chief, Moira served food all day yesterday, and nobody died," Nancy said.

"Any fresh baking done yesterday?" Jeff said.

"Yes, by your mother mostly. Are you going to haul her down to the station too?"

"I may have to," Jeff said, rubbing his temples. "That will go over even better than this is."

"I helped a little, but mostly with recipes. Tarts, muffins, and scones for the morning, and some cookies for the afternoon," Nancy said.

"Today is our leftover day. We weren't planning on baking anything new, only prepping for the rest of the week," Moira said. "Mondays are usually our slowest day."

Jeff and Moira kept staring at each other. It was as if they were daring each other to make the first move, but no one would blink. So I did.

"I'm going to go tell Ben and Freddie that we're closing down," I said.

"Freddie is here?" Jeff said, glaring at Ro.

"I didn't know she came in," Ro said steadily, refusing to take the blame.

"Ben pulled her right in to work the register," I said. "Do you want to talk to her?"

"You might say that," Jeff said. "Ro, could you go and get Freddie? Ask her to come out here. I'll wait."

"Jeff, what should I . . ." I asked.

"Ruth, go and help Ben get this place closed. Once the doors are shut, leave everything where it is. I'll come out to let you out, and seal the space."

My phone buzzed. "Kristen will meet you at the station," I said, reading the text. What she'd actually texted back was *Again? You need to put me on retainer.* She had been at the station for one reason or another a lot in the past few months. I leaned over and gave Nancy a hug. "Hang in there," I whispered.

"Pat, call me if you need anything," I said for everyone to hear. "Moira, are you going to go to the station?"

"No, she isn't," Pat said firmly.

"I guess I'm not. How about if I go and help you and Ben clear the house. Would that be all right?" she asked, glaring at Jeff. "Or am I still on some sort of death watch because of my muffins? Wait, correction. Your mother's muffins."

"That would be fine," Jeff said. "Just don't throw anything away."

Moira and I walked toward the swinging door that led out to the dining area. She stopped short before she pushed it open. Her hand was shaking, and she ran it down her pant leg.

"Want me to do this?" I said.

"Would you?" she whispered, seemingly paralyzed.

I pushed the door and took a deep breath. I walked over to Ben, who was steaming milk for a cup of coffee. The line was gone, and there were only a few people in the dining room. Moira grabbed the baskets of baked goods, which had been severely depleted, and brought them back to the kitchen.

"Make that to go," I whispered. "We've got to close down."

I walked over to the front door and turned the lock. I flipped the OPEN sign to CLOSED and pulled the front blinds closed. "Folks, we've had an emergency in the kitchen. I'm afraid we need to close the Sleeping Latte for the rest of the day. If you'd like to bring your mug up to the front, Ben will put your coffee in a to-go cup."

It took only a couple of minutes for the shop to clear. Once I'd closed the door for the last time, Ben turned to me.

"What the hell is going on?" he asked.

"How can he possibly think my mother had anything to do with Kim's death?" Moira said. The question was directed at me. She was making coffee in my kitchen, and I was setting the table for the three of us. Blue and Bezel didn't get to have breakfast again, as much as Blue begged.

"Do you know what happened to make them check the Sleeping Latte?" Ben said, chopping more ham and tossing it into a large fry pan, where it sputtered and splatted alongside the turkey and onion he'd been frying. He went back to the eggs he'd whisked and added a handful of cheese, and then poured them over the meat. He gently pushed and prodded the eggs.

"He's pulling stuff out of the air," Moira said. "Listening to anonymous tips that are called in."

"Moira, he's doing his job," I said quietly. "He has to let it take him where it leads."

"He can't think my mother—"

"Of course he can't. None of us do," I said. "But his job isn't to get the evidence to fit what he knows. His job is to follow the evidence and figure out what happened. Maybe they're crossing t's and dotting i's. Or maybe they found something that indicates that Kim didn't die of natural causes. Besides, if someone called, he had to check it out."

"How is a bell on her head natural causes?" Moira said. I winced. I took it personally when a clock part was implicated in a death. I put two more pieces of bread in the toaster. I moved the butter crock from the counter to the table.

"She didn't die from the bell," Ben said, still pushing his

eggs around. Ben's breakfasts were not to be rushed, but they were worth the wait. "She died from an allergic reaction. Not that I should know that, but that's Orchard for you. I wonder if that's what's going on? He has to be really careful to do due diligence in case her death wasn't an accident."

I went over to the cabinet and took out three plates, putting them on the counter beside Ben. "Can you be forced into an allergic reaction?" Moira said.

"Of course, if you knew what triggered it," I said. "She was allergic to nuts."

"There weren't any nuts in the food we brought over to the party," Moira said. "We were really careful about that. Too risky these days when so many people have allergy issues."

"But you do serve food with nuts at the Sleeping Latte."

"We do, but Kim doesn't eat food at the Sleeping Latte. Ever."

"Never?" Ben said. "How do you know?" He separated the plates and spooned eggs on each.

"She makes a point of it, though she lets my mother bake her cherry tarts. She hates the Reed family, plain and simple." Moira sat at the table and moved her juice glass around. "Hated. Yeesh, I keep talking about her in present tense."

"I keep forgetting too," Ben said. "Aunt Flo said Beckett is trying to get a committee together to plan a memorial service for her. He's having some trouble getting folks to step up."

"I wonder if they're going to find her family," Moira said. "It almost makes me feel sorry for her."

I took a bite of the eggs and closed my eyes in a food swoon. Included in Ben's many talents was his ability to cook. I opened my eyes and smiled at him. "These are amazing."

"Thanks, babe," he said. "What do you think, Moira?"

"I'm not that hungry. Maybe I should go down to the station?"

"You have to eat," Ben said. "I have a feeling it is going to be a long day." He pushed her plate a little closer to her, and she capitulated and took a small bite of eggs. Then a larger bite. "I'm going to check in with Jason and make sure he's set in the store," Ben said, handing us each a piece of toast. "Flo already said she's all set in the shop. Monday's she's usually closed, but she moved some of her Saturday regulars over, so they could go to the Signing Ceremony."

"I obviously have nothing to do today," Moira said, playing with her food sulkily.

"You could help out here in the shop until your dad gets back," I said.

"What could I do?" she asked. "I don't know anything about clocks."

"But you know about people," I said. I was improvising, but knew Moira well enough to know that she had to keep busy today. "Zane's coming in, and if nothing else, you can talk to him about the figures and what he needs to get them done."

"What do you mean, what he needs?"

"He's carving them to look like people. He made a model of my grandmother's figure already. Did you see it yesterday?"

"I did, but I didn't really look at it up close."

"He's probably going to have it with him and will show it to you. As he said, he's working on perfecting the solution that he wants to use on the figures— Did you move the test boards?"

"Checked this morning when I took Blue out for his run," Ben said. "Pat must have done it last night. Moira, I think you, Ruth, and I need to stay nimble today."

"What do you mean?" I said.

"You know what I mean," he said, pouring more coffee in my cup and then in his. "Something's happening. If Kim was killed, Jeff needs to follow the evidence. I keep wondering about that. There's a narrative arc—"

"Narrative arc? Who talks like that?" Moira said, smiling for the first time this morning.

"The English major with a computer minor," I said. "Go on, sweetie. Tell us about the arc."

"Are you both done? Good. The great thing about being an English major is that I look at the story line. What makes sense? What elements are missing? Who are the characters in the story? Ruth brings the clockmaker's careful eye," Ben said. "How does it all work? What isn't working, and why? How do we fix it?"

"What do I bring to the table?" Moira asked as she nibbled on a piece of toast.

"You bring heart," Ben said. "Ruth and I both care, but you are a fierce warrior."

"'Fierce warrior' is one way to put it," she said, almost to herself. "Jeff would probably use another phrase."

"I don't think so," Ben said.

"Jeff's crazy about you," I said. "He's got a strict moral code that makes him great at his job, which he puts first. He fights for the greater good at his own expense. This must be tough on him."

Moira looked down at her plate, blinking back the tears that had risen up.

"You know, ladies, together we have superpowers. Moira's passion, my love of story, and Ruth's innate ability to fix things. We need to make this right, not only for Kim, but for us all."

"That's pretty dramatic," I said.

"No, Ben's right," Moira said. "Things were so bleak for so long. It's gotten so much better . . ."

"Since Ruth came back." Ben finished her sentence and took my hand in his. With his other hand, he grabbed Moira's.

I squeezed Ben's hand. "Let's keep our eyes on this prize, my friends. Orchard needs us. We'll figure out what happened to Kim," I said.

One way or another.

chapter 17

Ben went to take Blue out for another walk and asked me to go with him. Much as I wanted to, I had to say no—too much to do and no time for distractions. Moira had the good grace to leave us alone for a few minutes, so at least he could kiss me good-bye. With a stupid grin on my face I finished loading the dishwasher.

I took out my notebook and made lists. I didn't have answers, but I had a lot of questions. Who had a motive to kill Kim? The list of people who considered her an enemy was long, but who was capable of murder? I'd need to think about that, much as I hated to go there. If I'd learned nothing else in the past few months, I'd learned that anyone was capable of anything, given the right push.

Next to motive was opportunity. Who could have killed her? I'd need some help with that, thinking about who was where when. I wish I'd paid more attention to Jeff's diagram yesterday, though I wasn't sure I'd make sense out of it. He had his methods, and I had mine. I jotted down a few more thoughts. How exactly did she die? Why was the bell used? Why was Kim back there in the first place? Lists and questions. No answers, not yet.

I knew myself well enough by now. I needed to stop thinking about murder and concentrate on clocks for a while. That always got my mind working.

I went downstairs and saw that Zane had already put Moira to work. He had three jars out on one of the worktables, and was taking out his box of rags. These were ratty-looking old sheets that he'd cut into squares, and washed regularly. I admired his frugality, but they weren't a pretty sight. He was taking out an old board. A staining lesson was about to happen. Moira lifted up a jar and swirled it around, holding it up to the light.

"Really? I never thought about making my own stains," she said. "Of course I'm not a woodworker, but my dad is. I think he's always bought stains."

"Nothing wrong with that, though I think I have him convinced to try these," Zane said. "They're water based. You take something, say a walnut—"

"Like you buy in the store?"

"No, more like you find dropped from a walnut tree. With the husks on. You want as much of the organic material as you can get. You boil it down, strain it, and voilà." He picked up a jar that was full of a thick brown liquid.

"Can you make a stain out of coffee? Or beets?"

"Sure. Listen, people used color for years before chemicals. I like the way these old stains look. They have a patina that brings a particular glow to the wood."

"That's why you want to use them on the tower figures," I said, leaning a hip against the workbench.

"Exactly. I want these figures to look like they were hiding in the tower all these years, and they came out to play when the tower was released."

"Released?" Moira asked.

"Released. The spirit of a clock tower remains a clock tower, even after the clock stops working. This one will be released soon. The rest of the glass is coming in this week, so we can install the windows and let the light in. That will help."

When the old clock tower had burned down, part of the reason it hadn't been restored right away was that the old clockface was wooden. Most of it had been burned beyond repair. It had been boarded up and weathered in time to a gray patina that matched the stone building. We'd talked about making the face wood again, but instead decided to put in plates of milky glass. Rather than a single pane, which would have been expensive, we decided to create a stained glass frame with three concentric circles on each window. Installation of the frames had started this winter. We decided to do it then, when folks needed the work, rather than later in the spring when the craftsmen we needed would be busier. We had to wait until the weather was a bit nicer to install the glass itself, since the glazing needed to cure correctly. Until then, tarps had been hiding the work being done, partly to keep the surprise, partly to try and be a barrier against the weather.

I'd been up in the tower a lot this winter, prepping the space, taking measurements, getting the frame for the clock tower mechanism itself installed. Right after the fire, my grandfather and his father had saved what they could. The

Seth Thomas clock piece, the guts of the tower, had fallen through the floor when it burned, crashing into the second mechanism below that ran the figurines. The only thing that stopped it from crashing into the Town Hall was the layer of slate that the original builders had used. I was grateful for those eighteenth-century builders, overbuilders really, of the Town Hall. Nothing would take this building down. Floods, fires, gentrification. Nothing.

Though they'd saved the old clock parts, we hadn't been able to use most of them. When I decided to focus on re-building the tower, Caroline asked me to come out to the cottage. She brought me out to the workshop and showed me a hidden door on the side of the main workroom. She had to move a shelf to the side to show me where it was. It was locked with a dead bolt, and Caroline handed me the keys with a flourish.

"This was Thom's pride and joy," she'd said. "Open the door."

"Must be top secret to be hidden like this," I said, going through the key ring to find the match.

"This room was where Thom locked away his dreams," she said just as I found the right key. I undid the lock and reached into the room, searching for the light. I turned it on and saw exactly what she meant by his dream. The clock tower had been part of G.T.'s DNA for a long time, and he'd been storing pieces of his dream in this room. Over in the corner I saw old wooden parts of a clock—maybe part of the original that had been salvaged? I walked over to take a closer look. The parts still smelled a bit like smoke. Resting up against the wall, on a frame that kept them upright, there was a sheet covering large poles. I lifted the sheet and saw clock arms.

"Thom did some work on a grandfather clock a few years ago in barter for getting these arms forged."

"They're beautiful," I said, running my hand along the sides. The pointer of each hand had an open-weave pattern that may not read from the ground during the day, but would be magical when the lights went on in the tower at night. "When did he paint them?"

"He didn't. He did work for someone who worked in an auto body shop. The hands got painted there. Thom thought they'd stand up better in the rain."

"More barter?"

"All of this is barter. Or, like in the case of that clock tower piece"—she pointed to another mound covered by a sheet, which I lifted up—"folks would keep an eye out for him. A friend let us know about a church that had decided to go electric and was getting rid of their Seth Thomas clock. The challenge was that it was in South Carolina, but that was a blip. We drove down one January, took it apart, loaded it up, and brought it back. Thom was thrilled. It was built the same year as the original clock, 1912. It desperately needed cleaning, and several parts needed to be replaced, but it gave Thom something to focus on."

"That's quite a trip! How long were you gone?"

"Two months. A long time, but we decided it was a good time to visit friends from around the country. I'm so grateful we made that trip. Wonderful memories."

Caroline's face changed as she remembered some of those happy moments. The smile she wore was one I rarely saw. When she and my grandfather had married, I was still in deep mourning over my grandmother. I didn't understand then that Caroline wasn't G.T.'s way of getting over my grandmother, it was his way of rejoining the living. I would never forgive myself for letting grief and G.T.'s obstinate nature drive a wedge in our relationship, a relationship that was never healed. He should have been able to call me and ask me to help out in the shop. He should have shown me this magical room and walked me through his dreams.

"Ruth?" Caroline said.

"Sorry, I was missing G.T.," I said to Caroline.

Caroline took my hands in both of hers and held on. "He's here. He was here when you looked at those clock hands. His light shines in you. I'm so grateful that you are carrying on his work."

I squeezed her hands and used my other hand to wipe the tear that had rolled down my cheek. "Thanks, Caroline."

"Don't you think so, Ruth?" I shook myself and focused on what Zane was saying.

"I'm so sorry," I said. "What did you say?"

"I asked if you finally agreed we should have a carillon so the figures could dance to a tune, rather than wobble to a bell."

"Zane, not again. Not today. Let's get one bell working, a new bell, and the clock installed. The dancers are a second-half-of-the-year project. I'm already worried about living with a clock bell every hour across the street. Not that I would admit that to anyone but the two of you."

"You live with clock chimes every hour. A new bell will have a finer sound—it will become part of your existence. You'll be fine," Zane said. "I'll stop pestering you until after the clock is set at the end of the month."

"And I'll stop asking you if the figures will all be done," I said.

"They are all going to be done," Zane said. "You'll have to trust me. Don't pester Pat either, mind you."

"Pat's been working on them? But you won't show me?"

"You need a surprise or two, Ruthie. Good surprises,"

Zane said. "Listen, are we still on schedule for the clock being set at the end of the month?"

I took a deep breath. "We are," I said. "But I want to get back to the tower."

"Will it take long to get the clock parts moved up?" Moira asked.

"It will take time, and assembly," I said. "But we need to finish getting the windows installed first. The arms have been welded, and we'll get them installed this week as well. Your dad is the foreman on this part of the project."

"He's been talking about it for weeks," Moira said.

"Ironic that this is where the last reinstallation stopped, with the fire," Zane said.

I glared at him, but he went on, oblivious. "I hope this business about Kim's death gets sorted out soon," he went on. "We don't need the distraction right now. 'Distraction' is an unfortunate way to say it, under the circumstances, but you know what I mean."

"You mean that we need to find out what happened to Kim so she can rest in peace," I said.

Zane looked at me and shrugged. "If you say so, Ruth. How's Jeff doing?" he asked Moira.

"I don't know," she said. "We aren't exactly on speaking terms right now." She took her phone out of her pocket and looked at the display. "I put it on vibrate just in case . . . This is my dad." She swiped the screen and walked over by the kitchenette.

"Janet's supposed to head back home today," Zane said. "Maybe I'll give her a call and tell her Jeff could use someone on his side. He's had a rough go of it these past few years."

"What do you mean?" I wasn't surprised that Zane and Janet had become friends during her short visits to Orchard.

He'd come down here early in the year to recover from some injuries. From the stories I'd been told, I expected him to be a recluse clockmaker. Nothing could be further from the truth, however. He was a clockmaker, first and foremost. He was also a kind and curious man who was able to get stories out of people. He'd become a cog in the gossip wheel, but understood what stories were meant to be shared, and when.

Zane looked over his shoulder at Moira talking on the phone, and then back at me. "Do you know why he came to Orchard?" he asked in a low, conspiratorial tone.

"Zane, you shouldn't—"

"I should. Listen, Janet's worried about Jeff."

"Isn't that a mother's job?" I said, instantly remembering that my own mother was less than concerned about me, mildly put. She and my father had been on an academic exploration for the past year and a half, with a quick e-mail check-in every few weeks. I'd given up on them playing the role of proper parents years ago and was a little jealous that Jeff had someone who played that role in his life.

"Jeff was a good cop who lost his job because of politics. Janet told me the story, but I don't remember the details. Something about him blowing a whistle on someone. Anyway, that's not the point. Grover Winter stepped in and offered him a five-year contract to come to Orchard. Janet says that he saved Jeff's life. She also says that he'd given up everything to be a good cop, including chances at a family. She's thrilled that Moira's wormed her way into his heart. Janet's phrase. She also said that if Jeff had to choose between Moira and the job, she hopes he'd choose Moira. But . . ."

"She isn't sure."

"Right. I'm going to give her a call, see if she can stay for a few more days."

"Jeff may not want her to," I said. "His place is pretty small."

"I don't care what he wants. It's what he needs. She can stay with Caroline. She'd probably be more comfortable there anyway. That way Jeff wouldn't have to sleep on the couch. I'm going to give her a call. In the meantime, make sure you stay on Jeff's side. He needs someone who can help him see the big picture."

"He's going to follow the evidence."

"Then find him different evidence," Zane said. "In the meantime, I'm calling his mother."

Moira got off the phone as Zane was about to hit send on his phone. Instead he turned it off and put it in his pocket.

"They let Mum go, of course," Moira said. "They're still questioning Freddie, though. Kristen is going to stay with her."

"Is Freddie's father there?" I asked.

"Yeah, he's waiting for her. Mum said Dad took him for a walk, so he could calm Fred down."

"Good luck to Pat. Fred's got a helluva temper," Zane said. "Pat and I were supposed to meet about the scaffolding. It's being delivered in a few days. Ruth, come with me over to the tower. I want to talk through the installation again." Walking through the installation was a daily routine, but that was fine with me. There were a lot of moving parts to this project, and rehearsal was necessary. For a lot of the work, we'd have only one chance to get it right.

"Is it reopened?" Moira asked.

"I have no idea. We'll check on that. In the meantime, I want to talk through how we are going to get the scaffolding down without trampling the new gardens," Zane said. I winced. I wouldn't want to cross Harriet's path if we ruined the gardens.

"Is Nadia coming in today?" Caroline asked. Whoa, my heart raced. I hadn't even seen her there. She'd been bent over a watch, and stood and stretched her back.

"You scared me, Caroline. Good morning. Nadia isn't coming in," I said. "Since she worked on Saturday I told her to work from home today. But Moira will be here in case anyone comes in." I looked at Moira, and she nodded. Phew. Caroline did not like dealing with customers now that she'd rehung her watchmaker shingle. She much preferred focusing on watches, and had a lot of work lined up. She was also determined to get a few pieces up on our website, thinking that they could help drive some more business to the shop.

Zane and I stepped out of the front door. Zane walked over to one of the rocking chairs on the front porch, sat, took his phone out, and hit send to call Jeff's mother. I stepped away from him and took one step down. I loved this view of Orchard. The current of the river humming behind me, and the town laid out in front of me. Honestly, I usually stopped my visual sweep at the edge of Been There, Read That, since Beckett Green sucked so much of the joy out of my life. Today I kept going, looking over at the Federal-style building.

One of the things I loved most about my town was that every building was different, with dozens of architectural styles represented one way or another. Been There, Read That had started life as a mansion of sorts, a Federal-style building complete with columns, a huge front porch, and a

U-shaped driveway. The driveway was empty this morning, more's the pity for Beckett. The original owners had built it in anticipation of a train route that was supposed to stop in Orchard, which would have made it a hub of the Berkshires. When plans changed, along with it the fortunes of Orchard for several years, the owners gave up on the house, which became a school, the police station, the library, and eventually a bank.

It had been empty for a few years or so when Beckett bought it and decided its next incarnation would be as a bookstore. He had been open for a few months and was hoping that the summer season would see a boom in business. So far it had been slow, but that was as much to do with Beckett's reputation in town as it had to do with the store itself. Tourists wouldn't know that Beckett had aligned himself with the wrong people and wouldn't hold it against him.

I glanced over at Zane, whose eyes were closed while he was having his conversation. He leaned forward with his elbows on his knees and nodded while listening. I turned back, just in time to see Jimmy Murphy come stomping around the side of Been There, Read That, followed closely by Beckett. I'd never seen Jimmy so angry. I stepped back up on the porch instinctively, stepping back into the shadows. Though I couldn't make out the words, I could hear Jimmy's voice raised above the river sounds. Beckett's wasn't audible, but his mouth was moving. Jimmy turned and faced Beckett directly, leaning in and poking his finger into the other man's chest. Beckett swatted it away, but Jimmy started poking again.

"Over my dead body," Jimmy said. That was loud and clear. Zane hung up his phone and stood next to me on the porch. Beckett responded, though the words weren't clear. Jimmy's response came not in words, but in actions. He hauled off and belted Beckett across the jaw. Beckett twisted as the blow landed, and fell over onto the ground. He didn't even try to get up and take a swing at Jimmy, which was just as well. I suspect Jimmy would have enjoyed hitting him again. Fighting in the streets. What was next?

Jimmy shook his fist over Beckett's face. He turned around, shaking his hand out in front of him. He saw us both on the porch and gave us a salute with his good hand. Zane laughed, loudly.

"He's got style, you've got to give him that. I wonder what the fight was about," Zane said, walking to the edge of the porch.

I watched Jimmy get into his car, which had been parked in front of the Town Hall. He pulled away, taking a right by the Corner Market without stopping first.

I stepped off the porch and walked toward Beckett.

"I'm fine, I'm fine. Don't come over here, Ruth. I'm fine," Beckett shouted as he stumbled back toward his store.

I stopped, feeling a little ridiculous.

"He's not a big fan of yours, is he?" Zane said. "Well, someone needs to make sure Beckett is all right. May as well be me." Zane walked down the three steps to the path in front of the store. "You go back in and let Caroline know she's going to have a houseguest. Janet is glad to stay with Caroline and be able to keep an eye on Jeff. I promised you had his back as well."

M oira signaled me to come over to the front counter as soon as I walked in.

She held up the phone. "Someone has a question about one of the clocks on the website," she said.

"Okay," I said, looking over at Caroline, bent over a watch.

Moira shook her head. "I think we need a salesman on the call. Sounds like a live one."

I smiled and took the phone. Moira knew very little about clocks, but she knew a lot about customer service. After a few minutes I realized she was right. The person on the phone was asking about two specific banjo clocks that we had on the website. She read the descriptions and asked if we still had them for sale.

"Yes, they're still for sale," I said.

"Don't you have to check your stock?"

"I'm the owner of the shop and know them both well. We have them." I walked to the showroom to make sure I wasn't inadvertently lying to her, but there they were, two stunning examples of Willard clocks, dating from the early 1800s. They were both on sale for $2,000 apiece. Selling them would hurt my heart, but it would also help me make the payroll for running the shop. Business was steady, but I had dreams of getting my nest egg feathered again before I turned forty.

"I'm interested, but would like to see them in person. I can't get there until tomorrow afternoon. Will you be open around three?"

"We will be," I said, marking the calendar on the wall over Caroline's work desk with a big red circle at three o'clock. Caroline preferred paper to technology, and we all put deliveries and appointments that everyone needed to know about on the calendar. Red was used for items everyone needed to pay attention to.

"You'll be there personally to show me the clocks?"

"I will," I said. "My name is Ruth Clagan. I look forward to meeting you, Ms. . . . ."

"Ms. Bloodsnow. I'll see you then." She hung up the phone.

"Bloodsnow?" I said to Moira. "Does that sound like a real name to you?"

"No, but why would she make it up?"

"Maybe she's a collector and doesn't want me to raise the prices. Or maybe she's a thief, and she's going to rob us." Moira looked over at me, and even Caroline stopped working. "I'm joking, gang. Moira, help me bring these up to my apartment. We can bring them back down tomorrow."

"How should I carry them? Isn't it bad to move them? Holy smokes, is this really worth two thousand dollars? I don't think I can do this, Ruth." Fortunately for Moira, the phone rang at that moment, and she went over to answer it. I sighed and picked up the first clock. I carried it upstairs and opened my apartment door. Carefully. A clockmaker's apartment always had space on the wall to hang clocks. Not just beauties in working order, like this one. Frequently I brought up clocks that I was working on, to see if a repair had worked, or to check on how the clock ran over a period of time. I went back downstairs and got the second clock.

After I hung the second one, I stepped back a step and watched them run. Ms. Bloodsnow had a good eye—these were real beauties. Lovelier in person than in photos, despite Nadia's abilities. I went to go back downstairs, but checked Bezel's food first. I topped off her dry food, and she looked up from her perch on the foot of my bed, giving me a slow blink of thanks. I slow-blinked back and closed the door behind me.

Both sides of the hallway outside my apartment had storage for clock parts in beautiful oak cabinetry that was five feet high. Running along the wall on top of them we'd hung a few clocks, part of the rotating stock for the shop. I took one of the other banjos down, a replica from the 1950s, and brought it to the shop. I hung it up and stepped back. I could obsessively rehang all the stock, but I let it go. This was a placeholder, and would be fine. If the other clocks sold, I'd rehang the room. I loved the artistry of our displays.

I opened the door of the clock and took out the key for winding. I checked my cell phone and set the time and then wound the clock carefully. A part of me admired the absolute precision of my cell phone time, but I still preferred the artistic craft of the clocks I worked on. Bits and pieces of metal, fitted together in such a way as to capture time with both precision and beauty. I loved that clocks didn't have extra pieces. Everything contributed to the whole, once it was understood. Sometimes you had to ferret out the explanation, but once you did, it all made sense.

I was heading back upstairs to get another clock when there was a sharp knock on the back door. "I'll get it," I said to Caroline, who had made no move to answer it, completely absorbed in her work. I walked around the Zane minefield of jars and opened the door, half expecting to see Ben. Instead I saw Pat and Nancy. I instinctively opened my arms, and Nancy stepped in for a hug. She rested her head on my shoulder for a moment, and I held her tight. When I let her go, she went over to Caroline, who also offered a hug. Moira had stopped working and was waiting her turn.

"Okay if we hang out here for a while?" Pat said.

"Of course," I said, closing the door after he stepped in.

"We could go home, but do what? Stare at each other all afternoon? Besides, better to be close to the Sleeping Latte so once they're done, we can get her ready to open tomorrow."

"You think they'll be done soon?" Moira said.

"Who knows?" Nancy said.

"You sound exhausted," I said to her. "Do you want to come upstairs and have a cup of tea?"

"I'd love that," she said, not waiting to walk up the stairs.

"Pat?" I asked.

"I'll make myself a cup down here. I've got some work I want to catch up on. Moira, you go upstairs with Ruth and your mother. It will make it easier if she doesn't have to repeat the story twice."

chapter 18

I filled up the kettle and turned it on. The basket of tea selections was sitting in the middle of the table, and I'd put my notebook on my seat. "Are either of you hungry?" I asked. "I have leftovers from last night."

"I'm still stuffed from breakfast," Moira said. "Ben made us an amazing omelet," she explained to her mother.

"Tea is fine for now," she said. "If I want more, I know where it is."

I took out the tin of cookies, putting them in the middle of the table. Cookies were always a good idea, in my opinion. The water was going to take another minute or so, so I sat.

"What did he say?" Moira said anxiously.

"Who he?" Nancy asked.

"Jeff he, that's who," Moira said.

"Typical Jeff, he didn't say a whole lot. Mostly asked questions. It didn't take long, but he wanted us to look over our statements and sign them. Then he took poor Freddie back."

"Why 'poor' Freddie? Aside from the obvious, I mean," Moira said. "That sounded mean. Sorry."

"She is a bit of a mess, is our Freddie," Nancy said. "But she means well and she certainly has her talents. And I can't imagine she'd do anything to hurt Kim, not intentionally."

"Hurt Kim?" I asked, getting up. The electric kettle had clicked off, and I poured hot water into three mugs. I carried two over to the table, putting them in front of Nancy and Moira. I brought my own mug back and moved my notebook to the side.

"From what I can gather, mostly from Ro, they think Kim died of some sort of allergic reaction. Since the bell was also on her, they seem to be thinking the allergic reaction could have been caused intentionally and the bell was insurance. Jeff kept asking me if any of the food at the party had nuts. Which, of course, it didn't. I never use nuts in food for large events where we can't make sure folks know what they're eating."

"What about cross-contamination?" I said.

"Possible, but not probable. We're really careful. Other than food, I wonder what else she was allergic to? Do either of you know?"

"Bees," I said.

Moira shook her head. "I don't remember seeing bees, but I guess there could have been," she said.

"I've been thinking about what you said last night, Ruthie," Nancy said. "About how little we knew her. There is a part of me who feels badly about that. Only a little part, though. I know, that makes me sound like a terrible human being. Maybe I am. But she was a miserable woman, no doubt about it. Question is, who hated her enough to commit murder?"

"Unless it was accidental?"

"And someone took the opportunity of her dying to drop a bell on her face?" Moira said. "Instead of helping her?"

"Maybe they wanted to make sure she was really dead, or make some sort of statement?" I said. "That's why they used the bell. It could be anyone, though. Maybe someone we don't even know. We need to figure this out. You had to go past the check-in table to get back there. But Kim didn't."

"Yes, she did," Moira said. "She came in late, tried to come in the side door, but it was blocked by the table. She was ticked off, but then her phone rang so she went out back to take the call."

"How do you know that?" I asked. "Huh. I'd been thinking that Kim had snuck into the portico somehow. I didn't realize anyone had seen her at all."

"Freddie told me."

"Freddie saw her go back? Did anyone else, I wonder?"

"I don't know," Moira said. "Jeff knows Freddie saw her. I made sure she told him."

"When was this?"

"Around two, I think," Moira said. "Why?"

"I'm just wondering who else went back there after Kim arrived. Those are the folks who would have known she was back there . . ." I said.

"And would have murdered her," Nancy said. "Yikes. Okay, at that point in the day the only people going back toward the vestibule were working the event."

"That means the both of you, me," Moira said.

I opened to a clean page in my notebook and made a list. "Ben, Jason, Fred, Freddie . . ."

Moira took out her phone and started to text.

"Who are you texting?"

"Nadia. Woman's got a memory like a steel trap."

"What are you asking her? Who killed Kim?" I asked.

"No, I'm asking her who went back out to the portico during the event. She'll know why I'm asking."

"Your father, me, Zane, Nadia, Caroline . . . who else? Jeff?" Nancy asked. She sounded like she was making a guest list for a dinner party instead of a list of murder suspects.

"No, Jeff and Janet stayed out front," Moira said. "Besides, I think they can be taken off the list, don't you?"

I flipped back in my notebook and looked at one of the timelines I'd been working on. I tried to visualize the day. I took out my phone and scrolled through pictures, trying to refresh my memory.

"So now let's figure out who should really be on this list. Moira and I were camped out by the tables that blocked folks from going back."

"Neither of you took a break?" I asked.

"No. It really wasn't that long an afternoon, especially when you're used to working a lunch shift at the Sleeping Latte," Nancy said. "So who else went past us? What about Jimmy? And Harriet?"

"Harriet stayed out front, watching over the clock parts, talking to folks about the gardens," Moira said. "I did see Jimmy go back."

"I saw Beckett," Nancy said.

"Beckett and Jimmy got into a fight today," I said, recalling the incident. "Jimmy hauled off and belted him."

"Belted him? Why?" Nancy said. "Not that we all haven't wanted to belt Beckett."

"Zane went over to try and find out," I said. "He isn't back yet."

"Zane? That should be interesting," Nancy said.

"Zane's a quiet one," Moira said. "But still waters run

deep. He'll find out anything there is to find out. So, who does that really leave on this list? Taking all of us off it—"

"Gee, thanks, Moira," Nancy said.

"Which Jeff can't do," I said. Both of the Reed women stared at me, but I forged ahead. "He has to rule us all out, and that is going to take time. Don't look at me like that. He's doing his job. I'm on his side on this. I know today has been hard for you, Nancy. But I think it's been pretty tough on Jeff too." Neither woman said anything, so I went on. "Let's keep trying to figure out who went back to the portico during the event and try and find out who may have had a motive we don't know about."

The three of us talked through the event. Moira and I both flipped through pictures on our phones, trying to remember who else was there. "Not just there, but went out to the portico," I said.

"Good thing the bathrooms aren't back there," Nancy said. "Otherwise the list would be longer."

We'd honed down the names, and Nadia finally texted back and confirmed what we'd been thinking. I looked down at the scrambled note, names, cross-outs, and circles. What a mess—I couldn't think like that. So I opened up a new page and wrote five names: Fred, Freddie, Jason, Beckett, Jimmy. Those were the only five people Moira, Nancy, and Nadia all agreed went past the tables. Five people I knew.

One of whom may have killed Kim Gray.

Once the list was made, there was no clear next step to take.

"I could use a nap," Nancy said.

"Me too," Moira said.

"Go ahead," I said. "Seriously. One of you take the couch,

the other one can take the bed. Close your eyes for a few minutes. I'll go downstairs and see if Zane is back."

"We could go home," Moira offered.

"Or you could relax, and then we'll regroup in a little while and talk through next steps. Whatever that means."

"Whatever that means. You can figure that out while I close my eyes for a bit," Nancy said. "Moira, you take the couch. I'll take the bed, and hope Bezel joins me."

I went downstairs and saw that Zane was back. He was over at his workstation, moving jars around. He'd unwrapped the figure he'd carved of my grandmother, and he was sanding it lightly.

"You're back," I said. "How's Beckett?"

"He'll live. What do you think of this color, Ruthie?" he asked. I walked over and looked at the deep brown hue. Zane did things his own way. I needed to let him drive this conversation. I knew we'd get to Beckett eventually.

"I like it, but it seems dark."

"Better for contrast," he said. "Remember, these will be about forty feet up."

"I need to see it finished, I guess."

"Next step," Zane said. "Just sanding this down to prep. The stain has a lot of water in it, so it raises the grain."

"This is the walnut stain?" I asked.

"It is," he said.

"If you're allergic to nuts, would you be allergic to the stain?"

"Well, you'd wear gloves while using it. I suppose if you drank it, it may affect you. But why would you drink it?" Why indeed? At least, on purpose.

"Trick will be," Zane said, "if we like it, to make enough

so that the stains are all the same color, though I don't mind a little bit of a difference."

"Especially since you'll be looking at them from a distance, in sunlight or at night. They'll be polished, right?"

"Been testing different polishes, got a board over in the clock tower. Looking forward to getting your thoughts. Me, I don't love high gloss, but I can be persuaded since it's—"

"Forty feet up," we said together. During this process we were constantly reminding ourselves that details didn't matter as much as they did on clocks. Forty feet required broader strokes. Though the mechanisms for the clock itself still required detail, the decorations required a different scale.

"One option I'm testing is bowling alley wax. May be best for standing up to the elements." Zane moved jars around again, and I realized these were all colors.

"Did you make these too?"

"Not all natural, but I did mix the colors. I think these will be the best ones to go for the look I want." Zane took out a felt parcel and laid it on the table. He unrolled it, showing a display of paintbrushes.

I had to stop myself from staring at Zane's rituals. As clockmakers, we are all fastidious and have a process. But I'd never seen anyone with such specific work habits. He had real talent, but as many tics. It was no wonder he worked alone for so many years.

He was fanning paintbrushes one by one and putting them down in front of the jars. I wanted to ask him how he decided which brush went with which jar, but I refrained.

"How was your conversation with Beckett?" I asked as he adjusted the brushes so the handles were all lined up.

"That man is a real piece of work," Zane said. "Has the backbone of a jellyfish."

"How so?" I asked.

"Jimmy Murphy's got twenty years on him, hit him once, and Beckett's a basket case."

"Is he going to bring Jimmy up on charges?"

"For a punch? I told him he'd be the laughingstock of Orchard if he did. Jimmy would be cashing in on that story at every bar in town for the rest of the summer. Beckett'll be fine. He's panicked because he's bleeding, but noses bleed. I remember once—"

"Do you think it's broken?" I asked. I knew better than to let Zane wander with his stories. His storytelling cast a spell I couldn't afford to get caught in.

"Nah, just bleeding. I got him some ice and got it packed so it would stop. Imagine if he'd really gotten hurt. He probably would have passed out cold." I looked over at Zane's scarred face. I thought again about the knife clock he tried to make several years ago—knives as arms, knives as weights, knives as handles. He'd lost a round while winding.

"Why did Jimmy hit him?" I asked.

"I asked him that. I wish I could say it was tough to get Beckett to talk, but I'd be lying. Simple as cracking a nut. Seems Beckett accused Jimmy of killing Kim."

"Really? Interesting. Did he say why?"

"I tried to get that out of him, but couldn't."

"That's a shame—"

"I misspoke. Beckett didn't know. He did say that Kim 'had something on Jimmy,' but he didn't know what it was."

"You think Kim was blackmailing Jimmy?"

"Sounds like. Can't think what over. I can't imagine Jimmy killing her, can you?"

I shook my head. "I really can't, but the list of people

who could have is pretty short, and he's on it. So's Beckett, for that matter."

"List?"

"Nancy, Moira, and I came up with a list." I shrugged with embarrassment, but Zane didn't seem fazed.

"Am I on it?" Zane asked.

"No. Moira was going between the sign-in table and the food stations. You couldn't get back to the portico unless you went past her, and you didn't go past her."

"I appreciate that, and you're right. So who did, besides those two?"

"Fred, Freddie, Jason."

"That's it?"

"That's what we came up with."

"And what if someone jumped the fence beside Beckett's store? They could have climbed up on his Dumpster and jumped down."

"Then they did it. But how did they get out? The fence is six feet high, which isn't easy to get over."

"Good point. Did she have some sort of allergic reaction? That's what killed her?"

"That's the rumor," I said.

"So maybe it was natural causes?"

"Except for the bell on her head," I said. I bit my tongue—that detail may have been a secret.

"Good riddance to that piece of junk. Any idea when we can get back up to the tower?"

"Hopefully tomorrow."

"We're cutting the installation close," he said. I wasn't sure if he was purposely changing the subject or not, but I decided to follow his lead.

"I know. I'm not as worried about getting the clock itself installed—"

"That makes one of us."

"But I am worried about getting the arms connected to the hands and everything synced up."

"I've been thinking about that. I wrote down some ideas I had, wanted to talk through them with you. Do you have time now?"

"Sure, that sounds like a plan. Let me grab my other notebook," I said. Clocks in one book. Murder in the other.

Zane and I talked through the installation plan twice. I'd never done a clock tower installation, and Zane had done only one. We'd both worked on our fair share of towers, though. Winding and maintaining—stock and trade for clockmakers. More and more towers, too many, were going electric these days, which made Zane and me double down on this project.

"I hope they didn't move the parts around too much," Zane said.

"I took pictures of the tables before we left. They're on my phone. Nadia put painter's tape on each piece so we'll know if something's missing."

"And if something *is* missing?"

"Then we go out to the cottage and get one of the backup pieces. G.T. had collected so many over the years we could build four clock towers."

"Wouldn't that be fun?" Zane asked.

"Let's get this one done first," I said, though I had to agree. "Do we have another zinc-wrapped rod—"

"You aren't going to freaking believe what—" Nadia said, bursting through the front door.

"Please, Nadia, I was about to reattach the crystal on this watch," Caroline said. She'd been so quiet I'd forgotten she was there. "Bad enough that these two are nattering on about the clock tower, men acting like hooligans and punching each other, lists of who might have killed—"

Freddie came in behind Nadia and closed the door behind herself. She walked to her right and flopped on the settee in the showroom. I walked out of the workroom and sat next to her. The tall, beautiful girl was sitting forward, her head resting between her legs.

"I might faint," she said, her voice slightly muffled as she spoke into her knees. "I feel sick."

"Don't puke," Nadia said. She ran behind the front counter and grabbed the wastebasket, putting it next to Freddie.

"Go get her a glass of water," I said. I put my hand on Freddie's upper back and rubbed it.

"What's the matter?" I said.

"Chief Paisley thinks I killed Ms. Gray," she said. She sat up slightly and looked at me. "And I think he may be right."

Then she started weeping.

chapter 19

"What are you talking about?" I said.

"I made the tarts," she said.

Nadia came over with a glass of water. "Sit up, Freddie. Drink this. Ruth says it will make you feel better." Freddie groaned. "She isn't making any sense. I was over at the Corner Market, dropping off Jack. I came out, and she was sitting in my car, crying. She wanted to see you. So here we are."

"Why don't we go up to the office?" I said. "Moira and Nancy are up in my apartment taking naps."

"Taking naps? What is this, a day care center?" Nadia said. "Where's Pat?"

"He went out to deliver a couple of clocks," Caroline said. "We haven't had a customer all day—no point in staying here."

"Nadia, pull a chair over," I said, lowering my voice. "Freddie, tell me what's going on."

"Nancy puts notes for me in a shared folder on the computer. Every day has its own folder. I used a tablet in the store, and keep track of what I'm doing there. I'm hopeless with paper. I lose it all the time. Anyway, one of the notes for that day was a special order for cherry tarts."

"What made it a special order?"

"The recipe had almonds in it."

"I've seen a lot of tarts with almonds on top," Nadia said.

"These almonds were in it, in the crust. The recipe called for almonds to be ground up and combined into the dough."

"Do you think it cross-contaminated the cookie dough?" asked Nadia.

"No, I was really careful. I made the doughs for the cookies first, then I made the cherry tarts while they were chilling."

"What happened to the tarts?" I asked.

"I did what the note told me to. I put them in a box and tied it up. I left it on the stool in the kitchen. Someone was coming by at ten to pick them up."

"Were there extra tarts?"

"No, I had to stretch to get an entire dozen made."

"Who picked them up?" Nadia asked.

"I don't know," she said. "I went out to bring a basket of muffins to the front, and when I came back they were gone. Someone must have come in the back."

"Nancy told you in the note, not in person," I asked.

"Right. Nancy leaves me notes on the computer all the time. My dad makes fun of me, because I spend so much time highlighting them with different colors so they make sense to me. But it's a system that works for both of us. Nancy can add stuff and check in even if she's not there. Plus she can remind me to do the everyday stuff I might forget otherwise," she said, finally sitting back and looking me in the eye.

"Are all the notes like this one?"

"No, not all the time. Most of the time they are more like lists. Lots and lots of lists. Like I said, they're online in a special folder. I come in, log into the computer, and print out any recipes that are special orders."

"So you printed out the cherry tart recipe?"

"Yes, I did."

"Who else has access to these online folders?"

"Who else? I don't know—anyone with the link to it, I guess. We use it to help run things. Sometimes Moria adds a note. Once in a while Pat adds something like 'leave the cutting board out, I'll fix the handle.' Wait, do you mean that you don't think the recipe was from Nancy?"

"No, I don't think so."

Freddie wept and lowered her head into her hands. "So that's why Chief Paisley was asking where the note is. Problem was, I wish I knew. I don't remember throwing it out."

"So maybe whoever picked up the tarts picked up the note as well?" I said. "You have no idea who picked them up?"

"None." Freddie put her head between her knees again.

"Is it still in the computer?" I asked.

"No, it's disappeared," Nadia said. "Nancy said she didn't add it to the folder."

"I swear it was there," Freddie said with a sob.

Freddie was inconsolable for the time being, so I left Nadia to try her best. Nadia had taken Freddie under her wing for the past few weeks and was obstinate enough to refuse to admit defeat in the progress she'd made. Freddie's talent lay in two areas: she was a genius baker and she could follow explicit directions. Very explicit. I'd never seen Nancy's lists for her, but I'm sure they included details like "put on an apron," "tie back your hair," "preheat the oven." I can't imagine what the directions were like to operate the industrial dishwasher—not an easy task, but the only aspect of the Sleeping Latte operation I could take on without driving away business with burned and uneven baked goods or overly strong coffee.

"Ruth, I'm going to bring Freddie home. That all right with you?" Nadia said.

"Sure," I said. "Freddie, call me if you need to talk." My phone buzzed in my pocket. I took it out, hoping to see Ben's smiling face peering up at me from the little screen. Instead I saw a police badge—the avatar I used for Jeff Paisley.

"Jeff, how are you?" I said. Cell phones were such an odd change to social convention. My parents always made me answer the phone "Clagan residence, how may I help you?" I gave that up once I went to high school, but I still answered the telephone "Hello," not sure of who was calling even if caller ID was available. These days cell phones brought a greater sense of informality. When certain people called, like Ben or Jeff, I assumed they were using their cell phone. So I answered it as if "hello" wasn't necessary. And they did the same. Social conventions were shifting, at least amongst friends.

"I'm doing a final walk-through of the Town Hall before we release it."

"So soon?"

"We'll keep the portico cordoned off for the foreseeable future. Thanks to the multitudes of cameras in action that day, we can confirm Kim never came into the hall itself. Just wish the outside camera you folks have rigged up was focused on the back of the hall, not the tower."

The streaming video! I gave myself a mental head slap. Nadia had installed a streaming video camera on the clock tower, so that people could check in on the progress that was being made. The camera was stationed in the attic/office of the Cog & Sprocket. Nadia was saving all of the video, planning on doing some time-lapse footage to put on the website.

"I'd forgotten about that camera! Obviously you and Nadia have been in touch."

"She's been helpful," Jeff said. "Gave me that video right away, and also video from the inside of the Town Hall."

"From the room?"

"She put a couple of cameras in the corners of the room for background shots. Didn't you know that?"

"No, I didn't. Kind of creepy, don't you think?"

"I don't know—filmmaking is not my area of expertise. It's helpful for me now though. Interesting footage on the journey of the clock tower. Should be an fascinating documentary."

"Documentary?" I said, turning toward Nadia. She had the good grace to look embarrassed, and turned back to Freddie.

"Class project. She didn't mention it? Anyway, not why I called. Can you come over and walk through the hall with me, this time coming into the space? I want to make sure I have the complete picture, and I'm not missing anything."

"Sure, though I'm not sure—"

"Ruth, spare me. Bring your notebook with you. Don't even try and pretend you haven't been writing furiously. Can you come over right now?"

"I can," I said, hanging up the phone. I walked over to Zane's workstation and grabbed the notebook in question. I also took the clock tower notebook Zane and I had been doodling in.

"Jeff wants me to walk through the Town Hall with him," I said.

"Again? Need help?" he said. Zane was more interested in this investigation than I realized.

"I'll call if I need you over there. In the meantime, keep an eye on this place, okay? Caroline's focusing on her watches today."

Zane looked around and shrugged his shoulders. "I'll do my best. But there's a storm a-brewing, and I'm only one man."

"I have complete faith," I said, putting my hand on his arm and squeezing it lightly.

I wasn't sure which entrance to use, but was saved a decision when Jeff opened the front door. "Thanks for coming right over, Ruth," he said, holding the door open for me. He closed and locked it after I was in.

All the lights were on, which didn't help the mood of the space. It looked like the set of a zombie movie—food half-eaten, paper strewn about, chairs in disarray, as if people had vanished mid-party. Which, in fact, they had.

"Can we clean up soon?" I asked. "We're asking for mice to come back."

"Come back?"

"Old building, underused, riddled with holes. Pat and Fred have spent the better part of the spring getting rid of the mice, then patching up the holes. We finally hired someone to come in and help. We had to rewire the building after we found the extent of the damage."

"More money to spend."

"More reasons for Kim Gray to complain. Problem for her was that the deferred maintenance was on her watch. The rewiring had been budgeted for two years, but she hadn't hired anyone to do it."

"This investigation has taken us on a number of paths so far," Jeff said, instinctively looking around. No one else was in the room. "Kim had some interesting business relationships."

"Interesting?"

"I suppose you're going to find out sooner rather than later. We're meeting with the Board of Selectmen later this week. She'd take a bid on a job, always the lowest. But then the job would come in with extra expenses, which the town would pay. Turns out that part of the overpayment was a kickback to Kim."

"Kickback?" I was shocked and angry. I felt my face getting warm and wondered what shade of red it was.

"She'd get money from the vendor for the overpayment—"

"I know what a kickback is," I said, the words coming out more sharply than I intended. "I can't believe no one caught on."

"It wasn't much. A few hundred here and there. Not enough to raise a flag, and it seems to have been considered the cost of doing business in Orchard for the vendors. Netted her about twenty-five thousand dollars last year."

"Cost of doing business in Orchard," I said. "That is terrible. Why didn't anyone say something? Or maybe . . ."

"What?" Jeff asked.

"I'm just thinking about something she said to me last week. She was wondering if the income we got for Signing Day was taxable. Started making noises about an investigation. I told her we were running a nonprofit, so we were all set. I also mentioned that I'd put her in touch with my lawyer if she had any questions."

"Not everyone has a lawyer," Jeff said.

"Not everyone has needed one as much as I have this past year," I said.

"Fair enough. But if you didn't have a lawyer, or wanted to cut some corners . . ."

"Maybe you'd be willing to pay a little extra. What a racket. Nancy's head's going to explode when she hears this one," I said.

"Ruth, this has to stay between us for now. After this week, it will be public knowledge. I'll make sure the selectmen know about it beforehand. Beckett's been doing some internal investigation, collecting evidence. He says he was about to blow the whistle."

"Beckett?" I said, not trusting my ears.

"Don't sound so dubious. He gave me the heads-up last week."

"Did he want her arrested?"

"He wasn't sure what the selectmen were going to do once he told them. He wanted me to be prepared, so we could try and keep it out of the press."

"Keep it out of the press? How? A summer scandal? After everything else that's gone on here?" I bit my lower lip. "How awful. My poor clock tower. I know that sounds terrible."

"Believe it or not, Beckett was worried about you, and about Orchard. If he wasn't sincere, he fooled me."

"Good for Beckett," I said.

"Yes, good for Beckett. Course, his business would be affected by bad publicity as well. He was trying to talk to Kim, get her to have a plan to pay restitution before he went to the Board of Selectmen."

"Was that really his call?"

"No, but he'd been talking in generalities, hadn't shown us proof. We had a meeting set for today to talk about next steps with the district attorney."

"So, Kim had reason to kill Beckett, but Beckett didn't have a reason to kill Kim that we know of."

"We?" Jeff asked, shaking his head. "No, he was worried about Orchard, first and foremost. That would have stopped him if nothing else did."

"He was worried about his business. I guess that could be motive, couldn't it? Can I ask you another question? I know you won't answer, but I should ask. Did she really die of an allergic reaction?"

"She died of a reaction," Jeff said.

"I suppose I should mention that Zane makes a home-made stain out of walnuts. We also use walnut oil on some of the wood in the building."

"Did he have some of the stain in the building?" he asked, suddenly very interested.

"Probably. He's been working over here a lot."

"Nuts are everywhere," Jeff said. "I'll make sure and let the lab know about that."

"Something's been bothering me, Jeff. Was Kim dead before the bell . . . I mean, the bell didn't kill her, did it?"

Jeff sighed. "Exact timing is tough to determine. But the ME thinks she was probably dead when the bell hit her."

"I hate to think of a clock part being used to kill someone again," I said. I was thinking about G.T., who had a heart attack after being struck by a pendulum. Jeff must have known what I was thinking, because he put his arm around my shoulder. He gave it a squeeze, then let go.

"We're going to need to keep the bell for a while."

"Keep it. We wouldn't . . . bad karma and all that. Besides, Zane always hated that bell. I may have a clock sale coming up. Two banjo clocks. If the sale goes through, I'll buy a new bell."

Jeff and I walked over to the podium. "What are those

things on the podium? They look like they belong on a barbell."

"They do, don't they? Those are like the clock weights we are going to be using. Pat, or was it Fred, made this model for folks to see what their nameplates would look like eventually. Clock weights can be anything, of course, as long as they fit in whatever shaft has been built to house them. Back in the day frugal folks would take the wooden packing crate the clock came in, fill it with field stones, and use that as the weight."

"Do clock weights have to add up to a particular amount?"

"No," I said. "The heavier the weight, the longer it will run without being wound, depending on the setup. But they can—"

"Whoa, wait a second, Ruth," Jeff said. "Much as I'd love to go off on this tangent, we need to move on. I'm assuming you want to look at the clock parts?"

"Yes, please," I said. We walked over to the signing stations, and I took a quick inventory. "You were telling me who else is on your suspect list," I said.

"I was not telling you that."

"How about if I tell you the names we came up with?"

"I'm not surprised that you've been thinking about this but I didn't realize you had a team. Who's 'we'?"

"Never mind who 'we' is. Do you want to hear the list?"

"Go ahead," Jeff said. I noticed he'd taken his notebook out and was jotting down notes. That made me oddly pleased with myself, so I kept talking.

"We tried to figure out who got past the table to head out back. We probably missed some folks. Let's see." I pretended to look for the list, but I knew it by heart. "Beckett. Fred. Freddie. Jason. Jimmy."

"Jimmy Murphy? He's on your list?"

"He isn't on yours?" I said, hopefully.

"Never mind. Just a comment on the thoroughness of your investigative skills."

"Did we miss anyone?" I asked.

"Ruth—"

"I know, I know. You can't blame a girl for trying. How else can I help you?"

"Walk through the day with me again. Go ahead, use your notes. I want to know if I missed anything."

"If *you* missed anything?" I asked.

"Listen, there's a lot of pressure to get this one solved. I've come to respect your keen powers of observation. A few things still don't make sense to me. Walk me through."

So, I did. For the next forty minutes Jeff and I walked through the day, starting with my call from Kim to when we all left.

"Kim not showing up for the press photos—that was odd, right?"

"I thought so. Must have been quite the meeting to have sidelined her."

"Must have been," Jeff said. "We're still working on that hole in her schedule."

"Then she arrived, but she must have come in the side door, and then gone out to the portico," I said. "That's weird too. Wouldn't she want to make an appearance? If she'd come in the front door, I would have seen her."

"Would you have called her over to make a speech? Even though she was late?"

"Of course," I said. "Listen, I wasn't a fan, but better to stay on her good side. But coming in the side? Maybe she was going to go to the party on the portico and figured she would get there early. Or maybe she was going to meet someone before she came into the event? The question is *who*? And *why*?"

"We've got lots of whys," Jeff said. "Working on the how. What we need is the who."

chapter 20

I walked back over to the Cog & Sprocket, thoughts spinning. Interesting news about Beckett. I wondered what got him onto the idea of investigating Kim's business practices? Was that why he was so friendly with her? Or did he want her to cut him in, and she refused? Beckett as a crusader for justice. Somehow that particular cape didn't seem to fit.

I walked up the porch steps and instinctively checked the mailbox beside the front door. Our old mail carrier had always come in the shop, but the new carrier's route took her by the Cog much earlier, so she left the mail in the box. I didn't mind the lack of human contact in this instance.

I sorted through the mail quickly, stopping when I saw a familiar name in the address. Another letter from Eric. I sat on the front porch and played with the envelope. The dove gray color, heavy linen stock. Professor Eric Evan. My old address. I took a measure of my pulse. Steady. Hands? Dry. I took a breath, and opened the back flap of the letter.

Without a letter opener. Eric would have hated that. I smiled at the jagged edge the rip made.

Ruth— it began. No salutation. Just *Ruth*. I read on.

Ruth—

I am sorry you weren't able to make it to the dinner with the dean I invited you to a few weeks ago. It is with some trepidation that I write to congratulate you on your newest adventure. I must admit, I was surprised that you decided to use your considerable talents in this fashion, but sentiment was always a driving force in your life.

As time has lapsed, I have reconsidered the way we left things. Your lawyer requested a split of assets, and my lawyer denied the request. Games. I would imagine that those assets would be useful for your business. Please accept this check as my attempt to honor our former relationship. My lawyer let me know that your cashing the check would be your agreement to terms. This seems a much better end to a mostly happy chapter in my life. I hope you agree.

With my highest regards,
Eric

With my highest regards. I wasn't sure what bothered me more. That I'd once desperately loved a man who used a phrase like "highest regards" to the woman he supposedly loved or that he was trying to make amends after being so horrid a year ago. I'd lived on campus with him, and we'd been banking money for a future home purchase. When we divorced, he refused to split all of the assets fifty-fifty, arguing that his income had constituted the majority of those assets, since most of my income had been spent on clock parts. I was left with the clocks I'd built, my tools, the couch and kitchen table (neither of which had been to Eric's taste), and my personal possessions. Clothes, books, and jewelry mostly. Fortunately, I was young enough to bounce back, thanks in no small part to the second chance the Cog & Sprocket, and G.T., had left me. Still, much as Eric's treatment of me had stung, I'd decided he'd done me a favor, and made it easier to close that chapter of my life. I hadn't fought him, feeling that my moral high ground was the last word.

I looked down at the check he had enclosed and lost my breath. Twenty-five thousand dollars. Twenty-five thousand dollars would go a long way in the clock tower dreams. But at what price?

I texted Kristen, asking to set up a call. Time for a lawyer's opinion.

"Penny for your thoughts."

I started, and looked up. Jimmy Murphy walked up and sat on the next rocking chair over. His tie was purple today, and his socks were also purple. I noticed them when he stretched his legs out in front of him and crossed his ankles. He leaned back on the chair and closed his eyes. Caroline told me that G.T. hadn't used the porch much in the years since she moved to Orchard, but I wasn't surprised. This was my grandmother's turf. I thought of her every time I sat here. When I was a kid, visiting my grandparents in the summer, I'd spend hours sitting on this porch, reading or watching my grandmother tend to her flower boxes. Now I was the one tending the flower boxes, but with far less artistry. At least the flowers were still alive. Well, most of them.

"Nice view, this," Jimmy said.

"It really is. Gives me a wonderful view of Orchard. Even the town fights." I looked over at Jimmy's bruised knuckles. He used his good hand to cover them. "You have a heck of a right hook."

"Didn't realize we had an audience," Jimmy said, squirming a little. "Anyone else witness that display?"

"Just Zane and me. Beckett finally pushed you over the edge, I guess."

"Beckett was on the receiving end of my frustration," Jimmy said. "They brought Nancy in for questioning too."

"Too?"

"Yeah. I'm on the short list. It isn't like I didn't have motive. Course, I didn't do it, but that's tougher to prove under the circumstances."

"What circumstances?"

Jimmy sighed and looked over at the clock tower. The sun was lower in the sky, and the building was playing its game of shadows on the grounds below. He looked back at me and shrugged his shoulders. "Kim Gray was a real piece of work, you know that? Once I got Nancy on the Board of Selectmen, Kim knew she was on borrowed time. I finally had enough votes to get rid of her. That's when she turned on the screws. Ends up she'd been doing business like that for years."

"Doing business like what?"

"Blackmail. She called it 'keeping secrets safe.' Horrible woman. Rest her soul, of course. But still, doubt she'll be spending time in the pearly gates playing a harp. No, she's in for a warm repose. Very warm."

"Jimmy, that's terrible," I said, and I meant it.

"The truth can be terrible. One indiscretion, years ago, mind you, should not be allowed to ruin your life."

"Indiscretion? Like breaking-the-law indiscretion?"

"No, the other kind," he said, sighing. "Three years ago. A lady friend."

"Didn't your wife pass away ten years ago?" I asked, feeling like I was missing something.

"The lady has a husband."

"Ah."

"Not something I'm proud of."

"So you let Kim blackmail you. To protect your, um, friend? That's pretty gallant of you."

"I have my moments," Jimmy said.

"That's why you voted not to fire her?"

"Ha! Guessing that little tidbit came from Beckett. That's so like him, going through the trash."

"Actually, I think he had good intentions."

"Come on—"

"No, really. I'm sure it was self-serving in *some* way, but—"

"You can take that to the bank."

"Anyway, you think Kim blackmailed other people."

"I do, though I don't know who."

"Did you ever give her money?"

"Money? No? The only thing she ever asked me to do was to not fire her, which I did. Now it's time to make it right. I'm offering my resignation from the Board of Selectmen, of course."

"Are you really sure that's what's best for the town? Beckett will run for your seat."

"He will. Probably get it unless I can get you or Ben to run. Any interest? We can have up to five people serve at any given time."

"None."

"Didn't think so, but I wanted to make sure. We've got to get a new town manager hired. I'd like to have a say in that."

"She's only been dead for two days," I said, a little shocked.

"But we've been planning on getting rid of her for months. Time to put that into motion." Jimmy looked at his watch and got up. "Look at the time. I've got someone I need to see—let her know what storm may be brewing in case Kim had a partner in crime. I don't look forward to this, but it has to be done." He stood and fixed the crease in his trousers.

"Do me a favor—don't resign before you talk things over with the rest of the board," I said. "There's a lot going on right now, and I think they need you."

"I'll consider it," he said, stepping off the porch. "You take good care, Ruth. Orchard needs *you*."

I went back into the shop. No one was behind the counter, though a voice said, "Hello? Can I help you?" Then Zane came through to the front counter. "Oh, it's you."

"Is Nadia back? Where is everybody?" I asked.

"She's upstairs with the rest of them, having tea."

"Tea?"

"More like a late lunch with airs. Flo came by a little while ago with a plate of sandwiches and a tray of desserts. Sent some down to me, but the gaggle is upstairs having a talk."

"Gaggle? Are you making a sexist comment?"

"Just observing that there are a lot of women upstairs, and I'm just as happy watching the shop."

"So Pat isn't back yet? Or Ben?"

"Pat got stuck doing another house call over in Marytown. Not sure where Ben is, but Flo will know."

"How about I turn on the bells so you can hear if a customer is coming in?" I said. We had an elaborate bell system on the ceiling, with a carillon of tinkling bells that were triggered every time the door opened. The system was invented by Pat, as was the turn-it-off option.

"Good idea."

"No customers today?" I asked.

"Not in person. Were you expecting any?"

"There was someone who called about coming in to look at two banjos. Ms. Bloodsnow. The clocks are upstairs. She said she was coming on Tuesday, but if she comes in today, let me know."

"Will do," Zane said.

I headed to the staircase and had gotten only a couple of steps up when a gale of laughter swept down the stairs. I looked back at Zane and put my hands under my armpits, then flapped. Zane laughed and winked at me.

chapter 21

My apartment was tiny. I dreamed of large and airy, but instead I had small and cramped. At least the ceilings were tall, well over ten feet. The kitchen table was too big for the space, but I was, once again, glad I hadn't sold it. It was the most-used piece of furniture in the entire apartment, including my bed. It was my desk when I was alone and my entertainment center when company was there. We kept a dozen folding chairs in the hallway and someone had brought a few in. Sitting around the table were Flo, Caroline, Nancy, and Nadia. Two empty bottles of wine were on the sideboard, and Moira was opening a third.

"Just in time," she said.

"Zane said you were having tea."

"My kind of tea," Flo said, lifting her glass in a toast. "Besides, I can't drink caffeine this late—I'd be up all night." She took a healthy swig of wine.

"You want some?" Moira asked.

"I think I'll stick with tea for the time being. What kind of wine is it?"

"Bubbling Burgundy."

"Bubbling . . ."

"Flo found it. It's not bad," Nancy said, swishing her glass around a bit.

"Make sure you eat something too," Caroline said. "There are wonderful sandwiches Flo brought."

"Not as good as the Sleeping Latte sandwiches," Flo added, eyeing Nancy.

"They're good," Nancy said, somewhat grudgingly. "Where did you get them? Hamilton's?"

"Hamilton's?" I took a sandwich. Fresh tomatoes and pesto oozed out of the sides of the fresh bread. I hadn't realized how hungry I was. "Same family as Fred and Freddie?" I asked with a full mouth. Delicious.

"Same. Fred's sister runs it. It's a little lunch place. Opened last fall, near the university. Great location. Does a pretty good business," Flo said.

"Course, it's hard not to make a good sandwich this simple," Nancy said. "Fresh bread, pesto, mozzarella, tomatoes. Hummus and cucumbers."

"Mum, that's not fair, and you know it," Moira said. "These are really good. Maybe we should think about asking her to make sandwiches for the Latte."

"Are you retiring, Nancy?" Caroline asked. She took another half a sandwich and a few chips.

"Not retiring. Coming to terms with the fact that I can only do so much. I was hoping Freddie could pick up the slack. She's a great baker, but a menace at anything else."

"You're not going to fire her, are you?" Nadia asked.

"Fire? No, not at all. In fact, we're getting more and more special orders in."

"Like the cherry tart order?" Nadia asked.

"I didn't have her make cherry tarts," Nancy said, in a way that sounded like she had said it many times before. "Can't say more about that—Jeff's orders."

"Oh, so they do think *tarts* are what killed Kim. Poor Freddie," Nadia said.

"So it was an allergic reaction?" Flo said. "Terrible way to go."

"Even more terrible that someone fed her the tarts knowing she was allergic, framing my mother and Freddie as they did it," Moira said, finally successfully removing the cork from the bottle of wine she'd been struggling with. "I think they call that murder."

"Perhaps it was an accident," Caroline said, holding out her glass.

"Someone conked her on the head with the bell too," Flo said. "Nothing accidental about that."

"Insurance policy that she was really gone, more like," Nadia said. "What are you all looking at? If I was going to kill someone I'd want to make sure I did the job. Maybe it was her ex-boyfriend."

"Ex-boyfriend?" Nancy, Moira, and I looked at one another. Had she been dating Beckett, Fred, Jason, or Jimmy? Because those were the only options on the suspect list. I mentally crossed Jimmy off that list. He may have a motive, but passion wasn't one of them.

"Yeah. She came by the Corner Market one day last spring. I'd broken up with Tuck again, so she was trying to make small talk. Mentioned that she'd had a relationship that went on for months before she'd finally gotten up enough steam to break up with him. From what she said, I think maybe he'd been married, and left his wife for her."

"How did you get her to tell you that?" I asked.

"I didn't get her to talk to me. I listened, and didn't judge."

"We don't judge," Flo said.

"Please," Nadia said. "You could be sitting on a jury, you're judging so hard."

I looked around the room and had to agree with the assessment. I wanted to let them all know about Kim's hypocrisy, blackmailing Jimmy for a sin that—by the sounds of it—she was also committing, but it wasn't my place. I'd put my notebook down on the counter when I'd come in, and my fingers itched to pick it up. I stood up, scooped up my notebook, and sat back down while everyone discussed the moral codes of Orchard.

"You know," I said, over the din of the conversation, "Kim had a few enemies. Seems like the Hamilton family, including Fred and Freddie, are on the list."

"Freddie couldn't have killed her," Nadia said, shaking her head. "She was so upset when she thought maybe she did."

"But Freddie would do anything for her father," Flo said, placing her glass down for emphasis. "Maybe *he* told her to make the tarts, and she's covering for him."

"I doubt it. First of all, she couldn't lie to save her soul. Secondly, Fred wouldn't mess around with a nut allergy. No guarantee it would work, for one thing. Kim was prepared to deal with her allergies. Even the bell isn't his style. He's more the blunt-object type," Nancy said.

"Fred's got a fierce temper, and there was no love lost with him and Kim. Still, I can't imagine him killing her, can you?" Flo said.

"What about Jason?" Moira said.

"What about him?" Flo said, pouring more wine. I pushed the bowl of chips over toward her.

"Did he and Kim get along?" I asked.

"So far as I know," Flo said. "He brought her prescriptions over from Marytown, and they always chatted when she came in to pick them up. Also took to picking up other things for her."

"He does that for Harriet as well," Caroline said. "Calls himself a sort of butler on call. Charges her a little bit extra, but she's happy to pay it. Saves her a trip."

"What does he pick up? Groceries?"

"No, health food stuff," Flo said. "He's got us carrying more homeopathic remedies and herbal medicine. He's even got some tonics he's adding to the stock. Says there's a demand for it."

"Herbs?" Nancy asked. "Harriet has him bring her herbs?"

"Swears it does her more good than the arthritis medicine the doctor prescribed. She's not the only one he's dosing with alternative medicine. Kim swore by his stress drops."

"Jason has a lot of irons in the fire, doesn't he?" Caroline said.

"Trying to forge a few more," Flo replied. "He wants to take over the Emporium, make it his own."

"Which leaves you and Ben where?" Nancy asked.

"Running the barbershop—"

"Are you going to stop calling it a barbershop soon?" Nancy said.

"We're working on naming both the shops." Flo sniffed. "Give us time. What are you, a sign maker looking for a job? Anyone who wants a haircut, they know where to come. We're plenty busy."

"Whoa, Flo, calm down. Don't get your dander up," Nancy said innocently.

Flo sighed, loudly and dramatically. The ruffles on the front of her blouse rustled when she exhaled.

"Ben and I had a long talk last night. I worry he's thinking about making some changes in his life that don't include running the store."

Everyone turned and looked at me.

"He's thinking about going back into the tech business," I said.

"Leaving Orchard?" asked Moira.

"He's working through a lot right now," I said.

"You're a smart woman, giving him space," Flo said.

"Just don't give him too much space," Nancy said. "I'd hate to see him leave. Why can't things just be the same for a while?"

The tea party broke up shortly after the third bottle of wine was empty. Nancy offered to stay and help me clean up, but I sent her home with Moira. Caroline went back downstairs to help Zane in the shop, and Nadia went upstairs to the office to check on the camera footage.

Flo wrapped up the leftover sandwiches and went to put them in the refrigerator.

"That's an impressive amount of leftovers," she said, holding the door open.

"I know. Most are from last night, though Ben used some to make an awesome omelet this morning."

"He said that you both had a good talk," she said.

"We did. You too?"

"Yeah. He's a good boy, always has been. We lost him for a while, back when his business took off and he married that woman."

"That woman?"

"That's what I call her. She Who Shall Not Be Named. Not good for Ben, not at all."

"Flo, we shouldn't talk about—"

"Of course we should. I'll blame it on the Bubbling Burgundy if anyone asks. She was self-centered and cared about herself first and foremost. Which worked out well, since Ben only cared about her too. Lost himself for a while, made himself what she wanted."

"Sounds like my ex and me."

"Something else the two of you have in common. Everything got wrapped up in her and the success of the business, not the business itself."

"What do you mean?" I asked, rinsing a wineglass and depositing it in the drying rack.

She shut the fridge. "The tech business suited Ben, you know? Ben loves developing ideas and hiring the right folks to make them work. It went well for a long time. Then he spent too much time working on a dud of an idea, and his investors got scared. He lost the business, and that woman left him."

"Broke his heart," I said quietly.

"More than that. She broke his spirit."

I took a deep breath and thought about my letter from Eric. He'd broken my heart, but he hadn't broken my spirit. Not by a long shot. My heart had healed, stronger than ever. Ben had wheedled his way into it. But what about Ben? Was he still in love with his ex? Did he miss his old life? Did he want it back?

"You're the best thing that's happened to him in a long time," Flo said, as if she'd been reading my mind. "Maybe ever. Promise me two things."

I knew better than to argue, so instead I asked her what the two things were.

"First, that you won't give up on Ben. Fight for him."

"I'll fight to make him happy," I said. I hoped I was part of the picture, but I didn't want to discuss that with Flo.

"Second," Flo said, "keep working on figuring out what happened to Kim. I've got a bad feeling about all of this and we need to get this solved as soon as possible."

"So do I," I said, nodding. "Jeff and I talked this afternoon. I'll help however I can, even though he'll never ask. He's going to figure it out."

"Jeff may figure out what happened to Kim, but I'm talking about getting to the roots of the influences around her. Figure them out, and made sure they're pulled out."

"Why do so many people think I've got this superpower to be able to fix things?" I said, drying my hands on a dish towel.

"Because you've got the mind for it. So did your grandfather. Where some people see bits of metal, you see the makings of a clock. You care about making things run, and run well. Kim was a broken cog. Let's get rid of the rest of them, otherwise Orchard will never run right again."

chapter 22

"How can I help you, Ruth?" Jason asked. He'd come out front a few seconds after the door chime went off in the Emporium.

"Are you still open?" I said. I'd decided to take a walk down the street and talk to Jason—he was one of the only people on my list I didn't have a whole ton of information about. I wondered why he'd gone into the vestibule, and the only way I'd find out is if I asked him.

"Till six."

I checked my watch. It was four thirty. "Whew. I remembered you said you have some allergy meds here. I usually don't have problems, but this year something is bothering me."

"We had a wet winter. Tough spring for allergies."

"Makes sense," I said. "I'm trying to train for a 5K this summer, and running is tough— What are you laughing at?"

He was covering his mouth, his shoulders shaking.

"I've been here for four months, and you've been training for a 5K the entire time I've known you."

I laughed. "I never get much past week two," I confessed. "This week I'm blaming it on allergies. Next month I'll blame it on the heat."

"Well, let's help you with the allergies. Any preferences? Side effects you worry about? Interactions with other drugs?"

"I don't take any other drugs. I don't like taking medicine unless I really have to. I hate pills, for one thing."

"You know, most pills come in a liquid form. Or your pharmacist can make them into a liquid. You just have to be really careful to shake them up every time, so you get the right dosage every time."

"Good to know."

"If you get this"—he pointed to a familiar brand name—"you'll be able to breathe, but it will make you tired."

"I don't want anything that makes me tired. Tired clock-makers are careless clockmakers. Harriet told me there are some natural alternatives I might try?"

"There are alternative medicines. Homeopathic meds give you a little bit of what you are allergic to so you build up an immunity. We carry a line of them. Those are the blue bottles over here. I've been experimenting with some myself, making them into drops that may help with immediate relief." We walked over to a section that featured blue bottles, brown bottles, and vats of protein powder. Jason handed me a little blue bottle.

"I thought you were a pharmacist," I said, leaning in to read one of the labels on the little bottles.

"I'm a realist. Folks are looking for other paths to health. I need to understand how they work, what the interactions are with traditional medicine."

"Interactions?"

"Just because something is natural doesn't mean it's safe. A lot of herbs have effects that are similar to drugs. If you are on a heart medicine, you need to make sure you don't take an herb that gives you high blood pressure. Sometimes people don't understand side effects, and they need to. Call it my new mission."

"I understand missions. I feel like that about clocks, though it is a little different. Clocks can't save people's lives."

"They can't kill people either," he said. "My sister was on antidepressants after her husband left her. Didn't understand the drug interaction they'd have with other things she was taking. She was driving home one night and got into a terrible accident. They say she fell asleep at the wheel. She never regained consciousness." Jason picked up a bottle of vitamins and started tossing it from hand to hand.

"That's terrible," I said, set slightly off-balance at his sudden openness. The pain of the memory was evident, and I was sorry to have brought it up.

"It is the worst thing that ever happened to me. Trust me, that's saying something. But it did give me a new mission. A couple of them, actually. One was to better understand medicine and explore what it can do more fully." Jason put the vitamins back on the shelf with more velocity than he expected—he bowled over a few other bottles.

"So, if I go the homeopathic route, will that get rid of the allergies?"

Jason nodded and forced a smile. "I don't know if it will get rid of them, but it would make it easier to live with them. If it works for you."

"It doesn't work for everyone?"

"Depends on the type of allergy, and how bad they are."

"Phew, that's a lot to think about." I picked up another bottle. "What does this do?"

"Good for migraines."

"Not a problem I have, thankfully."

"You're lucky. I sell a lot of this," he said. "I take it myself."

"Good to know. Do you use the allergy stuff?"

"I don't, but I do sell a lot of it." Jason started to straighten out the bottles of vitamins.

"I heard that Kim had pretty bad allergies," I said.

"Very bad ones, and all sorts. She carried an EpiPen with her at all times just in case. There was also one in her office, and in her car."

"What exactly do they do?"

"They are a shot to get someone through a bad reaction. Portable. Looks like a big plastic pen. It should have helped her, always had in the past. I've heard that she died of an allergic reaction. Is that right?"

"I don't know for sure, but I've heard the same thing."

"Such a shame. If only someone had been there to help her. To administer the medicine or call for help."

"You went back to the portico during the party, didn't you?" I asked, attempting to make this obvious interrogation seem more casual.

Jason looked at me, then walked over to the cash register and started moving things around on the countertop. "No, you must be mistaken."

"Really? I thought I saw you head back after the speeches were over."

"Oh yes, you're right. I didn't go to the portico, only to the kitchen. I went back to see if there was any more sweet iced tea. I love that stuff, though it is terrible for you. Sugar and caffeine. Still, my summer vice. Who made it? Please tell me it is a Sleeping Latte summer special."

"It is," I said. "Moira makes it from a secret family recipe Caroline gave her. It is one of my vices as well."

"Delicious. Anyway, I went looking for more in the kitchen."

"Did you see Kim?"

"Was she there then? I didn't see her." Jason looked right at me and didn't blink. Either he was telling the truth or was a good liar.

"That's a shame. You probably could have helped her. All right, let's try some of this homeopathic stuff," I said. "Might as well try and head this off at the pass."

"Let me pull what you need and write up some directions. Make sure you follow them exactly, otherwise it won't work the way it's supposed to. We can always make adjustments. Of course, if it gets too bad, there's always over-the-counter."

"Thanks, Jason," I said. I looked around the store, waiting for Jason to finish up. I looked over at the corner near the back office and noticed a bicycle wheel resting against the wall.

"How's the bicycling going?" I said.

"Good. I train for a century ride like you train for a 5K—never get much past the first month. But maybe this year will be the one where I do the hundred-mile ride."

"Why is your wheel in here? Did you need to get it fixed?"

"No, old habit from city living. Make it less attractive for a thief. The rest of the bike is chained up outside."

"Orchard isn't exactly a hotbed of bike thieves," I said.

"I know. Like I said, old habit. Like wearing my bike shorts under my pants."

I looked over at Jason, wearing his uniform of khakis and a button-down shirt. Red striped today. He caught me looking, and winked at me. "Nothing worse than bike grease on my pants," he said. "I hate not looking my best."

"You always do," I said, arranging my mouth into something I hoped resembled a smile. The image of him in bike shorts was now seared in my brain.

I walked back to the Cog & Sprocket and let myself in the front door. Nadia was working at the front counter and looked up when I came in.

"Where were you?" she asked.

"Went down to get allergy meds."

"I didn't know you had allergies," Nadia said.

"I don't."

"Why, Nancy Drew," she said, grinning, "were you sleuthing?"

"Stop. I thought that since Jason's on the list—"

"What list?"

I sighed deeply. Trying to act innocent around Nadia wasn't worth the effort. Actually, Nancy Drew was a bit of a badge of honor. She was one of my childhood favorites. I suspect Nadia knew that.

"Remember when Moira texted you asking for names of who went back past the tables into the vestibule? We're figuring that one of those people went out to the portico and killed Kim."

"Who's on your list?"

"Fred, Freddie, Jason, Beckett, Jimmy."

"Freddie? When did she go back?"

"About five minutes after the speeches were done."

"I didn't notice. But you saw her today. If she'd killed

Kim, she wouldn't have been able to function for the rest of the afternoon."

"I've been thinking about that. What about if Fred asked her to give Kim a tart? He hated Kim as much as anyone. Would Freddie be able to do it if she didn't know she was going to kill her? She would have done what her father told her." I hated the line of thought, but realized it made sense, so I went on. "And then Fred went back to make sure she was dead—"

"And dropped a bell on her to be sure. Ding-dong. That's cold," Nadia said. "I don't see it myself. Too much planning for Fred. That, and I don't think he'd use Freddie as his surrogate murder weapon. He adores Freddie."

"Maybe he just meant to get Kim sick?"

"Or maybe Kim died by accident, and then someone went back and dropped the bell onto her out of spite? I guess I can see Fred doing that."

"Dropping the bell out of spite," I said. "Maybe Kim wasn't killed at all? Maybe she died, and someone took advantage of it. Got his frustrations out by dropping a bell on her. It's pretty sick, but who can really know what people are capable of . . ."

"And there wasn't a house available . . ."

"Nadia—"

"Come on, Ruth, don't tell me you aren't thinking about *The Wizard of Oz* every time you think of a bell being dropped."

"You're the one who called her the Wicked Witch—"

"I'm not the only one," she said.

"You're right," I said. "Kim's death an accident? I'm not buying it. We don't have that kind of luck. Much as I hate to admit it, it looks like there's been another murder in Orchard."

Nadia looked down, and I knew she was thinking about Mark Pine. Time to change the subject.

"Zane said that no one came by today?" I asked.

"No one," Nadia confirmed. "But there were some calls. Where's that pad—here it is. Three calls to set up appointments for you or Zane to go look at sick grandfather clocks. The church over in Oakfield wants you to come over and look at their clock tower."

"Really?" I said, my ears practically perking up.

"Look at you, so excited. Yeah, it's intact, but hasn't been wound in fifteen years."

"Probably needs a good cleaning."

"Zane's first words too. They want to talk to you, specifically you, about how much it would cost to get it running again. I also talked to them about a winding and maintenance contract."

"That's exciting," I said, clapping my hands together with glee.

"You haven't even heard the best part. The church council was considering going electric, but then someone told them about our tower and suggested they try and save the original."

"How great is that?" I asked, meaning every word. While I understood why some folks decided to go electric, a small piece of my soul hurt every time an old clock tower was converted.

"There was a weird call on the voice mail. Someone calling on behalf of Lila Bloodsnow."

"The woman who wants the Willard banjo clocks?"

"Same woman, but her assistant was calling to follow up on the offer Ms. Bloodsnow had made on the clock collection at the Parker University."

"What offer?" I asked. I didn't need to ask which collection she was referring to. Back when I was a faculty wife, I'd lived in one of the houses on campus. I spent time getting all of the clocks in working order, showing the students in the house how they worked, getting a few of them to help me by being on the winding crew. The university was rehabbing one of the dorms, and they were selling two grandfather clocks. Neither of them had worked for years, or been taken care of for longer than that. The cases were scratched, the glass was dusty, the brass was dull. But they were both beauties. I made a low offer on them both, which was accepted, much to Eric's chagrin.

I had them moved to our apartment. It took me a year, but both of them got back to working order. We kept one of them in our apartment, but moved the other to the dining hall, where it became a showpiece for the university. When Eric and I broke up, I met with the dean and offered to put the clocks on loan until I settled down. I'd kept in touch with her, updating her on my new business ventures. At one point she'd written and asked if I wanted my clocks back. I told her no, that I didn't have room for them right now. That was a lie, of course. What I didn't want was to be tempted to sell them. I'd rather let the students enjoy them for a while longer, while I figured out other ways to finance my dreams.

"I called her back. Ms. Bloodsnow's assistant, Mary Stibal," Nadia said. "She wanted to know if you were going to accept the offer. It took me a while, but I finally got the details. She had offered a hundred thousand dollars for the two grandfather clocks. She also wanted to talk to you about some clock you made for the lobby? She'd love to commission one for her office."

"A hundred thousand dollars? Are you sure? That's a lot of money."

"That's what she said. It would go a long way toward keeping this place going, that's for sure."

"We're doing all right," I said weakly.

"You're forgetting that I am doing the books these days," Nadia said. "When's the last time you took a paycheck?"

"I get paid—"

"You pay yourself less than you pay me," she said. "You have to start—"

"Not now, Nadia. You haven't mentioned this to Caroline, have you?"

"You and I are the only two people who know how tight things are."

"Keep it that way, all right? We'll figure it out, I promise. Right after the clock tower is done, I can get back to making some money."

"Fair enough," Nadia said. "Unless you sell this woman the clocks she wants to buy. So what did the clock you made look like?"

"It had the university shield on one side, a calendar clock in the middle, and the house shield on the other side. The calendar clock was refurbished, but in full working order. Every hour a dove flew from one shield to the other, and then back. It was a fun piece. I had students help me with the install."

"Well, apparently she's an alum and fell in love with the clock when she went back for a reunion last fall. How much do you think it is worth?"

"Hard to say," I said. "The pieces were a few hundred, maybe more—"

"Ruth, we need to start getting you to value the art pieces you create. Can I try and figure out how much it might be worth?"

"Is it really art?" I said. I always felt odd talking about the clock creations I made. For me, they created another way to imagine a clock and gave me great joy to work on. Making money from them? Was that even possible?

"Just stop," Nadia said. "I'm going to do some research. Anyway, Ms. Bloodsnow's assistant says she's been trying to get hold of you for a while, but your husband—"

"Ex-husband."

"I explained that part to her. Your ex has been dodging her calls since alumni weekend. The dean gave her this number."

"Well, that explains the letter," I said.

"Letter?"

"My ex sent me a letter. Decided he was wrong not to split our assets last year when the divorce was finalized, so he sent me a check."

"Big of him," Nadia said.

"Isn't it though? He must have had a team of lawyers to help him phrase the letter in just a way that my cashing the check would have bound me to a new agreement. Probably some legal loophole my divorce lawyer didn't anticipate."

"So if you accept Ms. Bloodsnow's offer?"

"Eric will demand his share. Half of a hundred thousand dollars is fifty thousand, so he'd net twenty-five thousand."

"What a jerk," Nadia said.

"You have no idea," I said.

"Well, your taste has gotten better, that's for sure. Speaking of which, did I mention that Ben is upstairs?"

"You didn't," I said.

"Sorry about that, boss," she said a bit sheepishly. "Go ahead, I'll lock up down here. See you tomorrow."

I barely heard her, I was so focused on getting upstairs as quickly as possible. I opened the door, and Blue came bounding up to greet me. "Where's your dad?" I said, crouching down to rub his neck and return his kisses. I looked up and saw Ben stretched out on the couch, fast asleep.

"Ah well," I said to Blue. "Let me feed you guys, and then I've got some notes to write."

A half hour later I was sitting at the table, looking over my notes. Ben shuffled into the kitchen area and gave me a kiss on top of my head.

"Okay if I grab a beer? Do you want one?" he asked.

"No thanks," I said. "Would you like some dinner? We can cook, or there are sandwiches that Flo brought over in the fridge—oh, I see you found them."

Ben grabbed a sandwich, unwrapped it, and took a bite. "That's perfect. It will tide me over until we make dinner later. I have a pasta dish I want to make with the rest of the ham," he said, sitting at the head of the table. "What are you working on?"

"Notes from today."

"Clock notes?"

"No, notes about the weekend."

"Kim's death?"

"Yeah. It's been a busy day. Want me to tell you about it?"

"I do. I'd like to tell you about my day too," he said.

"You go first," I said, closing my notebook. I took a sip of water. My hand shook a bit.

"So, first thing I did was rent a car. I went back down to Hartford to talk to my buddy. I made a deal to license him the software I was telling you about."

"License? Are you going to go work with him?"

"Nah. May I see your phone?" I nodded and handed it to him. He scrolled through and then hit a few buttons. "As I said, I don't want to go back to the life I had before I moved here when I barely thought about anything other than work, constantly moving on to the next thing, and losing myself in the process. I can look back on it now and paint a rosy picture of the success I had, but the truth is, that success was ruining my life." He looked up and stared at me. "Of course, there are a couple of other things factoring into my decision. Okay, here you go. From now on you won't have to wonder where I am. I added a phone-finding app to your screen."

"You don't have to do that," I said, unsure of what this meant. "I trust you."

"I know you do, but I realize that I'm not always good about checking in, and I don't want you to wonder."

"I'm not going to use it."

"But you'll have it."

"Thanks, I guess," I said. I hoped he wasn't planning on tracking me. "Now, about the two other factors?"

"I kept coming back to two things that made me decide to stay here in Orchard, figuring out my new life." He put his beer down and reached over and closed my notebook. He reached out for my hand and pulled me toward him.

"Two things?" I said, getting up and moving toward him. He pushed himself back from the table so I could sit on his lap. I looped my arms around his neck.

"First, Orchard is home now. I don't want to leave." He kissed my jaw, the corners of my mouth, my temples.

"Second?" I asked, breathing heavily.

"You. Can't see that anything would be much fun if I couldn't see you every day." He smiled that smile, the one that took my breath away, and I leaned in and kissed him.

chapter 23

"Sorry, babe," Ben had said when I came back up from checking the locks on the shop. I trusted Nadia, but always double-checked. I'd bounded up the stairs, a spring in my step. "Pat texted, and needs help over at the Latte. They're going to reopen tomorrow."

"That's good news, at least."

"It is," he said. "Pat wants some help unloading a few things. I won't be gone long, I promise. Can you take Blue for a run? Don't wear yourself out." Another kiss, this one tinged with a little regret.

A run sounded like a good idea, and Blue agreed. "Thanks for coming with me," I said to Blue, quickening my pace to keep up. "Figure, given everything, I may as well get some sort of exercise in tonight, though this isn't what I had planned." I took a swig from my water bottle, trying to swallow the frustration that was welling up.

"Hey, Blue, slow down, buddy. I'm getting a stitch on my side." Blue did as I asked and stayed next to me. Maybe this 5K was going to get past week two after all. I'd decided to cross the bridge behind the Cog & Sprocket and run on the other side of the river. The change of scenery would do me good. I'd barely started when I ran by the first bridge, which was the half-mile mark. The next bridge meant it would be a two-mile run total. I decided to go for it. How I loved the long days of June. It was just past six, and I had plenty of daylight left. Blue was thrilled about the run, and I was trying to match his enthusiasm. Maybe he needed to be my new running coach.

It was a stunning night to be out. Coolish, around sixty-five degrees. Spring had been cold, so the trees were late, but the bright green was forcing itself out of the winter-gray branches. The river was running high and was more turbulent than usual. I loved the sound of the rushing water, ever mindful that the dam that kept it manageable also kept the Cog & Sprocket and the rest of the riverside businesses dry.

We finally got to the second bridge, and I stopped for a minute in the middle, eating a protein bar, looking back toward downtown. We were still in the town of Orchard. Aunt Flo lived in this part of town, as did the Clarks. These houses mostly dated from the mid-1800s—pretty summer cottages that were truly cottages, not the mansions of Newport. Porches that overlooked the river, clapboard and shingle sides, lovely but not ostentatious. Many of these houses had been split up into apartments over the years, including Flo's, though she owned the whole house. She'd left one apartment empty for Ben, and she rented the third for income. Mac and Ada's house was originally a gardener's cottage for a larger house that had long ago been razed for a post-WWII subdivision. Their house sat farther back, but I could see their gray roof from here. I loved this part of Orchard, and would consider living here if I ever needed more space.

"Ready, Blue?" I asked. Blue had been playing catch with the lapping water of the river, but as soon as I said his name he came bounding up. I stooped down, put his smiling face between my hands, and kissed the tip of his nose. Blue was quite possibly the sweetest dog I'd ever met. Ben was a smart man, leaving Blue with me. Being abandoned by both of them would have left me in quite a state.

I went running back down the other side of the river, toward downtown Orchard. I checked my watch. Quarter of seven. Not bad. Not good, but not bad.

I was running by the hardware store, looking in the window. Was someone in there? This late? Doubtful. But there were lights on inside. I went over and peered in the window. I couldn't see anyone. I walked around to the left of the shop. This is where the access road behind all of our shops dead-ended. No cars, no trucks. No one. Just the lineup of Dumpsters, for the use of the hardware shop only. That made extra clear by the lock the owner had installed on each of the lids. In the past the owners had all shared Dumpsters, but no longer. Now the Dumpsters were for sorting of recyclables and chemicals, the stock-in-trade of the store. Food items didn't mix in his specific system, so the Sleeping Latte had to get their own Dumpster out back. It had caused a bit of a kerfuffle. There'd been a lot of Dumpster angst this spring. Who knew getting rid of trash could be so fraught?

Someone didn't get the memo on "no Sleeping Latte stuff

in the hardware store Dumpster," despite the large sign he'd posted on the fence about them. The baker's box could have come from anywhere, until you noted the large turquoise, pink, and gray sticker on each side. Moira stuck them on everything that didn't move, part of the branding campaign Nadia had started for her.

Better I take the box than Henry, the owner of the hardware store, find it. It was resting on top of the closed lid of the Dumpster. The Latte had been closed, so where did this come from? If it was from the Latte itself, they would have used their own Dumpster so as not to set off a war. I walked over and came close to picking up the box, but then I saw the scrawl on top of the box.

Here are your cherry tarts. Hope you enjoy them. Thank you for your business!

I stepped back, fumbling for my phone, and called Jeff Paisley. He picked up on the second ring.

"You're not going to believe what I found."

I was dying to see what was inside the box, but refrained from taking a look. Partially because I didn't want to tamper with the evidence. But mostly because all three sides of the box were taped shut. I did take a few pictures with my phone while I was waiting. I'd tied Blue up by the street, since the last thing we needed was for him to dive on the box and open it for the police.

Finally Ro Troisi arrived.

"Causing trouble again, I see," she said, turning the corner into the alley. She bent down to say hello to Blue and then came down the alley. "Tell me. Step by step."

So I did. Step by step, I walked her through what had led me to finding the box.

"You were running? This late? With the best-looking boyfriend in Orchard? What's happened to you, Ruth?"

"Ben's helping Pat with something. Besides, that's all you have to say?" I asked, reddening slightly. "What about the fact that I found a key piece of evidence?"

"Nice job, that. I suspect you weren't meant to find it, though."

"Do you think Henry was supposed to find it?" I asked. "I doubt it would make it to the morning. There are a couple of raccoons living back there."

"I know. Been raising hell with the library's garbage cans."

"I'm sure. I'm surprised they didn't get at this box, especially since there was probably food inside."

"Presumably," Ro said. "You didn't sneak a peek, did you?"

"Of course not. I called you right away," I said, leaning a bit closer to take another look. "The box is in pretty good shape. If it is the box of tarts Freddie made, it mustn't have been outside all this time. The box looks brand new still."

"Good surface for prints, but I don't expect we'll be that lucky," Ro said. She turned to look at me.

"You'll probably find Freddie's," I said.

"Thanks for the tip, Ruth. I know where you are if we have any more questions. Head on home now before Blue gets into trouble."

I walked back out of the alley, toward Washington Street, past Ro's car, which was parked up on the curb. I untied Blue, and held onto his leash tightly so he wouldn't bound back down the alley. I needn't have worried. Blue pulled me down the street to greet one of his favorite people, Flo.

"Hi, Flo, need help with that?"

Flo loaded the box into her car. She turned back around, and bent down to say hello to Blue, and looked up at me. "No thanks, Ruthie. Just bringing some foil home so I can cut squares for the shop."

"Can't you buy them ready-cut?"

"You can, but I like to have different sizes. This way is cheaper, and it gives me something to do besides eat while I watch TV at night. Where are you coming from? You didn't find another body, did you, Ruth?" Flo asked, her forehead creased with concern.

"What would make you think I found a body?" I asked Flo, or rather Flo's backside, since she was reaching into her backseat to grab something. I may have had a bit of an edge to my voice, but honestly, who could blame me? She pulled herself out of the backseat and turned around to give Blue a couple of dog treats.

"Whoa, calm down. Just a question. Ro's parked crazy, and you've been back there awhile. I wondered what was going on."

"How do you know Ro came back to see me?"

"She told me when she got out of her car. Said you'd called something in. So I decided to wait around, see what happened."

"You would've found out sooner or later."

"I'd be up all night wondering. Besides, Jeff and Ro have been pretty tight-lipped lately. I was wondering if you had any more luck."

"None," I lied.

"Where's Ben?" she asked.

"Helping Pat with the Latte," I said.

"I heard they were going to reopen tomorrow," Flo said. "That's good. Nancy's probably home baking up a storm. I wonder what Pat needed help with."

"Got to admit, I didn't ask for details. I was a little ticked that he left."

Flo laughed. "Explains the run this late. Have you had dinner? Want to come over?"

"Thanks, Flo. I have so many leftovers. You're welcome to join me—"

"Laundry night. I've got to call Kim's sister back again tonight too—"

"You finally tracked her down?" I said. "Why wasn't Nancy calling her?"

"Nancy didn't know what to say. I can fake sympathy better than she can. We've already talked a couple of times. Her sister would rather not come out here to claim the body, so I'm trying to help her figure that out."

"That's a little cold, isn't it?"

"I would hate to imagine Ben not coming to get me if I passed somewhere else, that's for sure. The sisters weren't close. After Kim's husband died, it seems like Kim cut ties with everyone in that life."

"That's it? No other family?"

"Even I'm feeling sorry for Kim these days. No other family. Her sister's first question was about Kim's will," Flo said. "That's never a good sign. Then there's the way she died. I couldn't help Googling 'allergic reactions.' Terrible way to go. Can you imagine having an allergic reaction that bad?"

"I can't. Seems like more and more people have allergies these days."

"Isn't that the truth? Good thing Jason knows how to talk folks through different remedies. Not sure how I'm going to handle any tough questions for the next couple of days."

"Jason's taking a day off?"

"He works more hours than I can count, but I can't fault

him for taking a couple of days," Flo said. "He seems like he knows his stuff. He makes up these drops. Apparently they help with different ailments. A couple of drops here, a couple of drops there, bingo bongo, you're a new woman. Can you imagine?"

"He sold me some—"

"He's making us money," Flo said. She reached into the bag and took out another treat for Blue. "Back in the day, people would travel around and sell bottles of heaven knows what and pretend it was medicine. I hope we're not doing the same thing here."

"I've heard about homeopathy before. I'm impressed that Jason knows what he's doing."

"He got training up in upstate New York. He used to own a shop with his sister, until she passed a couple of years back. I shouldn't be so judgmental of him, I guess. He does bring in the business."

"Business is a good thing," I said. "Question is, is it the business you want?"

"That is the ten-thousand-dollar question, isn't it?"

chapter 24

I walked up the street, toward the Cog & Sprocket. Instinctively I looked over at the Town Hall. Buttoned up for the night. I couldn't wait to get over there, back to work. Clocks made sense. They didn't always work. But they made sense.

Blue lumbered along ahead of me, bounding up the stairs to the porch, then stopping. He leaned back and made a noise. I stayed back with him. The sun had dropped quickly, and my eyes were adjusting to the gray dusk filter. I should have left the lights on.

"Ms. Clagan?" Freddie said, getting off one of the rocking chairs and stepping into the shaft of light that the streetlight cast.

"Whoa, Freddie. I didn't see you at first."

"Sorry—we didn't know you were home. We needed a place to sit for a minute."

"We?"

"My dad and I."

I stepped up onto the porch and looked over to the left. Sure enough, Fred was sitting over in the corner, on one of the rocking chairs. He leaned forward, his elbows on his knees, head hanging forward.

"Fred?" I said. "Everything okay?"

Fred looked up at me, shadows playing on the planes of his face. He laughed, but there was no joy in it.

"About as far from okay as a man can get and still be standing. We didn't think you were home. Needed a place to sit and think."

"Do you want to come inside?" I said.

"Yes, please," Freddie said. "Come on, Daddy. Maybe Ruth can help us."

"Doubt it, but may as well."

I invited them both upstairs, but Fred declined. Blue wanted to go, probably to say hello to Bezel and get a drink, so I ran up to let him into the apartment. I grabbed the basket of tea and brought it back downstairs with me. I went over to the electric kettle in the shop kitchenette and turned it on. I gave the Hamiltons a minute to settle in. I watched as Fred went over to the windows and checked to make sure the blinds were closed, which they were. Standard closing procedure, as was triple-checking the locks on the windows. He turned toward his daughter and whispered something to her. I tried not to give in to my nerves. I couldn't imagine Freddie as a killer. Still, she and her father were on the list. I was glad I'd left the apartment door open and hoped Blue would come to the rescue if I called him. I double-checked that my phone was charged and in my pocket. Check on both. Jeff was on speed dial if need be.

"Would either of you like a cup of tea?" I asked.

"Did you find the box?" Freddie asked.

"What box?" I said. I hoped my face didn't betray me. I should have texted Jeff to come over.

"Freddie—" her father interrupted.

"We were on our way back to get the box," Freddie said, rubbing her eyes. "But then we saw that the police were there. So was Blue, so I guess you were there too? Did you find it? I didn't want to leave it by the Sleeping Latte. I'd already caused them so much trouble. Losing a whole day of business because of me."

"Wasn't because of you, sweetheart," Fred said. "This is all on me. Tell you what—why don't you go make us some tea? I'll tell Ruth about the tarts."

We both watched Freddie walk toward the back of the shop. Fred was sitting on the settee, watching his daughter. I stood by the front door, ready to bolt if I needed to.

"I wasn't really going to kill her," he said.

"Kim?" I said. My throat was dry. I reached into my pocket and pulled out my phone.

Fred nodded. "I knew she was allergic. Freddie told me that she was making some food for the party on Saturday, and I decided Kim needed a special treat."

"So you talked your daughter into making . . ."

"I didn't talk her into anything," Fred snapped. "She had no idea. None. I knew she had a special folder online that Nancy and she shared for a to-do list every day. I remembered that Nancy had sent a special order for cherry tarts, so I changed the date and added the almonds in the crust."

"Wouldn't Freddie question the change?"

"No, Nancy has her well trained. If she asks that a specific recipe be made, Freddie does it. Otherwise Nancy trusted Freddie to use her own recipe. Freddie is a helluva baker, but needs some guidance."

"So you had your daughter make cherry tarts that you gave to Kim, knowing that they would make her sick? Possibly kill her?" I asked. I stayed by the door, but put my phone back in my pocket.

"No, wait. No," he said, shaking his head. "Let me start again. I tricked Freddie into making the tarts but I didn't give them to Kim. All of them are still in that blasted box you've just found. Well, minus the two I ate, which were delicious."

"Okay . . . So you wanted to kill her, but you didn't?"

"Not kill. I figured she'd use that plastic pen thing of hers—"

"Her EpiPen?"

"She had them all over the place. I remember Nancy telling me about Kim making her learn how to use them. Kim was paranoid. I figured, worse came to worst, she'd have an attack and use the injector. Or someone would for her. I just wanted to give her a scare."

"That's terrible. Why would you do that?"

"I didn't go through with it. Couldn't. Not because I had second thoughts about serving them to Kim. I didn't. I wanted to make her sick. See her suffer." His hands were balled up at his sides—there was real anger there. "But when I saw Freddie's note on the box, I realized she'd be blamed. Even if I got them served to Kim without anyone knowing where they came from, Freddie would blame herself the minute she put it all together. If she put it together. I love my daughter, I couldn't take that risk. She'd never get over it."

I looked over at Freddie, who was sitting by the tea station. Blue had come down and was sitting in front of her. She was petting him with both hands, nuzzling his neck.

"She's all I've got left," Fred said softly. "I'd never hurt her."

"She's a good girl," I said, reassuringly.

"Baking is the only thing that she loves to do," Fred said. "I can't believe I almost took that away from her."

"She's really good at it. I've gained five pounds since she started working at the Latte." Fred didn't respond, so I decided to be more direct. "So you ate two of the tarts?"

"I did. They were delicious."

"Which means that when they look inside the box, two are going to be missing. Your fingerprints, and Freddie's, are probably on the box. Freddie is going to get blamed if a nut allergy killed Kim."

Fred nodded. He looked miserable. "She found the box in the back of my truck this afternoon. Panicked."

"And threw them out *on* a Dumpster," I said. Fred shrugged, and I could tell that we were both thinking the same thing. On a Dumpster, not in. What was she thinking?

"You have to believe me—I didn't kill Kim."

I looked at Fred. I believed he could have killed her. But use his daughter as the murder weapon? I couldn't believe that. "You need to tell the chief," I said.

"What happens if I get arrested?"

"I've got the name of a lawyer—"

"What will happen to Freddie?"

"We'll cross that bridge when we get to it," I said. I had no idea what I meant, but it sounded good. For now.

A few minutes later Jeff was downstairs with Fred and Freddie. I'd left them down there, talking. Blue kept looking at the door and then back at me.

"We need to give them space," I said to Blue. Bezel came out and looked at us both. "I figure it's a good sign that Jeff didn't arrest him outright. Don't you think?"

Bezel wound herself around my ankles. I knew it was less an "I agree" gesture than a "Gee, my food dish seems empty" challenge. I acquiesced by giving both Blue and Bezel some food. Then I hauled out the leftovers. It was getting late, and I was hungry. No word from Ben, so I assumed I was eating solo tonight. Not the first time, not the last. Though, truth to tell, I was more than a little disappointed. Where was Ben? I took my phone out of my pocket and texted him again. *Putting a plate of leftovers in the microwave. Want to join me?*

I turned to see who was coming up the stairs and was happy but a bit disappointed to see Jeff.

"You're having dinner," he said. "I was hoping to talk, but I don't want to interrupt. I'll check in with you later."

"Are you hungry? I'm microwaving leftovers, and I'd love the company."

"Where's Ben?"

"I don't know," I said, pouring myself a glass of water. "He went out to help Pat with something at the Latte, but I haven't heard from him. Probably got waylaid into another project. Zane and Pat are cooking something up. Maybe they've enlisted Ben. Anyway, about my desire not to eat alone? Can I get you a plate?"

"Actually, that sounds terrific," Jeff said. He checked his watch. "Eight thirty. It feels later. I can't remember which meal I had last, and it's going to be a long night."

"So you let Fred go?"

"Had him taken down to the station to make a statement, get his fingerprints."

"You aren't going to arrest him?"

"Not enough evidence. Yet." He went over to the kitchen sink and washed his hands.

I knew better than to push. Jeff was my friend, and I was

happy to give him a safe space to just be. I was extra glad that I held back when I watched him lean on the edge of the sink and close his eyes. Was there more gray in his hair today? The circles under his eyes were more pronounced, that was for sure.

"What would you like to drink?" I asked. "There's wine, some sweet tea Caroline made, lemonade—"

"Caroline's sweet tea sounds great. I'll get it out of the fridge. How about you?" he asked, keeping the door propped open.

"Will you think less of me if I have a glass of wine?"

"Of course not. The rosé here in the fridge?"

"Perfect," I said. "While you're at it, could you grab the two covered bowls on the second shelf? Salads."

"How did you end up with so much food?"

"A couple of impromptu dinners here at the Cog. You would have been here except, you know."

"Kim."

"Yeah. That." I put two serving spoons on the table and went over to the microwave as Jeff's plate was finishing up. I wasn't a great cook, but I was an excellent heater-upper. When it came to food, I was able to time things perfectly. It was a skill I'd developed and perfected over time. I put Jeff's plate in front of him. He waited until I sat to dig in, but dig in he did.

"Flo made the pasta, didn't she?"

"She did," I said. "There's plenty, so enjoy."

Jeff looked over at the clocks on the wall. "Weren't those downstairs?"

"Good eye. Yes, someone is coming to look at them tomorrow, so I brought them up here for safekeeping and to get them gussied up a bit."

"They look great to me," he said. He hit the screen on

his cell phone, which was sitting on the table face up. "Time is perfect. How much will they go for?"

"Around two thousand dollars. Each."

Jeff took a big swig of tea. "Each? Walk me through your safety protocols again."

"We have alarms on the doors and windows downstairs, as you know, since you helped me pick out the system. We turn it off during the hours we're open, unless we're working alone. Then we make sure the panic button is operating. The outside lights are on a timer, and the back door is on a motion detector. Plus, we have the outside cameras on the Town Hall pointing over here. If something happened, they may help."

"They may, though Nadia has them focused inside the Town Hall, specifically the clock tower."

"Nadia is scary with the technology. She's getting me set up on apps that will turn the lights on if we aren't here. Also an alert that will make it seem like I am home even if I'm not. She's getting the Town Hall hooked up, so we can turn the lights on the tower on and off in case the timers get screwed up."

"The lights in the tower are on a timer?"

"Yup. You know that the lights themselves are hanging lightbulbs, right? Nothing fancy, just an illumination behind the glass to let it glow."

"I need another tour of the tower. It's been a while."

"You deserve another tour, after the hours you spent helping us get it cleaned up."

"Those birds did some damage," he said, putting more potato salad on his plate.

"Don't remind me—I'll lose my appetite," I said. Five decades of a broken clockface had encouraged a lot of bird's nests. The cleanup was disgusting, and took weeks. "Want seconds?"

"I'll get it," he said. "You want more ham?"

"No thanks," I said. Jeff came over and sat back down. He cut the ham, but played around with it on his plate.

"What do you think of Fred and Freddie's story?" I said, finally acknowledging the elephant in the room.

"I don't know. It's so strange. Why would he order the tarts?"

"Because he wanted to make her sick. He thought better of it, though."

"He didn't want to get Freddie involved, more like," Jeff said.

"So you believe him?" I asked.

"I do, but it is a perfect frame. Or would be, if a nut allergy killed her."

"It didn't? You said she had an allergic reaction."

"I said she had a reaction."

"A reaction? What does that mean?"

Jeff hesitated.

"Jeff, I know you need to keep secrets," I said, regretting my overeager questions. "Sorry to ask. I completely understand that you can't talk about it."

"The thing is, we still don't know how she died. She did have an allergic reaction, but her EpiPen had been used, and the drug was in her bloodstream. The ME is running more tests, but it is going to take a while."

"Maybe she had a heart attack?"

Jeff shrugged. "It could be natural causes," he said.

"But you don't think so."

"I don't. It's a feeling I've got."

"Plus, the bell on her head."

"There's that," he said. "Though that may have been a crime of opportunity. Someone saw her lying there and decided to make sure she was dead. Rolled the bell stand over, lifted, and dropped. Possible, especially if they held such anger against her. The bell was one way of showing it."

"She had enemies," I said. Jeff nodded in agreement.

"They're running a battery of tests, but we may not know for weeks. It is easy to rule things out, harder to rule things in unless we have more information to help pinpoint the cause of death."

"Anything I can do to help?" I asked.

"Have you remembered any other details?" he asked.

"I've been thinking about it since we talked. Nothing so far."

"Well, keep taking your notes. Don't look so surprised. You notice details that a lot of folks miss." Jeff picked up his fork and took another bite of salad. "Hey, what's this?" He gestured to the assemblage of bottles in the middle of the table.

"Those? Homeopathic drops Jason gave me," I said. "For allergies."

"You have allergies?"

"Not really, but I stopped by to see him."

"To ask about allergies," Jeff said, shoveling another bite of pasta into his mouth.

"You caught me," I said. "But since then I've found out a lot of folks have allergies, so not really sure what I found out. Except that there are alternative ways to deal with them."

"These drops are the hottest thing in town," Jeff said. "Kim had two different kinds in her car. One for stress, another to help her sleep."

"I hate to even ask, but did you get the drops tested?"

"Both are in for testing, but seem to be what they say they are," he said. "She also took a bunch of vitamins, drank shakes, juiced. By all accounts, she was the picture of health."

"Until Saturday."

"Until Saturday," Jeff said, pushing his plate back. "I'm sorry to eat and run, but I want to check in with the lab one more time."

"I hate to ask, but can we still get back into the Town Hall tomorrow? We need to clean up and get back to work."

"We're done cataloging," he said. "I let Pat know he could bring a box by this afternoon. Tomorrow should be fine. I'll call you first thing. Now, let me help you clean up these dinner dishes; otherwise my mother will kill me for being a bad guest."

"Absolutely not. Thanks for keeping me company. And, Jeff?"

"Yes?"

"Call Moira tonight, before you go home. She needs to hear from you."

"Not sure she'll like hearing from me after today—"

"I'm sure. You need to talk to her tonight."

"Thank you for being a good friend, Ruth. To both of us. And let me know if you remember anything else."

chapter 25

Blue and I went for another walk along the river a little after nine. The sun had finally gone down, and then we headed back inside. I'd texted Ben and tried calling. I even sent an e-mail. It wasn't that I minded taking care of Blue. I didn't. It was only that he'd never left Blue with me before. Flo had always been the overnight sitter. I tried her next.

"What do you mean, where's Ben? Isn't he with you?"

"No, he left a few hours ago to help Pat with something. Maybe they're still together?"

"Not unless Pat's got a clone. Wait a minute. I'm going to put you on speakerphone. Pat and Nancy are here. Pat, where's Ben?"

"He helped me unload some groceries at the Sleeping Latte, and then he went over to leave a box of clock parts at the Town Hall. Jeff told us we could leave them in the office space he'd created. Last I saw him he was letting himself in the front door."

"Maybe Ben went back over to the Latte to help Moira," I said. I stepped out onto the front porch and went down the steps. I turned around and looked over at Moira's shop, which was dark. Maybe they were in back?

"I doubt that she's back from Marytown. She had her last accounting class tonight."

"Right, I forgot about that," I said. Moira had been taking small-business-owner classes over at Harris University. I turned and looked at the Corner Market, also closed. "Maybe he's helping Beckett with something? Looks like there is a light over at Been There, Read That. Oh, wait, it's just the light he leaves on in the shop. Maybe he went to return his rental car? Do you know what it looked like?" I tried to keep my voice calm, but I was getting worried. Where was Ben?

"A little red thing," Flo said. I looked around and saw a dark car parked near the Corner Market. Maybe that was red? It was the only car on the street.

"Where could he be?" I asked. "Maybe I should take a walk over toward the library? I'll check at the Town Hall, though there aren't any lights on over there."

"Listen, I'm worried," Flo said. "That boy is never more than five feet away from his cell phone. Maybe it ran out of power?"

"He charged his phone in the car," Pat said. "Listen, Ruth, hang tight. I'm on my way."

"No, Pat, I'm sure he's—"

"I'm on my way. I'll be there in fifteen minutes."

"I'm calling Jeff," Flo said. "Maybe he knows where Ben is." She hung up before I could tell her that Jeff had just left.

I walked back up the stairs and went back into the Cog. "Hey, Blue, I'm going to take a walk over toward the library. Let Pat know I'll be right back, okay?" I said, pulling my

Pocasset sweatshirt over my head. I put a flashlight and my cell in the front pocket. Orchard was quiet on a Monday night, but at least the library was open for a few more minutes. I set the alarm and closed the front door.

As I stepped off the front porch I glanced over at the Town Hall. I couldn't wait until the clock in the tower was my own moon, shining every day. My eyes swept down, and I saw something next to the Town Hall, by the path toward the back. Maybe it was a firefly? But if it was, why wasn't it moving? Why was it so low on the ground? And why was it blue?

I crept across the street, my feet familiar with the path. I made my way over to the flashing light, slowly, steadily, not even daring to turn on my flashlight. Why was I being so quiet? I had every right to be over here at the Town Hall. Still, I put my phone on vibrate and took another small step, trying to locate the source of the beacon. I finally hit a wall of dark I couldn't navigate without help, and I took the flashlight out of my pocket and turned it on. I swept it across the gardens, and it flashed on something. I made my way over and picked it up.

The flashing light was a message indicator. I recognized the phone. The messages were probably from me. The phone was Ben's.

I took out my own phone and tried to call Jeff. No answer. I texted him: *Come to town hall.* I looked up and down the street. Where was Pat? Pat would help me find Ben. But what if Ben was hurt? Maybe he'd gone exploring in the Town Hall and fallen? How did his phone end up out here? I wished I'd brought my own keys to the building. Best to go back and wait for Pat.

What was that noise? It was coming from the side of

the building. I looked around, but no one was coming to my rescue. There was another sound, this one louder. It sounded like an animal grunting. Was that Ben? Maybe he really was hurt. I walked over to the right of the building. I swept the flashlight over in an arc and caught a reflector from a bike, pushed into the bushes. I crept forward and took a closer look. Jason's bike. I recognized the red and black paint job. A water bottle was strapped to the frame— not his Been Here, Read That bottle, but one from a local radio station. Was Jason here? Why was his bike in the bushes?

Another sound, this time a crash. I went back around the front of the building. I moved to the left and moved around toward the back of the Town Hall.

"Ben, are you here?" I called out. The fence door to the portico was slightly ajar.

I crept forward and peered around the trellis. Jason came around the corner, his pants clipped at the ankles with reflecting wraps. His shirt was untucked, and there was dirt down the front of it. He was disheveled and looked distracted to see me. I took a deep breath and made sure there was distance between us.

"Jason, what are you doing here?" I said. "I heard a sound and worried that someone was hurt. How did you get the trellis door open?"

"It was already open."

"Really? That seems careless, doesn't it?" I walked past him. I looked around and noticed that the planters were all a bit askew. I thought back to Saturday night, and Jason walking out with his bike tire. And his dress shirt. Had he stashed his bike back here on Saturday? What had he seen?

"I was surprised too," he said. No more information. His eyes darted around, and he was bouncing on his left foot.

"You haven't seen Ben, have you?" I asked, filling the time, hoping that Jeff got here quickly.

"Have you lost him again, Ruth? You really need to keep track of him. He's a real catch, that one." Jason walked over and lifted a pot out of its base and then put it back, slightly askew.

"Are you all right?" I asked Jason. He wasn't holding eye contact tonight. Instead, his eyes were darting around.

"This is going to seem odd," Jason said, "but I've been racking my brain, trying to remember the last time I used my bike lock. It was here, and since the crime scene tape was down, I figured it would be safe to look. You haven't seen it, have you?"

"No, I haven't, but I haven't been back here since Saturday. Why are you looking for it tonight?"

"Heading out tomorrow, and I need to be able to lock the bike to the car. Not all places are like Orchard, you know. Safe enough to leave houses open and bikes unlocked."

"I saw your bike out in the bushes."

"You caught me. Don't tell Harriet. She'll be furious that I broke a few branches. But that side shrub, it is a great hiding spot for bikes."

"You've used it before?"

"Not me. I know, I know, I should use the new bike rack. I was just being lazy. Trying to get packed and prepped for the weekend."

"Going for a ride as part of your training?" Where was Jeff? My fingers itched to take out my phone and see if he'd texted back, but I refrained. Jason was acting squirrelly, and Jeff needed to be here in case it meant something more than that Jason was odd. He was still on the list, after all.

Jason looked puzzled for a moment, but then his brow cleared up. "I'm heading up north. Some family business that is finally getting settled," he said.

"Ruth?" Jeff called out.

"Back here," I said. Jeff came running back and looked at me, then at Jason.

"I found this out front," I said, handing Jeff Ben's cell phone. "I don't know where he is. Jason hasn't seen him either."

"Jason, what are you doing? How did you get back here?" Jeff said.

"The trellis door was open. I'm looking for my bike lock," he said. He ran his hands along his pant legs. "Sorry to have been a bother. I'll head home, come back in the daylight."

"You want more light?" I said, taking my phone out of my pocket. I pulled up the app Nadia had installed, and hit "clock tower" and "all." Next thing I knew, all the outdoor lights were on. I stepped away from Jeff and walked toward the gardens. Jason moved to follow me, but Jeff put his hand on his arm.

"Is Ben back there?" Jeff said.

"No," I said, scanning the back area. I looked over toward Been There, Read That and noticed that the Dumpster had been moved aside. Had Jason come through there? Was he lying about the trellis door? Jeff stepped next to me and looked around. I pointed to the Dumpster next door.

"Where's Ben?" Jeff asked Jason.

"I have no idea," Jason said.

"Why don't we all try and look for him?"

"Maybe he's in the Town Hall. He was going to drop something off," I said. "I'm going to see if I can find him. Okay, Chief?" Jeff nodded, but didn't leave Jason's side. I swallowed the fear that was rising up and walked in the side door.

"Ben!" I yelled. "Are you in here?" There was pounding coming from somewhere, and a muffled sound. Ben? I ran across the hall, toward the storage area. I turned to the closet on my right. The key was in the lock. I turned it and opened the door.

"Ruth!" Ben said, sounding muffled. I opened the door, and he came out, practically falling into my arms.

"Are you all right?" I said, holding him up and hugging him at the same time.

"I am now. Did you know that door locks from the outside? Whose big idea was that? Stuff of nightmares—getting locked in a closet."

"The doors over here are tricky," I said. "Probably got stuck."

"How did you find me anyway?" he asked.

"I found your phone out front."

"It must have fallen out of my pocket. I was about to text you when I came back here. Glad the phone-finder app worked."

"I told you, I won't use it." Of course I might have if I'd remembered I had it. "Your phone was flashing and I saw it."

"Eagle Eye Clagan," he said, hugging me close. "Is Jason still here?"

"Jeff's with him out back. Why?"

"It was weird," Ben said. "I was heading back to your place and I saw Jason over here, by the gate door. I couldn't figure out how he got there. He said he'd come by to look for a lock he lost on Saturday—"

"He told me the same thing," I said.

"Maybe he is," Ben said. "But something seemed off. So I pretended to leave and came back in here to see what he was up to. The garden gate was open."

"Why?"

"Maybe for the streetlight to spill in? It's pretty dark back there. Anyway, I snuck in and noticed the side door was open. I think he jimmied the lock."

"So you decided to follow him in there?"

"Luckily, I've spent a lot of time back here, so I know the ins and outs. When he was turned around I snuck in and stood in the alcove near the kitchen."

"You spied on him?" I said, half-horrified, half-impressed.

"Shh. Keep your voice down. I did. I'm not proud of it, but I did. He stayed in the vestibule area. He was reaching up, running his hand along the wainscoting. You know how it kind of dips with the trim? There's space for stuff up there. He was looking for something. Then I heard you calling my name. So did he, and he went outside for a moment. He came back in and went back to searching, so I hid. Next thing I knew I couldn't get the door open again."

"Why did you hide?" I asked.

"Because I went over to where he'd been looking, and found this." He pulled a blue bottle out of his front pocket. It looked a lot like the one Jason had given me.

"Jason, didn't you come back here on Saturday?" Jeff said. I'd texted Jeff: *Keep Jason here. Play along. I think I have an idea.*

"Maybe you dropped the lock in here," I said, leading Jason away from Jeff and Ben so that Ben could tell Jeff what he told me. "Let's take a look. Now, where did you go?" We stood in the side vestibule. The clock tower steps were to the right, but I knew that was locked up. Pat, Zane, and I had the only keys.

We went into the kitchen area, which looked like a hurricane hit it.

"This is a bigger mess than I remember," I said, knowing that I sounded like an imbecile, but I needed to play dumb.

That was critical. Ideas were coming together, but we wouldn't find the answer in here. "I'll tell you what—I have a bike lock over at the shop. Why don't I loan it to you for your trip?"

"You don't have to—"

"Please. Happy to. I know right where it is and won't need to use it for a while."

Jason stood and looked at me. "Okay, thanks," he said. I stepped aside and followed Jason back into the vestibule area. His head turned slightly toward the wainscoting, but he caught me watching him and turned away.

"Any luck?" Ben asked when we stepped back outside.

"Nope. Once we can get back inside and clean up, I'm sure the lock will show up," I said. "I'm going to loan Jason my bike lock for his trip."

"Great. That will give Jason and me a chance to talk about what he was doing in a restricted area. First, let me get this place closed up again," Jeff said. "Ruth, you need a better lock on this door. You can pick it with a credit card. I hate to leave it wide open. Let me call Officer Wilson and have him come down and keep an eye on things." Jeff ran his hand over his closely cropped head, from front to back. He jaw was set in a straight line.

"Can we go back to the Cog & Sprocket? Pat is probably frantic," I said.

"Pat?" Ben said.

"When I couldn't find you, I called Flo. Pat and Nancy were there. Pat was coming into town to help me."

"You were that worried?" Ben said. "That's sweet." He put his arm around my shoulder, and Jeff rolled his eyes.

"Tell you what. This place is lit up like a Christmas tree, plus Nadia's cameras are rolling. It should be all right for a few minutes. Why don't we all head over to the Cog?" Jeff said.

"Nadia's cameras?" Jason asked.

"The locks may be low-tech, but the security is pretty high tech," Jeff said. "State-of-the-art cameras all over the building. Lots of video, from lots of different angles."

"So, you have video of the back portico?" Ben said.

"No, unfortunately those cameras aren't in place. Otherwise we'd know who killed Kim."

"Ruth, do you have the keys for this door?" asked Jeff. "Ben, Jason, you can head on over. We'll catch up."

"Did Ben show you the bottle?" I whispered. "Do you think that could be what killed Kim?"

"I have no idea. Maybe. But we have no proof of anything," Jeff said. "Even if that bottle is what killed her, Ben found it. No proof of whom it belonged to."

"No proof yet, but we're close. I can feel it."

chapter 26

When we opened the door to the Cog & Sprocket we were met with a full house. Flo and Nancy hadn't let Pat come in alone. Moira was there as well. Nadia was standing behind the customer counter, her phone in hand. Caroline and Zane were also there, along with Janet. Jimmy Murphy was sitting in the customer area, his phone to his ear. Beckett was standing off to the side, looking at the grandfather clock. When we first walked in there was dead silence, and then a cacophony of voices.

"Where have you been?"

"You had us worried sick."

"Ben, do you not listen to voice mails anymore?"

"Jason, what happened to your clothes?"

"Chief, are you all right? You look a little—"

"What is everyone doing here?" I asked. The answer was silence, but then Pat spoke up.

"Nancy was going to meet Jimmy and Beckett anyway,

so she came with me. When you weren't here, and Harriet hadn't seen you . . ."

"We called Caroline and Zane," Nancy said.

"I'm so sorry they worried you," I said to Caroline.

"I'm not. If something ever happened to you—"

I went over and gave Caroline a hug. "Nothing is going to happen to me. What's this?"

"Cookies. From Nancy."

"I bake when I'm stressed," Nancy said. "Sue me. Try one, Ruthie. Tell me what you think."

I took a bite out of the pink cookie. A sweet and tart sandwich cookie. "Yum. What is it?" I chewed while I tried to make sense of the threads of an idea that were trying to form in my brain. For some reason they wouldn't all catch. Maybe a cookie would help.

"Grapefruit cookie. I'm glad you could take it for a test drive. Most of the folks here can't."

"Why not?" I asked.

"Grapefruit is a no-no if you are taking certain medicines. Makes them less effective. So Pat and Flo won't try the cookies."

"Better safe than sorry," Pat said.

"I do hate this, since I love grapefruit," Flo said. "Maybe if I get my cholesterol under control."

"Good luck with that," Nancy said. "Some folks are predestined."

"And others enjoy bacon, cheese, and wine too much," Flo said. "Still, I can try." She picked up her water bottle and went to take a swig.

"Wait, that one's mine," Caroline said. "See the *C* in the *B* of Been? I marked my bottle so I could recognize it. Here's your bottle," Caroline said, handing Flo the other bottle on the table. "In the meantime, have one of these sugar cookies."

Pink grapefruit cookies. Water bottles. Unexpected interactions. Or perhaps, some interactions could be expected? Even encouraged? I wondered if—

"Jeff, can I talk to you for a minute?" I said.

"Ruth, I wonder if I could get that bike lock now? I want to get home and finish packing," Jason said.

"Sure. Ben, could you get the bike lock? It's in the staircase going down to the basement, hanging up. To the left of the doorway, second spot down," I said. I looked at Jeff and tapped my temple a couple of times. I hoped he read "I have an idea" rather than "Someone is nuts." He gave me a nod.

"Ruth, do you always know where everything is?" Jimmy said.

"Old habit. Know where things are and make sure you put it away when you're done. Precision. It is a clockmaker's trait. Jason has a similar trait, don't you? Pharmacy. Homeopathy. You need to get it precisely right," I said. I wandered over to make sure I was standing near Jason.

I thought about water bottles. Drops in blue bottles. Tolerance buildups. Unexpected side effects.

"What do you mean?" Jason asked.

"Your medicines. Compounding of some meds for folks who can't take pills, and your warning that folks need to shake up the meds, otherwise they won't get the right levels. Homeopathy, and the idea of building up a tolerance over time."

"It is important to follow directions," Jason said, picking up a cookie. "You're right. These are delicious."

"Would there be enough grapefruit in them to be a problem for folks?" I asked. "I hate that Flo can't try them. They really are good."

"Hard to say. Better to avoid foods that may have interactions with drugs," he said through a bite of cookie.

"I used to be a housemaster with my ex-husband," I said, nibbling the corner of my cookie. "I spent a lot of time with students. I remember one student, Lydia, who struggled with depression. She finally found meds that worked, but she couldn't eat specific foods. Surprising foods, like certain cheeses, and soybeans. Pickles. She was a kombucha fan, till she realized it was on the list."

"Kombucha?" Pat asked.

"It is a fermented drink," Moira said. "Supposed to have health benefits. I drink it every day."

"So did Kim. I tried it a couple of times, but couldn't get it down," Beckett said.

"You need to try different types. I like the ginger lemon flavor," Moira said.

"Are you talking about that mold drink?" Nancy said. "Disgusting."

"It isn't mold, Mum. You haven't even—" I watched as Jason's face relaxed. The conversation had moved on. Then he saw me looking at him.

"Kim was taking stress drops, wasn't she?" I asked, raising my voice a bit so that Jeff could hear me. "She suggested I try them at one point."

"Course, she was the reason you needed them," Nancy said. Flo laughed aloud.

"She swore by them," Beckett said, artfully ignoring Nancy. He was good at ignoring Nancy, which drove her crazy. "She started taking them three, four months ago. Isn't that right, Jason? It didn't take long for them to make her feel a lot better. Even I noticed a difference."

"Me too," Jimmy said. "I called her Queen Drip. Not to her face, mind you. She had alarms set on her phone. When they went off, no matter what we were doing, she'd stop and take a drop or two. Some of them straight up. Others she'd add to a glass of water."

"Must have been hard to keep them all straight," I said. "How many blue bottles did she have?"

"Three or four," Jimmy said. "She wrote on each bottle and used nail polish to paint the caps different colors."

"Blue was stress, red was for headaches. Green was for sleep. White was for general health," Beckett said.

"Good thing that nail polish comes in so many colors these days," Flo said. "Back in my day she would have had shades of red and pink. A lot harder to keep track of on the fly. I used to get distracted in the middle of a pedicure, and then I'd go back and pick up another pink, not realizing it was wrong. I remember one time—"

"You gave them all to her—right, Jason?" I said. "It must have been a lot for both of you to keep track of. You needed to make sure they all worked together. And not against each other."

"That's my job," he said, shrugging. Jason looked up at the clocks on the wall.

I noticed Jeff stood in front of the door. He lifted the blue bottle we'd found over in the Town Hall out of his front pocket, holding it by his side. If folks noticed, they didn't say anything. I looked over at Jason, who stared at the bottle, transfixed.

"What do you put in them? The drops?" I asked.

Jason started, and then looked back at me. "Some of them were off the shelf. Others were tonics I'd concocted over time. Chief Paisley knows all this. I gave him samples. They were mostly herbs. Nothing dangerous."

"Did she like to have all of her medicines in liquid form? Sounds like she did, from what folks have been saying."

"She didn't like pills," Jason whispered. A bead of sweat rolled down his face and he took a half step toward the door. "I really need to get going."

"Just one more question. You know how much I hate unanswered questions," I said. "I've been wondering, what would have happened if someone knew Kim was taking something that helped her with stress? Say, a depression medication like that student I knew did."

"Depression and stress aren't the same thing," Jason said.

"Of course they're not. But if someone doesn't feel well, would they really care what helped? If she wasn't paying attention to the side effects, that could be a problem, especially if she was using other drops that may have an interaction. An interaction, like, say, high blood pressure. That was what my student had to worry about. Certain foods could trigger an episode, since the medicine made her vulnerable. Maybe some of her other drops added to the problem."

"I was always careful to warn her about side effects," Jason said. "I can show you the printouts."

"Of course you were," I said. "But what if someone wanted to do her harm? Is there something they could give her that would be a fatal blow? Cause a reaction of some sort? Or a heart attack? Maybe her allergy meds caused an interaction?"

Jason was silent for a moment. No one else was talking in the room now. They were all listening to us.

"It wouldn't be an efficient way of killing someone. It would take a lot of patience. It might never work," Jason said.

"It might take a long time," I said. "And you're right. It might never work. But suppose someone wanted to rush it, for whatever reason. Then what would they do?"

Jason didn't answer. I looked over at Nadia, who had her phone out. The red recording light was visible.

"What would they do, Jason? They would probably give the person a huge shot of something that would cause a heart attack. I'd imagine if you went to all that work, you'd want to be there when it happened, don't you think?"

"Why would this person do this terrible, difficult thing?" he asked, swallowing.

"Well, maybe this person hated Kim not for what she's doing in Orchard, but for what she did in another life." I looked over at Nancy. "Nancy's been trying to find next of kin and has been uncovering a pretty checkered past. She left a lot of carnage in her wake."

"Why did they hire her here, then?" Jason said. "If she was so terrible."

"She came with good references," Jimmy said.

"Folks were afraid of her," Nancy said. "I think they were willing to give her a good reference to get her out of their lives. One guy I talked to today over in Binghamton, he sounded relieved. He'd moved there after his divorce, a divorce he got so he could marry Kim."

"I thought her husband was dead?" Beckett said.

"She didn't marry this one. He wasn't much use to her after his divorce. His wife got half of everything, and he had high child support payments. After she left, he made a few phone calls, dug up some of Kim's past. He told me stories about the games she'd been playing that wrecked families. One woman even killed herself. Course, there wasn't any proof, and Kim moved on when it got too hot to stay put. I don't want to speak ill of the dead, but she was a truly terrible person."

"Binghamton. Your family is from upstate New York. Is that right?" I said to Jason. I hadn't taken my eyes off him. The story threads were becoming a rope, and I imagined them snaking toward Jason. "Didn't you say that your sister died in a car crash? After being depressed when her husband left her for another woman?"

"You think Jason . . ." Flo said. She sat on one of the settees. Caroline ran over to grab her hand, and Nancy sat on the couch arm and put her arm around Flo.

"I'm afraid I do," I said.

"You can't prove anything," he said, his face a mask. "Thanks for the cookie. I have to be going now." He picked up a water bottle, then he dropped it back on the counter.

"All of the bottles look alike, don't they?" I said. "So easy to get them confused. Looking back, I never saw Kim without hers the past few weeks."

"Neither did I," Beckett said. "She had a couple of them. Left them everywhere."

"You found her water bottle at the scene, didn't you, Chief?"

Jeff nodded. "It was full of water."

"Of course it was. I'll bet if you checked the DNA on the part you drink from, though, you'll find it was actually Jason's bottle. I remember him leaving with a bottle on Saturday. That was probably Kim's."

"You think that he switched bottles with Kim?" Moira said.

"I think he met her in back, on the portico. Maybe he gave her a special set of drops, told her they would help with stress. She added them to her water, as directed by Jason."

"So you think she died from some chemical reaction?" Jimmy said.

"You can't prove anything," Jason said, his eyes still fixed on the water bottle.

"I'm not trying to prove anything. I'm only telling a story. Suppose you went back and found her dead. You grabbed your water bottle. Then you rolled the bell stand over and knocked it on top of her."

"Why drop the bell if it wasn't to kill her?" Flo asked. "Seems like a horrible thing to do. Never mind heavy lifting."

"I've been thinking a lot about that," I said. "Kim had a lot of enemies here in Orchard, that's for sure. Sounds like she left a wake of misery behind her. If she was killed over time, that takes visceral hate. Also planning, and knowledge. Think about the weight of that hate, and how it would corrode someone's soul over time. Maybe that's what the clock bell was about. A final act that gave her killer satisfaction? What do you think, Jason? Maybe murder wasn't enough?"

Jason looked at me and started a slow clap. "Nice story, Ruth. Let me offer an alternate solution. Maybe her killer had nothing to lose? He had some health issues that gave him limited time left to right a few wrongs? Maybe a relatively painless heart attack wasn't as satisfying as he expected it would be? Maybe he wanted her to suffer, even after she was dead, by taking away the one thing she used every day in a million different ways: that coldly beautiful face of hers? She cast a powerful spell on men. The bell took that away. I didn't want her to seem in peaceful slumber at an open casket funeral. No, she was going to have a closed casket. Just like my poor sister who—"

"That's enough," Jeff said, stopping Jason cold. "Let's continue this conversation down at the station, Jason."

chapter 27

"Once Jason filled in the gaps, the picture became a lot clearer," Jeff told me when he came by Tuesday night to let me know we could move back into the Town Hall. He and his team had spent the day in the Town Hall, reexamining evidence in light of Jason's confession. Jeff had agreed to sit down for dinner with Ben and me and help us get rid of the rest of the leftovers. Moira and her mother were over in Marytown, buying new baking supplies for the Sleeping Latte.

"That bottle I found?" Ben asked. "What was in it?" He scooped out another serving of corn salad and dug in.

"Adrenaline. Herb based, but effective. He'd set her up with a series of drugs that left her vulnerable to a heart attack. The elixir he offered her that afternoon delivered on that promise. His words. Anyway, she died instantly."

"The bell was a mistake? If they'd found her dead, they might have assumed it was a heart attack," Ben said.

"The ME never thought it was just a heart attack," Jeff said. "But figuring out the how, and then proving the who—that was tough."

"You must have suspected Jason," I said.

"There were a lot of suspects," Jeff said. "He was on the list. But you homed in on him. Why?"

"A combination of things. I'd been trying to remember if he was carrying his bike lock when he left on Saturday. I remembered his wheel. Then I remembered him carrying his water bottle when Caroline and Nancy almost mixed their bottles up tonight. But he had a different bottle on his bike. So what if the bottle he had on Saturday wasn't his bottle?"

"How did you decide the drops were the culprit?" Jeff said. "This was a fairly complicated plot. I'm not sure we would have made the connection."

"I'm sure you would have," I said. "It wasn't only the drops. It was the knowledge that went with the drops. When you are trying to cure an ailment, you tell the person helping you a lot of information. It is pretty intimate knowledge, when you think about it."

"After she and Beckett had a falling-out, Kim really confided in Jason," Jeff said. "She trusted him with her health, and he gave her magic tonics to cure her ills. How did you guess that he was setting her up to die?"

"I remembered you said that Kim had a lot of health food drinks and elixirs in her house and in her office. Jason's printouts told me to watch taking certain allergy drugs if I had thyroid issues, or high blood pressure. All of a sudden I wondered, what if this was more of a long-term plan? Then Caroline and Flo got their water bottles mixed up, and it all became clear to me."

"But you must have focused on Jason earlier than that," Jeff said.

"He was acting weird at the Town Hall, for sure. But it didn't all come together until I tasted the grapefruit cookie."

"That's a pretty terrible way to think," Ben said. "Cookies and water help you solve a murder?"

"Ruth puts pieces of a puzzle together in a unique way," Jeff said. "She doesn't try and fit the pieces together the way they work best for us. She fits them together the way they need to go."

"What does that mean?" Ben said.

"How about if I use a clock metaphor? We were all looking at these pieces of evidence and thinking we were looking at a grandfather clock. Ruth saw them and realized they worked in a clock tower. They may have looked the same, but the scale was different. We were all focused on Orchard, and the motives here. But Ruth pieced together information about Kim's life and realized that the picture was a lot bigger. Still not sure how she narrowed it down to Jason though."

"I saw the pain in his eyes when he talked about his sister," I said. "That came from real love, and loss. I've thought about how far someone might go to avenge a loved one, probably because I've been thinking about my grandfather so much lately."

"You wouldn't kill anyone to avenge him," Jeff said with a certainty that warmed my heart.

"I wouldn't, no. My way of remembering him, and letting him live on in my heart, is working on the clock tower. I do think that, and this shop, and other things"—I grabbed Ben's hand and gave it a squeeze—"have helped hate from taking up residence in my heart. But what would have happened if I hadn't had the Cog & Sprocket, or all of you? I hate to think."

"You hate to think?" Ben said, his eyebrows raised.

"What would have happened to all of us? You've healed this town, Ruth."

"I second that," Jeff said. "I'm in charge of law and order, but you've been helping me with real justice. I'm glad you're here."

I leaned over and gave Jeff a peck on the cheek. "We make a good team," I said.

"That's enough of that," Jeff said. "And don't get any ideas about becoming a citizen crime solver."

"What, me? Never," I said.

Jeff looked over at the wall. "The banjo clocks are gone."

"Ruth sold them to a collector from Boston this afternoon. Lila Blood-something-or-other," Ben said.

"She is an alum from the school where my ex-husband works. She tracked me down after she saw some of the clocks I'd left in the house," I said.

"Apparently a few of the students told her stories about Ruth's work. They spoke so highly of her, she wanted to meet her in person," Ben said. "Her ex hadn't told Mrs. Blood-whatever that his ex-wife was a clockmaker."

"Her name is Lila. Eric never would have referred to me as a clockmaker," I said. "Not nearly pretentious enough. He would have called me a horologist." I smiled and played a bit with my food. When I thought about how much happier I was this June than last? I looked up at Jeff to tell him the rest of the story. "They're doing some renovations to the house where my ex is still housemaster. At his suggestion, they're thinking about putting the clocks in permanent storage. Lila wanted to buy them, and my ex was willing to sell them to her. But then the dean cleared up the ownership. So she came to see me."

"Test you first, more like it."

"She didn't know about his offer to me," I said. "She loves

clocks and wanted to see if I was the real deal. After a few conversations with my ex, she realized he wasn't a great lover of horology."

"You were pretty elegant at describing your ex and his offer," Ben said. "You could have made his life pretty miserable. Though it sounds like your ex-husband has some juice at the school."

"I'm sure he does," I said. "Eric never lacked ambition. I appreciate her coming out here to talk to me."

"Put it this way, Jeff. Ruth's got a new fan. She agreed to loan Lila the clocks for her corporate offices and to go to Boston to help supervise the move."

"She made a nice contribution to the project, which will go to the new bell. She also bought both the banjo clocks. A good day overall."

"Not for your ex-husband," Ben said. "He missed out on a nice paycheck. Wasn't he setting himself up for half the proceeds if you sold them to her?"

"He was. Might have even had a case. Which is why I loaned them to her for a dollar."

"Well, I for one am glad to see that you aren't perfect, Ruth," Jeff said. "You are capable of spite. I'm relieved, frankly. Perfect people make me nervous."

"My lack of perfection is robust," I said, laughing.

"Not from where I sit," Ben said, kissing my hand and then grabbing the bowl of salad. "Try this corn salad, Jeff. New recipe I'm trying out, inspired by a conversation with your mother. Pretty good, if I do say so myself, but it's missing something."

chapter 28

"**T**his is ridiculous," Pat said for the tenth time in as many minutes. "The scaffolding is being delivered in a few minutes. We don't have time for this."

"Indulge me, Pat. Please," I said.

He walked around the perimeter of the Town Hall and pointed the fans up toward the ceiling, hoping to get more air circulating. A team of volunteers had arrived at seven o'clock Wednesday morning to help get the Town Hall cleaned up. Harris University also sent over some staff and had a couple of Dumpsters delivered. We'd been talking about doing this later in the summer, but today was so full of energy and forward momentum, we just couldn't wait. Old carpets were torn up, revealing more slate floors. Broken furniture was tossed, as were the piles of junk that had been accumulating, waiting for this moment. Walls and floors were washed. Zane spent time walking folks through techniques for covering scratches with the stain he had made. All the wood was getting the Pat treatment of oil and TLC.

By five o'clock the entire building had been refreshed. Nothing hadn't been cleaned. Finally, we were ready for the last step. Nadia called all the volunteers into a circle in the middle of the Town Hall.

"I can't believe you are willing to go along with this," Pat said to Zane. Though different in so many ways, the two men were bound by a love of all things clocks. They were both filthy after a day of cleaning, staining, and polishing. But where Pat looked aggravated, Zane looked at peace.

"I think it is a terrific idea. Something had to be done, don't you think?"

Nadia stepped into the middle of the circle of people and held up a green bundle tied with red string. "My grandmother passed on a lot of knowledge to me. I wish she was here in person to do this, but she couldn't get here physically. So she's here virtually. Here, Ruth, can you hold my grandmother?" Nadia handed me her phone, and I smiled and said hello before turning her so she could watch her granddaughter.

"There is an ancient practice called smudging. It requires burning something. We're using sage, and using the smoke to cleanse a space. There are steps we take, and things we say, as part of this ritual. But before I begin, I want to talk about why this is important.

"This old building has seen a lot," Nadia said. "Today, all of you took the time to clean her up so she can meet the next chapter in her history looking her best. In a couple of weeks, we're going to be setting the clock tower, winding her up, and letting her watch over us for the rest of our lives. Seriously, Ruth said these clocks can last a hundred years if they are maintained. And you know that a Clagan living across the street means that this baby will be maintained."

Everyone laughed, and I felt myself blush. "Last weekend, some terrible things happened here," Nadia continued, and everyone stopped laughing at once. "So the space needs to be cleansed. If you don't want to participate, you don't have to. But I hope that you all do. We need your good vibes to help release the sadness this space holds, and to bring in the light."

Nadia looked around, but no one left the circle. "Let's begin," she said, lighting the bundle of sage.

"Let's begin," I agreed.

"That was really wonderful," Moira said a little while later. We were sitting on the floor of the Town Hall, sipping the wine that Nancy had brought out after the ceremony. Flo and Caroline brought in trays of fruit, cheese, and finger sandwiches. Zane and Pat helped set up the tables. It was a lot like last Saturday's Signing Ceremony, with many of the same people. But where last weekend had started off as joyous, today had a somber tone. Peaceful because of the resolution but somber.

"It was exactly what was needed," I agreed.

"Are you going to be able to pull the installation off? You've only got two weeks until—"

"Don't remind me! Yes, I can pull it off, but not alone."

"You're not alone," Moira said. "If nothing else, I'll keep you fed."

"That's not nothing. An army runs on its stomach. Or something like that."

"Ruth's Army? Nah. The Clagan Corps. I like the sound of that."

"You like the sound of what?" Nancy asked her daughter. She had brought over a folding chair in one hand, a bottle

of wine under her arm, and a plate of food in her other hand.
I took the food, and Moira grabbed the wine so that Nancy
could set up the chair. "I don't know how you girls can sit
on that cold floor like that."

"Yoga and youth," Moira said. "I thought you had a
Board of Selectmen meeting tonight?"

"We do. We're going to meet here, in one of the rooms
in the back."

"Should you be drinking?"

"Please. I'm saving two bottles for the meeting. We need
to decide on an interim town manager."

"Interim?" I asked.

"We're going to need to post the job. But we'd like to get
someone in place who can help us get things settled. Or at
least put a brave face on it, and put out fires. Kim left a real
mess."

"Are you going to offer it to Beckett?" Moira asked. "He
obviously wants it."

"We've got someone else in mind. Never you mind who.
You'll find out soon enough. Now, where's that handsome
boyfriend of yours, Moira?"

"Not sure I'd call him a boyfriend, especially after this
past week. He's arrested both my parents in the past year.
How am I supposed to make that okay?"

"By knowing he was doing his job," Nancy said, firmly
placing a hand on her daughter's shoulder. "I would have
brought me in for questioning too."

"Mum—"

"Don't 'Mum' me. Here he comes now. Go get a chair
for his mother, and bring it over here. Looks like she brought
a plate of patties, bless her. I'd never had Jamaican patties
before. The meat ones are my favorite. You have to try them,
Moira, they're delicious. They'd be perfect to sell at the

Sleeping Latte. Now, go grab a plate, get some food, and take Jeff somewhere quiet to talk."

Moira didn't move, so I nudged her with my elbow. "Go. He's a good guy," I said.

Moira looked over toward Jeff. He was helping his mother set up her trays of food and laughing as Ben took a bite out of a patty, put his hand on his heart, and pretended to swoon. Jeff leaned down and gave his mother a kiss on her cheek.

"That he is," Moira said, getting up.

chapter 29

"You ready?" Ben said.

"I am, though I'd rather be up in the tower," I said.

"Of course you'd rather be up there. But you're going to be down here, so get used to it. Come on, it's a quarter of. Time to speechify."

June 21. The big day had finally arrived. In some ways, time had crept towards this day, which I'd been dreaming of for so long. In other ways, it had flown by in a flurry of details that I kept trying to keep track of, like feathers flying from a pillow with a small hole. But finally, we were going to set and wind the clock. Ben and I both stepped up onto the platform that we'd set up on one end of Washington Street. Traffic had to be rerouted for a few hours, but what little traffic there was were people looking for a parking place. Since eleven, people had been walking around Orchard visiting the shops, getting ready for the big show that was set for noon. At five after eleven Zane, Pat, and I had made a great show of climbing up to the tower and winding the clock. Nadia followed us, along with two interns from Harris University who were documenting the event as part of a summer school project. Other interns were peppered throughout the crowd, getting ready to record and social media the entire day. I still couldn't believe that there was enough interest to livestream it, but Nadia did. I hoped she got my best side. Winding a clock in a hot tower wasn't a pretty business. There were a couple of screens downstairs, and it had been disconcerting as the crowd began to chant when we got closer to one hundred turns on the winding crank. We knew that would get us through only two days, since it required fifty revolutions a day to keep running, but today was all about the show.

When I came down, Flo was waiting for me. She fixed my makeup and my hair before she let me go outside again.

"Thank you, Flo," I said. "You are a miracle worker with this mop of mine." I leaned over and gave her a hug.

"You are a beauty, Ruth Clagan. You're the image of your grandmother, you know that? She'd be so proud of you. We all know that Thom's genes made you love clocks. But Mae passed on her generous spirit. Having you here, I miss her a lot less."

I wiped a tear from my eye.

"Now, none of that," Flo said. "You have speeches to make. Let me fix your mascara. Here you go." She turned me around and pushed me out the side door of the Town Hall.

The crowds were out front, as was the platform. First things first, though. I looked up at the clock and pulled out my cell to check the time. Whew. So far, so good. We'd had several test runs over the past week, adjusting the pendulum as needed so it would keep good time. I had no doubt that we'd continue to do that for months, but for today, I wished for accuracy till noon. Zane and Pat had gone down to the level below the clock itself. In a few months the mechanisms down there would be connected to the clock mechanism, but for today Pat and Zane were going to manually run the figures out so they could take a bow. Zane hadn't let me look at the final figures, insisting that I should have some surprises. I wasn't looking forward to seeing how the figure of Beckett came out. I hoped he hadn't insisted on a Been There, Read That T-shirt as part of his figure. I so didn't want my clock to be an advertisement.

"It's showtime," Nadia said, coming around the corner and grabbing my hand. I took a step up on the platform. Ben winked at me and stepped forward, tapping the microphone.

"Good morning," he said. A few people mumbled a greeting. "Let's try that again. Good morning!" Now the response was loud and followed by applause.

"I don't want to take too much time, but I wanted to welcome you all to Orchard! My name is Ben Clover, and I am the acting town manager for this fabulous town. We know there's a lot going on in the Berkshires, and we appreciate you taking a trip here on this lovely Saturday morning as we welcome in a new chapter in the history of Orchard. We have several members of the Board of Selectmen here, and I'd like to ask them to wave when I say their names. Harriet Wimsey, Nancy Reed, Jimmy Murphy, and Beckett Green, thank you all for your service and leadership to the town." A hearty round of applause followed.

"Now, I'd like to introduce Ruth Clagan. The Clagan family is one of the oldest in Orchard. They've been running the Cog & Sprocket for over a hundred years. Ruth's grandfather, the late and greatly missed Thomas Clagan, had a dream that the clock tower would get rebuilt. His granddaughter, Ruth, came to Orchard last fall after he died to take over his shop and to make his dream a reality. She's the best thing that's happened to this town in a long time. Here's Ruth Clagan herself to let us know what is going to happen today."

Ben stepped aside, and I walked up to the microphone. There were people as far as the eye could see. My heart pounded in my chest. The crowds alone didn't make me nervous. I looked down at my cell phone. Five minutes to go.

"Friends, I echo Ben in thanking you for being here. On behalf of my family, Caroline and Levi right over there." Caroline was so glad her son could be there, she was beaming as she looped her arm through his. They both waved, and the crowd cheered. "In memory of my grandparents, Mae and Thom, and their friend Grover Winter, who shared the dream of rebuilding this clock, we're thrilled that in less than three minutes the bell in the clock tower will chime for the first time in over sixty years."

The crowd clapped loudly, but I interrupted them. "As a special treat, we are giving you a preview of New Year's Eve here on the first day of summer. On the hour, not only will the bell chime, but four"—Nadia held up her hand, showing all her fingers—"sorry, five figures will come out from that door, do a turn, and go back in. On New Year's Eve, they'll do that automatically with the rest of the clock. Today, the great team of Pat Reed and Zane Phillips, the dynamic duo who have been working with me on the tower, will manually show you what it is going to look like. The first two figures will be my grandparents, Mae and Thom Clagan. Beckett Green sponsored the third figure. And the fourth figure was chosen by Caroline Adler. I have no idea what the fifth figure is, but I look forward to seeing it.

Thanks to Nadia Wint, you'll be able to see close-ups of the figures on our website as soon as the clock strikes noon. But for now, enjoy the preview of the big show. Which will happen in thirty, twenty-nine, twenty-eight . . ."

The crowd joined in and helped us all count down to five, four, three, two, one. There was silence as we all watched the clock hands come together, and then the bell ringing its slow, methodical clang. Twelve bells. The new bell was a vast improvement over the old one. It was much louder too, though I didn't really mind. The Clagan Clock Tower should be heard for miles around. When the last bell chimed I let go of my breath. I turned around and threw my arms around Ben's neck. He picked me up and swung me around.

"We did it!" I said to him breathlessly.

"You did it, Ruth. The bells will never be quiet again. Wait. Here comes the rest of the show."

The doors opened, and the figure of my grandfather came out. If you didn't know him, you would have seen a craftsman wearing a buffalo plaid work shirt, with a cog in one hand and a hammer in the other. The arms moved around in their sockets, and I suspected they would be doing more before January. Next out was my grandmother, wearing her flowered dress, a cog in one hand and flywheel in the other. I loved that Zane had made her an active participant to the clock making. Zane and Pat gave each figure a minute to be out there by itself, to get its own applause. The crowd was roaring. Next out was the Beckett figure—except it wasn't.

"That's you!" Ben said.

I looked up at the zany red curls, magnifying work glasses, and string of cogs and wheels that wove around me as if I were a living Christmas tree. I hopped off the platform and jogged over to Beckett.

"That's me," I said. I couldn't believe it. My heart was

bursting, and I impulsively gave Beckett a hug. He returned it, then let me go.

"Of course it is," Beckett said. "I hope you'll forgive the whimsy of the piece. You look a bit like a mad scientist up there."

"It looks like me. Thank you, Beckett. I'm really honored."

"My absolute pleasure, Ruth. Congratulations on today. Thank you for including me in it."

"Of course," I said. "You're a business owner. And a member of the Board of Selectmen now. Congratulations on that, by the way."

"An honor you helped with by not accepting the job."

"Listen, I have my hands full with the tower, and the business."

"And dating the new town manager would be a conflict of interest."

"There's that. But he's only interim town manager."

"As far as I'm concerned, he's got the job if he wants it. Moving to Orchard has changed me, Ruth. Took me a while to accept that. I kept thinking I needed to change Orchard. Kim had me convinced that hers was the only path forward. I was wrong. You and Ben have a better vision for what this town can be. Should be."

I linked my arm through Beckett's. "We're in it together."

Ben jumped down and stood next to me. "How great is that?"

I looked back at the clock tower. I'd missed the emergence of the fourth figure, Caroline's choice. Harry Clagan came out, white shirt and tie, holding a large cog. The smile was the one the photo on the shop had, and I couldn't have been more thrilled that Caroline had included him. The final figure came out. It was a figure of Bezel, carrying a cog in her mouth. The five figures weren't moving, but they would be by New Year's. Maybe Zane was right, and we needed to add some music for them to dance to.

I clapped along with everyone else. Ben scooped me back into his arms, and I gave him a big kiss.

"Whoever would have guessed?" I said, hugging him tight. "Dreams do come true."

about the author

Julianne Holmes is the author of *Just Killing Time*, the Agatha-nominated debut novel in the Clock Shop Mysteries, and is the pseudonym for J. A. (Julie) Hennrikus, whose short stories have appeared in the award-winning Level Best Books. She serves on the boards of Sisters in Crime and Sisters in Crime New England, and is a member of Mystery Writers of America. She lives in Somerville, Massachusetts, and blogs with the Wicked Cozy Authors at wickedcozyauthors.com. Visit the author at julianneholmes.com.

Ready to find
your next great read?

Let us help.

Visit prh.com/nextread